W9-CRD-308

COLOR ME
A KILLER
A SUSAN CHASE MYSTERY

STEVE BROWN

ibooks
new york
www.ibooks.net

DISTRIBUTED BY SIMON & SCHUSTER, INC.

For Patricia Cornwell

A Publication of ibooks, inc.

An ibooks, inc. Book

ibooks, inc.
24 West 25th Street
New York, NY 10010

The ibooks World Wide Web Site Address is:
http://www.ibooks.net

The Chick Springs Publishing World Wide Web Site Address is:
http://www.chicksprings.com

ISBN 0-7434-8688-9
First ibooks, inc. printing August 2004
10 9 8 7 6 5 4 3 2 1

Printed in the U.S.A.

ACKNOWLEDGMENTS

For their assistance with this book, I thank Missy Johnson, Mark Brown, Bill Jenkins, Ellen Smith, Kate Lehman, Cathy Wiggins and Lesta Sue Hardee of the Chapin Memorial Library, Lieutenant Jackie Kellett of the Greenville County Forensics Division, and my favorite Generation Xer, Stacey, who helps me sound slightly hip, and, of course, Mary Ella.

1

The day things began to go wrong was the day I was scheduled to go through the door with a guy who didn't believe I should be going through any door unless it was held open by a man. After all my training, and despite my having more nerve than thought good for me, this guy still didn't want me tagging along. Thankfully, my boss didn't agree. He said Earl Tackett would have to get used to it. Women were here to stay. I don't know about other women, but I needed this job and not only for the money.

The guy who didn't want to be paired with me was stocky, baldheaded, and a twenty-year veteran of the military police. When the army began allowing women into its ranks, Tackett was outta there. He cashed in a twenty-year marker and took a job with the Myrtle Beach police force along the Grand Strand. He also taught self-defense two nights a week at the local Y. Earl Tackett was a pretty good instructor. For a guy.

In the Sunnydale Motel, at the southern end of the Strand, some bad guys were selling crank, the working man's drug of choice, and the Chamber wanted the beach cleaned up for the approaching Season. Today's weather was breezy, but my boss had told me to lose the jacket. He wanted the bad guys to notice that I was a woman. Earl Tackett's jacket, however, concealed several guns, plus a wire, knife, and sap.

The dealers operated out of a room at the far end of a motel built in the shape of an "L." The letter's base contained

1

the office near the street. The remainder of the two-story building was filled with rooms and sat off the street behind a swimming pool. To bolster their defenses, the bad guys had a minicam mounted on the dashboard of their van parked in the last slot of the motel's parking lot. A black-and-white monitor sat on top of the TV inside their room, giving the dealers a pretty decent look down the side of the building.

Tackett and I were tooling down the Boulevard in my jeep, an old red thing now closer to pink. For the drug bust I wore a yellow cropped top and cutoff jeans with a fanny pack. Inside the fanny pack was a Smith & Wesson Model 36 with a hammer shroud. The shroud kept the pistol from hooking on all the stuff we gals tote around, and the fanny pack was Velcroed together for quick access. It was a little chilly without a jacket, but, hey, when you're the resident sex object . . . .

Tackett stopped at a light while I hugged myself for warmth and watched the annual ritual so important to the Grand Strand's success. In one business after another layers of dust and grease were being removed, water pipes checked for leaks, and windows inspected for cracks from the latest storm. Owners rolled out awnings or swept off sidewalks. Everyone waved. I waved back. I'm sure I appeared to be the same gal they'd always known, this time taking up with a man old enough to be my father. That wasn't true. Things had changed from the days when I worked as a lifeguard and finder of runaways.

"You talk tough, Susan, because you're so unhappy."

"Am I, Earl?" For the first time I held a year-round job, and one where the boss didn't come on to me.

"You need to get married. It'll fill in the cracks, especially the ones around your soul." Earl Tackett was a Promise Keeper, and they can be worse than a reformed drunk.

"I'm only in my twenties. Can't I have some fun?"

"This isn't women's work and you know it."

"What about vice?"

"Vice is too degrading for a woman."

"So you have to be a guy to be a cop?"

"Susan, don't mock me."

"That's not women's work either?"

The light changed and the jeep pulled away.

"I know about your mother walking out on your family, your father lost at sea. You need a family, not some job."

Finally, I faced him. "Earl, *this* isn't some job. I work for the South Carolina Law Enforcement Division. At any crime scene I outrank you. Isn't that what really chaps you?"

"It's in the Bible, Susan. God first, then man, then woman, and finally the children."

"Man as the head of the household. Funny, I don't remember that in the catechism."

He shot me a look. "Don't be blasphemous. You know you won't be truly happy until you have a family."

"And accept the leadership of some guy."

"Not just any guy. One who truly loves you."

"I'll bet you guys really get off on being the leader of the pack."

"Actually, it's a rather awesome responsibility."

About the time we arrived at the motel, Mickey DeShields would be climbing out of our boss's car in the parking lot of a pancake house behind the target location. There, Mickey, an attractive black man, today dressed as a bum, would become a staggering drunk, first investigating the contents of the dumpster behind the pancake house, then moving on to the dumpster at the Sunnydale.

This was why the bad guys had chosen the room at the end of the L-shaped motel. If they smelled trouble, all they had to do was throw a few bags into their van and drive across the alley into the parking lot of the pancake house and be on their way. Our boss was parked there to block their escape route.

As Earl Tackett turned into the parking lot of the Sunnydale, a van approached from the other direction and turned in behind us. The van had been confiscated from a pool-cleaning service that had been distributing a multitude of drugs along the Grand Strand. The van stopped at the motel office and the driver got out. Slipping out the rear of the van was another cop. His job? To baby-sit the manager. Around any dealer's crib you never know who's on the pad.

"Oh, this is nice," I said, glancing at the pool-cleaning van. "They were supposed to be here already."

"I'm sure everything will work out just fine."

Tackett drove to the far end of the parking lot and pulled into the slot in front of the bad guys' unit. The curtain was pulled back, but only slightly. So we sat there, waiting for our backup, hung up at the motel's office. To tell you the truth, it kinda got on my nerves.

Turning to Earl, I said, "Slap me."

"What?"

"We've got to distract them."

"Susan, I can't hit a woman."

I slapped him hard enough to make his teeth rattle.

A moment later he returned the favor. After bursting into tears, I begged him to give me some money.

"Push me out of the jeep. I'm going inside."

"Susan, that wasn't the plan."

I stumbled from the jeep, then over to the door and knocked. That got Earl moving. Down the sidewalk a maid was catching the late checker-outers. She was a he, also a cop, pushing a cart and looking the part, a scrawny fellow with delicate features. No wonder Earl didn't think they needed women in vice. This guy had hips narrower than mine. Another cop baby-sat the remaining maids in the store-room. It was hard to see how anything could go wrong, but that's when things usually did.

Earl joined me at the door. "I don't like the way you're doing this."

The cop-dressed-like-a-maid glanced at the pool-cleaning cops, whose van had parked alongside the fence encircling the pool. Ah, nothing like more than one vehicle, and more than one person, converging on the same location at the same time.

The pool-cleaning cops were my age, wore jeans, tee shirts, and what looked like headphones for a couple of DiscMans. They got out of the van, arguing over who'd climb down into the pool. After that they began to discuss the weather. You'd think they were up for an Oscar.

"It's warming up," said one.

"Wait 'til July," said the other. "Then you'll really see some heat."

The rest of what they said was lost in the clatter of equipment hauled out of the van. About now Mickey DeShields should be stumbling across the alley separating the Sunnydale from the pancake house.

Earl knocked on the door.

No answer, just some rattling around. They wouldn't be hiding the stuff, would they?

No, Susan, but they could be gathering up their Uzis.

The door opened and a pair of blue eyes squinted through the crack. This had to be the big guy we'd been briefed about: blue eyes and a deep tan. Blond bangs fell across his forehead.

"Yeah—what you want?"

"I was told you could . . . I could—"

"We were told to ask for Leon," cut in Earl.

"What you want with Leon?"

"What the devil you think . . . ?" Earl tried to look inside but Ole Blue Eyes blocked the way. "Maybe this isn't the right place."

"But—but it's got to be." I trembled. "You've got the shit, haven't you?"

The big guy gave me another look, then opened the door. When I tried to go inside, Earl stopped me.

"You stay out here."

"Earl, I've got to have—"

"Let the girl in," said Ole Blue Eyes.

Like there was any doubt the blonde wouldn't be allowed inside? I went ahead of Tackett into the darkened room.

A wall lamp between the double beds had a towel draped over it. Any other light came through the space between the curtains at the window or from the bathroom. A second guy sat at a table in the rear with an open briefcase on the table in front of him. The lid of the briefcase hid one hand; with the other he was smoking a cigarette. From a nearly closed bathroom door, a narrow slice of light cast across his shoulder and the table.

He gave me the once-over as I approached him. The table had been moved from near the window to the rear, between the last double bed and the washbasin. Ole Blue Eyes stood behind me and beside Earl Tackett, towering over both of us. A pistol was jammed into his belt, but it was his arms that drew my attention. This guy could do major damage without any frigging weapon.

"What can we do for you, honey?" asked the guy sitting behind the table.

"Is this the place?" asked Tackett.

"What place?"

The second guy's legs stretched out in front of him and crossed at the ankles under the table. Brown, curly hair hung to his shoulders, and his beard grew thick. He wore jeans and a short-sleeved shirt open at the chest, a gold chain around his neck, earrings in both ears. Behind the briefcase lay a pistol. I could barely see the weapon, but, hey, when you're in a room full of testosterone, a gal tends to pick up on such things.

I stood near the space between the two double beds, their sheets and covers in a mad tangle. Empty boxes of Chinese takeout sat on the nightstand, as did the motel's telephone. Newspapers had collected between the beds and been trampled repeatedly.

"You guys selling or what?" asked Tackett.

Ole Blue Eyes ran his hand up and down my arm. A tattoo encircled those biceps: decorative barbed-wire. Sorority girls are fascinated by tattoos—when they should be strapping on their running shoes.

"Why you with him?" the guy at the table asked me. He inclined his head in the direction of Tackett.

"I—I needed a fix."

"Yeah, right, but that still don't answer the question. Why'd you bring him along?"

"She don't sleep with you guys. She just wants a hit."

The long-legged guy regarded Tackett. "You don't do shit, do you?"

Tackett worked out daily in the department's gym. Upper body one day, lower body the next. He inclined his head toward the huge guy behind him. "Like your friend—I juice up." Inferring he used steroids.

"But you don't mind your woman doing a little hooking, do you?" asked the guy at the table.

Tackett shrugged.

"Hey," I asked, stepping forward and seeing the briefcase was full of money, "you got the stuff or do we gotta go somewhere else?" Thinking that might be something I shouldn't see, I glanced behind me. It was then I saw Ole Blue Eyes pull his pistol.

Sticking it in the small of Tackett's back, he ran the barrel up Earl's back until the barrel ran into something. The wire.

"What's this?" The big guy backed away, leveling his weapon at Tackett.

Very slowly Tackett turned around, and as he did, pulled back his jacket, revealing his shoulder harness. "So I carry. I've got a permit."

"Sure you're not cops?" asked Leon, pulling his legs in under him.

"If I was cops, I wouldn't be here."

Leon stood up behind the table and pointed his weapon at us. "And that might be why you're here."

Tackett turned to Leon, hands still open in surrender. "Hey, you want us out of here, we're gone."

With Leon's pistol on us, Ole Blue Eyes returned to the door and opened it. He saw the maintenance men in the pool area, then stuck his head farther out and looked down the sidewalk, where he probably saw the cop-dressed-as-a-maid or her cart.

Ole Blue Eyes closed the door. "Nobody out there." He glanced at the monitor feeding a signal from the minicam on the dashboard of their van. On the screen a bum was digging through the Sunnydale's dumpster.

Leon was around the table now, running the barrel of his

pistol up my tummy until it ran into my cropped top. His weapon was a fourteen-round little monster that could rip you in half with a single burst, if you could keep it steady.

Tackett stepped toward Leon. "Hey, we didn't come here for—"

A blow to the back of his head knocked Earl to the floor. Startled, I stepped back. Ole Blue Eyes had split Earl's scalp open with the butt of his pistol, and because Tackett was bald, you could see the skull until the blood pooled up and began to run down his head.

"Why—why you'd do that?" I didn't have to pretend to shudder.

Ole Blue Eyes kicked Tackett in the back, then kicked him again. Tackett never moved.

Why are you kicking him? That should be enough to get the pool-cleaning guys in here, shouldn't it?

"Take off your clothes, bitch!" This from Leon.

"No, no!" I backed away, into the space between the double beds. The pool-cleaning guys could hear all this over the wire, couldn't they?

"Honey," Leon said, "get those clothes off. You've got work to do."

"But—but I didn't get my hit."

"You ain't gonna get one unless you perform." He looked me over. "We're leaving tonight, but if you're any good we might take you along. Looks like you're built for screwing. Look at them hips."

What a terrible thing to say. Oh well, I've always been rather sensitive about the size of my hips.

Stepping over Tackett, Ole Blue Eyes reached for me.

Where were the pool guys?

The huge guy grabbed my cropped top. When he did, I went limp. The motion caused me to almost lose my top as I went down. Still, Ole Blue Eyes had no other choice than to let me slide to the floor.

"Get up, bitch!"

"Please—please don't hurt me." Where was our frigging backup?

Not a sound from outside.

Oh, well, it looked like we were going to have to do this the old-fashioned way: one bad guy at a time.

On my knees, I slapped the Velcroed side of the fanny pack and my pistol fell into my hand. With my other hand I pulled down my top. When Ole Blue Eyes hauled me to my feet, I put a bullet through his heart.

And felt the powder burn.

Damn. I knew I should've worn a bra. Whirling around, I stuck my pistol in Leon's face. "Drop the weapon!"

The best Leon could do was gape at me, so I knocked the pistol out of his hand. The Glock hit the wall, then clunked to the floor.

"Up against the wall! Now!"

Leon didn't move. Well, how many gals did he know who could take out someone the size of his partner?

"Against the wall! Assume the position!"

Leon blinked, but before he could move, a hand gripped my shoulder and turned me around. It was Ole Blue Eyes back from the dead. What was this guy on? His pump should've shut down already.

Outside someone shouted that they were the police and to open up or they'd knock down the door. Ole Blue Eyes glanced over his shoulder.

Something hit the door once, then again, knocking it back and out of the way. The pool-cleaning cops tumbled into the room. More than one of them said, "Drop your weapons and release the girl!"

The cops glanced at Tackett lying unconscious at our feet, then double-gripped their pistols and trained them on Ole Blue Eyes, who dropped his weapon, went to his knees, and collapsed across Earl.

The cop-dressed-as-a-maid finally appeared at the door. He, too, had his weapon drawn. All three cops stared at me, as well they should. A forearm had been wrapped around my throat.

Leon pointed his pistol around me. "You drop yours!"

In his bum's clothing, Mickey DeShields appeared at the

door, pistol drawn. The air was full of sirens and the room smelled of cordite. The cops standing in the doorway glanced at each other, not knowing what to do. About that time I remembered the pistol in my hand.

Duh.

I reached around my body, hugged myself tight, and pulled the trigger . . . over and over again.

The arm came off my neck and Leon fell across the table, knocking off the briefcase. Money flew everywhere, pieces of mirror clattered into the washbasin, and Leon knocked over the chair on his way to the floor.

I checked on the status of Ole Blue Eyes, then staggered over to one of the beds, sat down, and dropped my weapon. The pistol hit the carpeted floor with a muffled clunk.

Mickey Dee rushed over. "Susan, are you all right?"

"Check Earl. The big guy hit him with the butt of his pistol. He might be dead."

2

The next thing I knew I was on admin leave. Oh, yeah, and I had to be counseled by a shrink. Since the departmental shrink was in Columbia and I was at the beach, Lt. Warden agreed I could see my own doc. SLED did not want civilians thinking some newly-hired was blowing away people without giving it another thought.

Puhhhh-lease! I gave it a thought, considering what those bastards had in mind for me!

Okay, okay, I'll take a deep breath, relax, and tell you where I'm coming from.

My name is Susan Chase and I live along the Grand Strand. Nowadays I'm an agent of the State Law Enforcement Division—SLED—and considering where I boot-strapped myself up from, it feels like the top of the world.

My family used to fish the Florida Keys, and Daddy pursued that career up the East Coast until finally reaching the Grand Strand, one step ahead of the bill collectors. After my mom walked out on us, that left Daddy and me, fussing and fighting until one night he fell overboard and drowned. Pirates boarded us, thinking they could claim the boat as salvage. They didn't know about me sleeping below. Their "Ahoy theres" woke me, and I was lucky there were only two of them.

I stabbed the first one with a galley knife when he turned around to tell the other guy they were in luck. There was a young thing below, and when they'd had their fill, it'd be

11

over the side with me. When the pirate with the knife in his back stumbled topside, the second guy came below. The bastard was smoking a cigar and bragging he was bigger than any cigar.

Come on out and get what you've got coming, girlie, and if you're real nice, I'll make it quick and easy.

He wasn't talking about the rape.

I left the propane on and climbed out the forward hatch. The sorry bastard blew himself up the ladder and into the pilothouse. I kicked both of them over the side and got the hell out of there, only to learn that was just the beginning of my problems. Being fifteen, my next stop was a foster home, where it only took a few weeks to gauge my chances of becoming the next Cinderella. I hit the streets and lived by my wits. As far as I know, the bastards are still collecting my per diem.

Later on I worked out a deal to step-and-fetch-it at Wacca Wache Landing for the privilege of mooring *Daddy's Girl* there. Several friends from the street moved in. At the time I thought they were my friends, but they turned out to be moochers, panhandling or turning tricks for their next blow. I threw them all out. I had to get on with my life, whatever that might be.

Since *Daddy's Girl* was in no shape for shrimping, and me no Forrest Gump, I took a job guarding the beach. Steady work but seasonal. Still, I didn't want to sell dope or my body. Not that I'm knocking it, but dopers and prostitutes are just changing the old boss for a new one. For the next several years I lifeguarded during the Season and waited tables during the off-season. Then came my big break.

Some Baby Boomer asked me to find his kid who'd run away from home. Boomers' kids think they've been abused when their parents don't buy them a new car every year or enough condoms to last through the weekend. Made five hundred bucks for a couple of days' work. More money than several weeks of lifeguarding—because all *that* money's reported! Then, while private-eyeing, the second most important man in my life came along. J.D. Warden sent me to school to learn how to profile men who rape, murder, and mutilate women. In other words, sex crimes. Along the Grand Strand we have our hands full of jerks forcing themselves on the public, and I don't mean the ones trying to sell you another tee shirt.

It seemed like a pretty cool gig until I trained at Quantico. All I can say is you're better off running for your life than being taken by one of those weirdos. I mean, can you believe the asshole can still get it up after murdering someone? And ejaculate! Inside his victim! In one of the gazillion holes he's stabbed in your frigging body.

And still be able to go!

Anyway, you learn your parents were right. There are some frigging weirdos out there, and the worst of it is, they can snatch you off the street anytime they want. Talk about power. That's what it's all about. Some wimp controlling a woman, any woman—as long as he wants! The pervert is obsessed with being powerful, not only for the moment, but later when he replays the scene in his head over and over. How these guys can remember every gruesome little detail when they had trouble remembering dates in high school history is beyond me.

Okay, okay. Bad example. Anyway, don't be fooled when the perv tells you he can't remember anything about the crime. Tell him to save it for the parole board. Wackos remember every detail. That's part of the kick, and why they go so long between kills. Thank heavens for small blessings!

Anyway, while I was learning all the ways you can slice and dice the female body, M.J. Dawkins disappeared from the parking lot of the Pottery Warehouse. M.J. was a dish-water blonde, slender as only some of us wish we could be. She sold shoes in the outlet mall. In her mid-twenties, she was not known to be sexually active or have anyone stalking her. Truth be known, said a neighbor, M.J. was a rather dull sort who lived with two other silly girls. The night she disappeared M.J. hadn't waited for the shuttle that drops you off at your car and waits to make sure your engine starts. She was in a hurry to get home. Her roomies had rented the latest Johnny Depp flick and had plans to watch, drool, and eat popcorn late into the night. Her body was never found.

This happened while I was at Quantico, where I had little on my mind but returning to the Grand Strand and Chad Rivers. My main man had come into my life while I was making a name for myself as a private eye. The dead girl was never mentioned, perhaps because Chad had other things on his mind.

Me! Or perhaps he'd heard too much from his mother about girls who worked the mean streets of Myrtle Beach. What'd she have to worry about? If things went according to her way of thinking I'd disappear, too.

Bottom line: The Grand Strand had its first serial killer, but we didn't know it until the following Season—which was now, and despite everything I'd learned at Quantico, not even the FBI was prepared for how this killer would use his victims.

"How'd you feel after shooting those two men?"

My therapist is usually paid by my boyfriend, but today's session was on SLED. Chad says I have issues to work out. I say guys have their own issues, like overcoming an attachment to their mothers.

"How'd I feel after shooting those guys?" Already I needed a cigarette. "I felt safe."

"Nothing else?"

"Er—relief?"

"Is that a question or an answer?"

"You're the one pushing for another answer. All I felt was safe."

The shrink leaned backed in her chair. I sat across from her in another straight-backed chair. There was a sofa, but I didn't lie on it, not since the time I'd fallen asleep while we were getting down to the nitty-gritty. The shrink was too tall for a woman, and she needed to cut her hair. Or perhaps she thought she could get away with long hair because of her height. Oh, Jesus, but I hate coming here. It makes me curious about the most trivial shit.

"Do you mind if I smoke?" At first the woman had

resisted, but soon learned what a bear I can be when I need a cigarette.

"If you feel a need."

"I need to relax and a cigarette does that for me."

"Does your anxiety have to do with the shooting?"

"No. Just you." I took my cigarettes out of my backpack. No gun in there now.

"I make you tense?"

"Your questions do."

"Why's that?"

"You want answers I can't give you."

"Could you please elaborate?"

"The answers you want don't make sense. To me."

After shaking out a smoke, I returned the cigarettes to my backpack. I missed having my gun along, but I wasn't about to tell the shrink that. I didn't want a lecture on penis envy. Lighting up, I drew the smoke deep into my chest. By then the shrink had returned to her seat. She'd turned on the air filter.

"You think I expect certain answers?"

"Well, you don't accept my first answer."

"I shouldn't probe?"

Shrugging, I settled into my seat. "I've gotten used to it."

"Then you don't mind if we continue?"

I looked away.

"Susan?"

After a moment, I returned my attention to her. "Remember when I first came to see you and you had me take all those tests so you could get a handle on me? You said I'd done lots of work on my own, but you didn't know where my head was."

The woman nodded.

"You still haven't been able to figure me out. Like when I told you I was relieved to have killed those two drug dealers, you didn't get it, did you?"

"I don't understand your reaction, that's true."

"And I don't understand the question. I planned to kill those bastards the moment I hit the floor."

"You had no trouble making that decision?"

"Absolutely not." I took another drag off the cigarette. When would this hour ever end! The woman had only one clock and the son of a bitch was way across the room where you had to squint to see it. When you did, she jumped you for being antsy. Well, what'd she expect? Nobody wants to be shrunk. Therapists make you face what you don't want to know about yourself. Shrinks think that's good for you. I say get on with your life.

"How are you sleeping?"

"Okay."

"Need any medication?"

"I don't have any trouble sleeping." I smiled. "Unless Chad stays over."

"And how is he with this?"

"The sleeping over or the shootings?"

Now she smiled. "The shootings, of course."

"He wants me to quit SLED."

"And how do you feel about that?"

"I'm just getting started. But if I keep on killing people, I'll be history."

"Because the killing will get to you?"

I shook my head. "Warden said he couldn't keep me on if I kept on killing people."

The woman's face turned white, which looked pretty weird for someone who lived at the beach. Man oh man, I couldn't wait to escape this Bizarro World.

"Susan, how many people have you killed?"

Oops.

I took a drag and let the smoke out through my nose. "Just the two, the other day."

"What about the ones who boarded your boat when your father got drunk, fell overboard, and drowned?"

"Yeah. There were those, too."

"And the woman who drowned when you were trying to arrest her"—she glanced at her notes—"when you were a private eye?"

"Uh—they never found the body."

"So she doesn't count?"

I shrugged.

"What about the boy who leaped off the pier?"

"I was after his girlfriend, not him."

"But he's still dead."

"Look," I said, shaking the cigarette at her. "The girl's parents wanted her to call home." I sat back in my chair. "Really, that was it. After she called home, I was history. Just one phone call, that's all they wanted. That kid jumped to his death for nothing."

"Do you feel in any way responsible for his death?"

"The kid was a frigging idiot."

"So you don't think his death was any big deal?"

"I think you'd have to be my age to have a clue how my generation feels about drugs."

"People my age wouldn't understand?"

After snubbing out my cigarette, I said, "Boomers started the drug craze, not the CIA, and I have to deal with the consequences. My older sister was nothing to write home about, but she might've taken longer to die if her only choice had been different brands of booze to choose from. I can't tell you the number of times I've been panhandled by someone looking for their next snort or almost mugged for the same reason."

"But is it fair to hold a whole generation responsible for the actions of a few? For example, you were in a situation where you killed two men even though very few people in law enforcement ever draw their guns in the discharge of their duties."

"Wait a minute. Are you switching sides here?"

"I'm simply trying to get you to examine some issues," she said with a smile. "That's what I do."

I returned the smile—because the hour was up, which is only fifty minutes, thank the Lord! I stood up, taking my backpack with me.

She watched me go. "Next week you may feel differently after you've had a chance to process all this."

"Okay, but you'll be doing all the talking. I'm moving on." With another smile, I added, "That's something else I learned in this office."

Color Me A Killer

I left the shrink's office but only made it as far as the local McDonald's. A cup of coffee at McDonald's was more appealing than one at the law enforcement center. One of my gal pals stopped by, but when I showed little interest in her problems with her live-in lover, she gulped down her coffee and left me sitting there alone. Too many people had been poking around inside my head in the past twenty-four hours. The first had been Mickey DeShields, after making sure both drug dealers were dead.

"You okay?"

"Yeah." I heard the flatness in my voice, despite the ringing in my ears. Near the door the pool cops huddled, outside the maid-cop stood, and all of us could hear a car racing around the side of the building, then screeching to a stop. Another one screeched in behind it.

"You're trembling."

"It happens, Mickey. It happens." Shrugging off his concern, I about tossed myself off the side of the bed as another tremor shook me. Under any other circumstances it would've been comical.

DeShields shouldered his weapon, sat down, and put his arm around me. Mickey usually dressed to the nines, not like some bum. "Better?"

I nodded, leaned into him but continued to stare at the floor, actually at the few feet of carpet clear of bodies and blood.

Our boss came through the door and stopped cold. What J.D. Warden saw must've rivaled anything he'd seen while policing New York City. Earl Tackett lay on the floor with a towel wrapped around his head, a blanket covering the rest of his body. Near him lay a large fellow with a blackened hole in his chest, and beyond them another guy in a bed of dead presidents. Blood spattered a wall where a mirror had once hung, its glass littering the washbasin.

"Chase, what in the world have you done?"

"Saved Earl Tackett's life, it would appear."

Warden stared at me, glanced at Tackett, and then asked, "Has anyone called the paramedics?"

One of the pool guys said he had.

Warden tried not to contaminate the crime scene as he stepped over bodies to where DeShields and I sat at the end of the bed. I resumed staring at the floor.

J.D. Warden is a stocky guy with a broad chest and not much of a pot gut. He wears off-the-rack suits, and I'd never seen him in anything less than a long-sleeved shirt and tie during the hottest summers. J.D. had taken a bullet in the line of duty, then moved south, living on disability, playing golf, and attending to his grandkids. SLED learned he was available and hired him to head up their field office along the Grand Strand. Evidently there's a limit to how much golf one can play. In J.D. Warden, SLED possessed a competent, yet unambitious man who ran a tight ship along the Grand Strand and left politics to the folks farther inland.

"Are you injured?" he asked.

"No." I trembled again.

"Tell me what happened."

"They made us."

He glanced at the overturned table, the dead Leon, and the money scattered all over the floor. "Why do you say that?"

"Because they didn't want to deal. They weren't the least bit interested."

"Why not?"

"I told you. They made us."

"What gave you away?"

"I don't have a clue. I was in front of Earl, trying to make the buy and all of a sudden he went down." Glancing at the door, I added, "And there was no backup."

"No backup?"

"Well, they took forever."

One of the pool cops said, "The last thing we saw was the big guy come to the door and look out."

"And the last thing we heard was Chase asking 'why're you doing that?'" chimed in his partner. "It didn't sound like she was in trouble."

"Yeah," said the other pool guy.

"We didn't know there was any problem."

"It took a minute to figure that out."

"Not a minute," he said, looking at his partner. "It was less than that."

Behind them the maid joined in this foolishness. "It was more than a minute. I was coming out of the room next door when our guys came charging out of the pool and across the parking lot. And the girl's being straight with you, Lieutenant. They didn't want to deal."

"What about you, DeShields?"

"I came in when the shooting started."

"What did you hear?"

"I didn't know Susan was in trouble until they started knocking down the door. There was a thump, probably when Earl hit the floor, but that sounded like someone hitting the microphone."

Warden stooped down beside Tackett and removed the wire from the unconscious man. He turned over the apparatus, examining it. "Did they kick him?"

I was staring at the floor.

"Chase, did they kick him?"

Without looking at him, I said, "Yes."

"Did they try to rape you?" he asked, scanning a roomful of bodies, blood, and greenbacks. "Is that why all this happened?"

"Something was said about me going along. It's on the tape." Straightening up on the end of the bed, I asked, "Why didn't you hear anything?"

He dropped the wire to the floor. "Something's wrong with my machine."

"Something was wrong with this whole fucking operation."

"Watch your language, Chase."

Outside another siren wound down.

I glanced at the pool-cleaning cops. "We pulled in together. It probably tipped them off."

"We were held up in traffic."

"Save that for the summertime."

"J.D.," asked Mickey, "is it possible you could finish interviewing Susan at the law enforcement center?"

The cops in the door made way for the EMS techs with their bags and stretcher.

"The guy with the towel is one of ours," Warden said. "Get him to Grand Strand Regional. Leave the dead guys for the coroner."

The techs nodded, then laid their stretcher beside Earl.

"Chase, can you drive?"

I shuddered. "Of . . . course."

"DeShields, drive her over to the pancake house and buy her a cup of coffee."

Which gave me plenty of time to figure out what I was going to tell my boyfriend.

"It was on the news, Susan."

"Sure you didn't hear it from your mother?"

Chad was doing his imitation of my boss, towering over me while I sat cross-legged on the sofa in the pilothouse of *Daddy's Girl*. Max the Wonder Dog lay on the sofa, head in my lap. Chad is slightly taller than my five-foot-ten, and his brown hair was wet and slicked back from a quick shower and rushing over to my place. Good shoulders, a rugged, tanned face, and good hands. Very good hands. Tonight I wasn't likely to feel those hands. I trembled, and it was no come-on. Time to stroke the dog again. When I did Max looked at me with mournful eyes.

"Why does my mother always have to come up in our discussions?"

"Because we haven't called it quits, I would imagine."

"Just because you don't have a family, you can't begrudge me mine." When I said nothing, Chad went to the sink and fixed a drink. "You know my family will be yours one day."

"What a pleasant thought."

He faced me. "Take your best shot, Suze. I'm not letting you build a wall between us tonight."

Max watched with great interest. When Chad had the drink right, he took a seat in the rocking chair across from me. The chair was a gift from my berth mate, Harry Poinsett. Harry thinks a rocker makes people more reflective, but a rocker on the water? I looked back into my lap. Why couldn't everyone just go away and leave me alone? Uh-huh. Chad had done that before, so had Harry, and it had broken me in a matter of days. Once you allow people into your life, you end up needing them.

"People kept coming up to me, Susan, asking about the shoot-out, asking about you."

"Ignorance is bliss."

"Look," he said, leaning forward on his knees, "I know how badly you want to be a SLED agent and I have to get used to it, but all that blood and gore . . . learning you were the one . . . what did they do, try to rape you?"

My head jerked up. "Don't go there, Chad!"

He finished his drink in one long pull, then clunked the glass on the worn coffee table. "Those assholes don't know what they missed."

Huh?

Chad left the rocker, crossed the room, and pulled me into his arms. Time for the dog to go out and do his business— while Chad attended to mine.

Afterwards he still wanted to talk. "Are you okay?"

I sighed and stretched out my naked frame. "Never better."

Evidently Chad wasn't.

"What's the problem, my man?"

He sat up, cross-legged on the bunk bed. There's not much room in the pilothouse of a former shrimp boat so I sleep in bunk beds. We were on the lower bunk, me against the wall.

"I thought you'd be safer working with SLED. I ought to call J.D. and give him a piece of my mind."

Rather firmly, I said, "I wouldn't do that if I were you."

"Suze, we have to talk this out."

With another stretch, the sheet fell away from my chest. "Really?"

He looked away. "I can't talk to you with your breasts staring at me."

"Breasts can't stare, only you can."

He snorted and climbed out of the bunk.

"Does this mean we're not going to play any more?"

Finding his pants, he pulled them on. "Not until we talk this thing out."

I turned toward the bulkhead. "There's nothing to talk about. My boyfriend serviced me and—"

A hand grabbed my shoulder and rolled me over. Covers were pulled up to my neck, then down tight, trapping my arms alongside me. When Chad straddled me, I had no advantage, none whatsoever.

"Tell me what you were feeling during the shoot-out."

"Like I told the shrink: better them than me." Working my hand under the sheet, I found his groin. "I was thinking they ain't gonna get none tonight. Not like me!"

An elbow knocked away my hand. "Suze, this is serious."

"I don't bug you about how to build your boats." Chad's father builds boats farther inland where the property values are lower and the profits higher.

"People don't usually shoot at me when I arrive for work."

"Not yet, they haven't."

Rather than argue the point, he let go of the sheet, climbed off, and stalked across the cabin. Like I said, the pilothouse isn't all that wide, so it wasn't a very lengthy stalk. Through the screened door separating us from the deck, Max whined.

I thumped my feet to the deck. "Okay, let's get this over with." I found my top, a blue-and-gold sweatshirt from the justice academy, and slid into it.

Chad stood at the bar, facing the mirror on the bulkhead. He had not mixed another drink. Chad didn't usually drink more than a couple of beers, so he was well over his limit. "Suze, it's perfectly normal for me to be worried about you. You could've been killed."

"You want me to quit?" I stood up, pulling on my underpants. "Is that what this is all about?"

Now he looked at me. "Of course I want you to quit. So does my dad. We all want you to quit."

"And your mom?"

"Yes, but let's not go chasing that rabbit."

Snatching up the jeans he'd peeled me out of only a half-hour earlier, I did some stalking of my own—over to the door to let Max in. "Chad, I'm just getting started with SLED." I plopped down on the sofa, jeans across my lap. Max quickly joined me, head across the jeans.

My boyfriend picked up a glass and examined it. "Maybe I was watching someone else almost get herself killed this afternoon on TV."

"And maybe that's how you'll have to treat it."

Down went the glass. "Susan—"

"Chad, don't deny it. You wanted me to take this job so your mother would think better of me."

"I wanted no such thing!"

"Be straight with me. This job makes me more acceptable."

"I can't help it if she's such a snob."

"She should move to Charleston."

"Then my father wouldn't fit in."

"I know the feeling." I gazed at the pilothouse with its home entertainment center and PC, which was among the older stuff. With a regular paycheck I should be able to upgrade. Or move in with my boyfriend and fight over my job. "I never had the chance to make any serious money, or be taken seriously, but with SLED I will."

"I don't care about the money!"

"I do."

"Then come to work for my father."

"I'm not going to sell boats and I don't know where you got the idea I would."

"Then tell me why it upset you so much when I asked about those guys wanting to rape you? They didn't and they paid with their lives."

And that's when the discussion really heated up. It was pretty damn obvious what was wrong with those a-holes trying to rape me. It makes men think women have to be protected. That's a close cousin to women not being able to do the job—whatever the hell the job is—and I wanted to keep this job. Of course, that was before some scumbag started killing and mutilating friends of mine. Then I wanted to break all the rules and go looking for the asshole myself.

3

While I sat in McDonald's, drinking coffee and wondering what to do, Harry Poinsett walked in. After picking up a coffee, along with sugar, he strolled over to my table. A balding fellow in his mid-sixties with a gray beard, Harry wore a navy blue windbreaker over a long-sleeved shirt with slacks. The collar of the shirt was crisp, as was the crease in his pants. On his feet were a pair of highly polished loafers. Harry is a descendent of the fellow who christened the scarlet-leafed plant that so many people decorate their homes with at Christmas, the poinsettia.

"Good morning, Susan. May I join you?"

"Of course."

Harry put down his coffee, took a seat, and moved the chair one way, then the other. "Amazing, isn't it? They know exactly how many inches to give each customer."

"Never thought about it."

"No. Something like that you'd take for granted, like the telephone."

"Like you did the horseless carriage?" I wasn't put off by Harry. Fact was, his gentle taunting was how he'd gotten me to read, and if I could write a decent e-mail, I had Harry Poinsett to thank for it. His schooner is moored forward of mine at Wacca Wache Landing.

After watching his boss be blown to bits by a car bomb in Greece and being held hostage in Iran, Harry said he'd had enough of diplomatic life. But early retirement wasn't his wife's idea. She moved inland and runs with the former James

Dickey crowd—you know, trying to get laid by someone who can diagram a sentence. Occasionally, the old bat shows up and spends a few days on the schooner. I don't go over when she's there, and Harry's always in a funk once she leaves. I never have the nerve to ask why.

"How'd it go with the therapist?" he asked me.

"Dads, how come you always show up after each session?"

"I trust it was productive."

"Not really."

"What's the problem?"

"I wasn't raised in suburbia."

"I'm sure the doctor has your best interests at heart." After a sip of coffee, Harry made a face. "Doesn't anything they make taste good?"

"The fries. Everybody thinks McDonald's has the best fries, even Julia Child."

"Ah, yes." Dads put down his cup. "I remember Miss Child from when she worked for the CIA during World War Two."

"Dads!"

"Oh, sorry. That's something you wouldn't know—"

"Yes, I know. Without reading a damn book. I'll catch her on *Biography*."

After adding more sugar to the coffee, he asked, "So how's Earl Tackett? Should I stop by and see him?"

"There're so many visitors you might not get in. Earl's a deacon in his church."

One of Harry's eyebrows arched. "Did you get in?"

I looked into my cup. "The doctors think there may've been brain damage. That was an awfully big guy who hit him."

"Is that something you feel responsible for?"

Looking up, I said, "Earl shouldn't have let that big guy get behind him."

"Good God, Susan, but that's cold. I hope you didn't tell that to the therapist."

"'Fraid so."

"My dear, you may never complete treatment."

"Whatever." I returned to my coffee.

"I have great faith in fools; self-confidence, my friends call it."

"Huh?"

"Something by Edgar Allan Poe."

"Someone *else* you were on a first-name basis with?"

"So what are your plans for the rest of the day?"

"SLED's sending some agents to interview me. By rule they have to come from a different region." I took a sip of my coffee, not understanding Dads' complaint. At least we didn't have to brew the stuff. "Until the investigation's over I'll probably be assigned to the cold cases." The State Law Enforcement Division breaks in new people on unsolved murders, running them past a new set of eyes, along with making an example of what SLED doesn't want to happen to newbies: agents being unable to close a case.

"Glad to hear you won't be on the street."

I stared at him, puzzled.

"Er—since you did so well on the last one."

I shrugged. "We got a cold hit." A cold hit is when the computer discovers the identity of a killer or rapist by matching his DNA from blood, semen, or saliva left at the crime scene. Those samples are compared with DNA profiles in a humongous database. This particular suspect turned out to be an inmate only a week away from parole in Indiana. We'd been lucky, really lucky. Some girl, down the road, had been real lucky.

After wrestling himself out of the swivel chair, Harry said, "Well, I have errands to run."

"Don't forget the mahogany. That pocket of dry rot's not going away."

He patted a pants pocket. "I have it on my list, as I do food for three. Will Chad be joining us tonight?"

"As far as I know."

Harry leaned over and kissed the cheek I offered. And this was a guy whose wife had dumped him because he had become disenchanted with his job? Would Chad dump me because of my work? Better question: Would I dump my work to keep Chad? I really did love that guy.

At the law enforcement center in downtown Myrtle Beach, the squad room was busy, folks having time only to nod or give a quick "hello." All this activity and the Season had yet to begin? What was up with that?

I dropped my backpack on a desk and wandered into the office assigned to SLED. It was shared by both Warden and DeShields. Each was on his phone: my boss telling the director of the Chamber of Commerce that he didn't have anything yet. Warden motioned me to one of the two metal chairs in front of his desk.

Because I'd be saddled with a desk job, I'd worn a white, short-sleeved blouse and navy blue skirt. Not as short as I liked them, but I was doing my damnedest to fit in. And though I had a better tan than most of the legs in the squad room, I wore hose. But no heels. You can take this dress-for-success stuff a bit too far.

Mickey Dee was on the phone with my former boss, Marvin Valente. Marvin runs one of the lifeguard services along the Strand, and in the days when I hadn't worn hose, I'd been one of his regulars. Marvin had not been pleased when I'd quit. Besides knowing how to keep his piece-of-shit truck running, I would guard any section of the beach. I also posted assignments for the other guards when Marvin got slammed, especially during the Season.

Warden put down his phone. "Chase, do you know a girl by the name of Lucy Leslie?"

I nodded. Lucy was a couple of years older than me. During the Season she guarded the beach and met guys. During the off-season she waitressed for an uncle who owned a place along Restaurant Row. The uncle was okay. I'd even worked for him when I needed some extra cash.

Warden got to his feet and pulled his suit jacket off the rack in the corner of the small room. Beside his coat hung a white fedora. Mickey Dee's. Mickey didn't look like any bum today. He wore black pants and matching jacket over a white silk shirt. His tie was black, as was a pair of half-boots.

"Let's go," said my boss, coming around his desk.

"But I have that appointment." I was a government cop now, and if a cop so much as took the strap off his weapon, there was paperwork to fill out.

"If you do anything today, it'll be with me."

Mickey put down his phone as I stood up.

Warden stopped at the door. "What'd you get?"

"Morning, Susan." DeShields crossed the small office and reached for his hat. "Lucy Leslie is on the schedule." He took down the fedora.

"To guard the beach?" That didn't sound like Lucy. Lucy put off any kind of work until the last minute, and she was usually late for her shift.

"Come on, Chase," said Warden, heading out the door of his office. "This is your case."

Outside the office, I picked up my backpack. "What case?"

It was left to Mickey to explain as he came out of the office behind us. "Lucy Leslie was found dead on the beach between here and North Myrtle."

"You're kidding." I'd just seen her. Actually, I didn't remember the last time I'd seen Lucy, but she couldn't be dead.

"She was found in a lifeguard stand."

"In a . . . stand?"

"Like she was working."

"Obviously staged." Warden cleared his throat. "We've been told the body is nude."

"She's naked?" I stared at him.

"Not even a bathing suit," explained Mickey.

My backpack slid off my shoulder and somehow I found a way to plop my butt on the edge of a desk. "But why would anyone kill Lucy?"

"That's what you're going to find out. Unless you want the county police to handle it?"

I continued to stare at Warden.

"Well?"

"No, no. I can do it."

Around the squad room cops hustled hither and yon. With a body on the beach nobody wanted to appear idle.

My hand found my backpack and I slung it over my shoulder, missing it the first time, finding the shoulder with the second try. This couldn't be right. Everybody liked Lucy. I mean, she loved to party. Often she *was* the party. She'd go anywhere, do anything. Lucy was the person Harry Poinsett used as an example of where my life was headed if I didn't get myself on track. I don't know about that. Lucy seemed to have it figured out: work all day, party at night.

"Susan, are you going to be all right?" asked Mickey as he steered me across the room.

"When . . . when do I meet with SLED?"

Warden was ahead of us. "You really want to talk with those people?"

"I thought I had to talk to them before returning to the street."

Warden went through the glass doors ahead of us and outside. DeShields opened one for me, then handed me a weapon. My Smith & Wesson.

"I'm to carry?"

DeShields nodded to me, then to a patrolman who stared at us as we passed by.

Outside the building, I said, "I don't understand why I'm carrying." To our left and right were patrol cars. Farther out, the unmarked ones.

As we crossed the parking lot, Warden explained. "This morning I presented the findings of our investigation into the incident at the Sunnydale Motel to the Horry County solicitor. He signed off on you and that's good enough for me." Warden glanced over his shoulder. "Just try not to shoot anyone in the next few days. It would reflect badly on the judgment of the county solicitor."

We followed Warden to a sedan parked in the shade of a palmetto palm. He opened the door with a key, then slid in behind the wheel. Mickey Dee opened the rear door and slid in behind him. I went around to the other side and took the seat beside Warden, who was rolling down his window to catch the breeze. The law enforcement center is only a few blocks off the beach. Warden put the car into reverse, and laying his arm across the seat behind me, jammed on the brakes and muttered a curse.

The car rocked to a stop, causing me to turn around. Another sedan had pulled in behind us. We waited until a red-faced man hauled his heavy frame from behind the wheel and walked over. He left the door open, and through it you could see a middle-aged woman in the passenger seat: dark blue pants, pale skin, and short black hair. She looked vaguely familiar.

The red-faced man wore a suit whose jacket would never button across his stomach and probably hadn't for a good many years. He leaned down on the windowsill. "Where you headed, J.D.? You knew we were driving down this morning."

"Got a body on the beach. Be back after lunch."

He looked at me. "This the Chase girl?"

"Right."

"I thought she was on admin leave."

"Not when the victim was someone she knew."

The red-faced man regarded me. "You think Chase had something to do with the death?"

Warden sighed.

From the back seat, Mickey asked, "How you doing, Paul?"

The heavy man shifted around. "Oh, yeah, DeShields. I'm okay."

"Can you move your car? This is a tourist town and we have a body on the beach."

"If you leave Chase with me."

"Paul," Warden said, "I said we'd be back after lunch."

"Uh-uh. Chase can't work the street until we finish our investigation."

"Friddle, are you going to move your car or not?"

"Not unless you give up Chase."

"Suit yourself."

Putting the car into gear, Warden moved forward until he had the front tires snug against the concrete curb stop.

"Hey!" exclaimed Friddle, stepping back. "What you doing?"

Warden gave the car a measured amount of gas, then eased the front tires over the curb stop, across the sidewalk, the curb, and down into the street. Friddle followed us as far as the curb.

"J.D., you can't do this! You're not in New York anymore."

Everyone in our car looked both ways. Headed toward us was a patrol car. When our car rolled across the sidewalk into the street, a female patrolman turned on her light bar. After seeing who it was, she held up her hands in a gesture of helplessness, then shook her head. Paul Friddle was left standing on the curb, shouting expletives.

"I'm to be interviewed by that guy? Give me a break."

Warden drove a few blocks before turning north on the bypass. When he did, Mickey gripped the front seat and leaned forward.

"Susan, you need to know there were no drugs found at the Sunnydale Motel."

"What are you talking about?" Turning around to face him, the seat belt and harness bit into me. "Everybody was there. I saw the money."

"Chase," Warden said, "no one's under suspicion for missing drugs or money. DeShields is simply informing you there were no drugs found at the crime scene."

"I—I don't understand."

"The manager of the Sunnydale said the dealers had checked out. Their suitcases were in the van. No significant amount of crank was found in the van, just paraphernalia. Probably why they had all that money."

"But surveillance said customers were able to make a buy as late as midnight last night."

"It was just bad luck," said Mickey, sitting back in his seat.

Facing the windshield, I said, "Earl Tackett's bad luck, you mean."

4

We drove north, toward an unincorporated section of the beach filled with restaurants, hotels, and other businesses, such as places where you can load up on fireworks. For some reason Northies always seem to find their way to this part of the beach. The Horry County Police Department has jurisdiction in these slivers of beach where one city government ends before another begins. This was where Lucy's body was found.

The press had not yet arrived, but several county vehicles clustered in a sand parking lot, spaces lined by weather-treated four-by-sixes. An EMS vehicle sat beside the Horry County Mobile Crime Unit and a group of locals lined the dune. In one of the slots was Lucy's old gray Nissan sedan, a bright yellow crime scene tape around it. The forensics people were working on the car, taking samples, snapping pictures, and bagging portions of anything in sight. Two Horry County homicide detectives were interviewing people, and on the street a rollback wrecker waited to haul Lucy's car away. EMS techs sat in the rear of their vehicle, smoking cigarettes and waiting for their chance to haul the body away. The number of hands you can keep off the chain of evidence is always a plus when you have to go to court.

Jacqueline Marion, a latent prints expert, gave us the 411 before we went over the dune. "The car was driven here from wherever she was abducted. She was strangled."

"Her passenger killed her?" asked Warden.

Marion shook her head. "She was done through the

33

driver's side window, then pushed over into the passenger seat. The killer forgot to return the seat to a position that would accommodate a victim of her leg length." Marion gestured at the car. "Then she was hauled out through the passenger side door, hoisted over the killer's shoulder, and carried down to the beach." The fingerprint expert shook her head. "And that's something you have to see to believe."

Warden nodded. He and DeShields left the forensics people to their work, but I lingered behind, studying the car for anything forensics might've missed, or perhaps I was reluctant to go over the dune, a low sand wall with a fence made of wired-together pieces of weather-treated wood. Faded signs posted on the flimsy-looking fence told people to stay off the dune. Still, people stood there, mostly retirees, probably relieved by the Grim Reaper's choice of victims.

Warden and DeShields made their way through the crowd and crossed the wooden walkway over the dune. A cop stopped me, however. Her name was Vance and we'd competed for the same guy friends while growing up along the Grand Strand.

Vance gave me the once-over. "Never seen you in a skirt and blouse before. What's the deal?"

"I'm with them." I pointed at Warden and DeShields, who were walking down the stairs to the beach.

Vance glanced in their direction. "No shit?"

I opened my pack and showed her my new ID.

She took the SLED ID and studied it, head canting to one side. "This another one of your scams?"

For once I didn't know what to say.

Another patrolman crossed the walkway and told the people they had to move off the dune. He smiled when he saw me. "Susan, heard you survived the academy."

Eddie Tooney was tall, broad-shouldered, and as clumsy a dance partner as you could find. Tooney wore the colors of the Horry County Police Department, but along with a shirt, he wore a sweater and utility belt with thirty pounds of equipment. My interrogator, Vance, carried the same equipment and had the hips to hold it up.

"What you doing?" Tooney asked Vance, who still held

my SLED identification in her hand.

"Er—just looking at Susan's new ID." Vance returned the laminated card.

"What's up with you being on the street?" asked Tooney.

"You know me," I said, putting away the ID. "I just do as I'm told."

Tooney threw back his head and laughed as I crossed the walkway.

From the raised walkway I could see up and down the Strand: Myrtle Beach's high-rises to the south, North Myrtle's houses to the north. In front of me was a taped-off crime scene with a lifeguard stand in the middle, and in that stand sat a woman, her back to me. A towel had been draped over her head as if to protect her from the sun.

Farther out, the sky was clear and blue, the line between horizon and ocean sharp and clear. The tide was out, and beyond the high-tide mark, litter from the off-season lined the beach: seaweed, shells, plastic milk cartons, and the occasional piece of underpinning from someone's pier. Down the beach a flock of laughing gulls waited for an opportunity to pick over whatever we left behind.

Flanking the lifeguard stand were two four-wheelers used to patrol the beach. The county coroner stood on the seat of one of the vehicles. Beneath him stood Teddy Ingles, a rather large and dense fellow who did all the heavy lifting for the coroner's office.

A patrolman nodded me into the crime scene when I flashed my ID, and I wandered over to where DeShields, Warden, and the police chief were standing. Horry County is the only county with a police force. Something to do with politics back in the fifties. It only took a glance to scope out the scene; then I looked out to sea. There, I'd find no naked dead girls, with something jammed between their legs.

The chief of police was an average-sized fellow with red hair and a trimmed mustache. He wore thin, wire-rimmed glasses. His black Stetson matched the piping on his gray uniform and he carried little in the way of extra pounds. He frowned as I strolled over to join them. Jennings and I went back a ways. I'd once run with his daughter, you know, doing chick things, like I'd done with the dead girl in the lifeguard stand.

"Does Susan have to be here?" asked the chief.

"Of course she does," said my boss. "Where've you been, Chase? You're on the job, not here to visit old friends."

"Congratulations," said Jennings, offering his hand. "I saw the write-up in the paper."

"Thank you, Chief. I think Mickey Dee was responsible for that."

DeShields looked down the beach as Warden glanced his way.

"Your boss wants you here," said the chief. "I don't agree, but I'm from the old school."

I faced my dead friend: arms on the armrests, towel over her head, and legs spread. Protruding from between her legs was a bright red plastic shovel. "After this I may join your school. May I go up?"

"That's why you're here, Chase."

Jennings glanced at my boss, who definitely wasn't from the old school; then the chief gave me a hand up on the four-wheeler. But the chief didn't stay there long. I imagine he had seen farther up my short skirt than he cared to. Jennings *was* from the old school.

The coroner nodded across Lucy. Albert Greave and I were fishing chums, running into each other in places we didn't think the other knew about. Returning from Quantico, I'd offered him my expertise regarding the slicing and dicing of young women by serial killers.

"Sorry," Greave had said, "but you of all people should know I'm not going to look at your photographs." Greave's daughter had been robbed, raped, and murdered in the parking lot of a Charlotte mall. The attack had been so vicious the funeral required a closed casket.

Because I had the skinny on some seriously deranged guys, I became irritated at his lack of cooperation. Didn't he know I was doing this so fewer women would be robbed, raped, and murdered in the parking lots of other shopping malls?

Albert Greave was a thin man who wore black, horn-rimmed glasses and had an extended neck that appeared to push his emaciated face forward. He wore a white, short-sleeved shirt, and a string tie that would not contaminate the crime scene. What little hair he had was jet black and whipped around in the breeze off the ocean. Around his thin neck hung a camera. Greave had the habit of snapping a few shots at the crime scene, and he had a pretty good eye for someone untrained in forensics. In his shirt was a pocket recorder.

"I'm genuinely sorry about this, Susan."

"Thank you, Albert."

After steadying myself on the four-wheeler, I took a pair of latex gloves from my backpack. Despite the towel, I could see where blood had leaked from Lucy's nose and caked across her upper lip. Lucy always wore too much lipstick, but today those lips were much too pale. Nails gash-red, a couple chipped and broken, probably from where she'd struggled with her attacker. Her hands had yet to be bagged.

Greave was saying, ". . . how you must feel, but this is business now."

I finished pulling on the gloves. "No, no. I'm all right."

"Then let's proceed." He clicked on the recorder in his pocket. Greave gestured at a row of footprints coming and going inside the yellow-ringed crime scene. "Combat boots. That's what the killer wore."

A member of the forensic team walked back and forth, examining the crime scene. As he passed by, he glanced up at the new kid on the block. And that new kid's legs felt weak. I was having a hard time breathing. I gripped the stand and stared at the boot prints. Another tech was making casts of them.

"He's a big fellow, Susan. Six-and-a-half feet tall, if the boots match his frame. Size fourteen or more."

I shivered. "Sounds like some kind of monster." But aren't they all when they're in that frame of mind.

"Could you speak up?" Warden had his notebook out and was jotting down what was being said.

I scanned the beach, taking in the hotels farther down, the houses in the opposite direction, and the rubberneckers on the dune. "And nobody saw anything?" I asked, raising my voice.

"I have people canvassing the area," said Jennings from below.

"Somebody had to have seen something with the size of this guy," said Greave. "Combat boots make a good bit of noise when they hit pavement, and the only way he could've left the crime scene was to have walked out to the road. There are no corresponding prints in the sand the forensics people have been able to find."

"Or he had an accomplice," injected Warden. "Or another vehicle waiting for him."

"I don't know," mused Greave. "It appears to be a crime of passion, someone simply snapped, but then there are the gloves . . . ."

"The shovel is a crime of passion?" asked Jennings.

At the mention of the shovel, I looked inland. "A cold front passed through last night and the Season hasn't started. I don't know who would've seen anything. How long's she been here?"

"My guess is she was left after midnight, but we'll have to let Vickers make that determination." Benjamin Vickers was a surgeon at Grand Strand Regional. He did "quickie" autopsy work for the county. For a body found on the beach you'd want a quick autopsy before it was sent on to the county seat in Conway.

"You said something about gloves," reminded Warden.

Greave used the eraser end of a pencil to lift the towel. "You see these marks around the neck where she was strangled?"

I did, but there was also blood on Lucy's shoulders, mixed with her blond hair. Now why would there be blood on her shoulders if she'd been strangled?

"Jacqueline Marion said they found a thread on the handle that moves the front seat of Lucy's car back and forth. I found another thread on the body. I imagine they're from an old pair of work gloves."

"Was she violated—besides the shovel?"

Jennings answered that. "Forensics found no semen outside the body."

"I see," I said, faking nonchalance. Women have a basic reaction to something like this: stark raving terror. Men react schizophrenically. On the one hand they want to catch the bastard and string him up by the gonads. On the other, the damsel-in-distress, if she survives, is a lady no more.

I took a pencil of my own from my backpack and lifted the towel. Though I'd braced myself I still shuddered. Lucy's eyes were wide open, but nobody was home.

"You okay?" asked a voice from below.

"She's okay, Chief. Let her do her job."

"But she looks like—Susan, are you okay?"

"I'm fine." After clearing my throat, I asked, "Who found her?"

"DeShields is talking to them now."

I glanced around for Mickey Dee, and the beach tilted to one side. I gripped the stand tighter.

"J.D., I think—"

"Chase is tough enough to handle this. If she wasn't, SLED wouldn't've hired her."

Greave leaned over. "Are you, Susan? It gets worse."

Repositioning my feet on the spongy seat of the four-wheeler brought the world back into focus. "Anything special about this thing?"

"Agent Chase is referring to the shovel in the groin," said Greave for the benefit of the recorder. "As to your question, nothing at all. The shovel could've been purchased anywhere along the Grand Strand. There's no blood on it, though I'm sure Vickers will find contusions when he examines the body." When I didn't comment or question him further, Greave asked, "Time to bag the towel, then the hands and feet?"

"Er—yes." The coroner and the chief of police were being quite generous. Only last year I'd been in their faces about the sorry job they were doing protecting young women from predators along the Grand Strand.

"I'm going to lift off the towel," Greave said. "Is that okay with you?"

I stared at him. Certainly I could lift a towel off a dead person's head, even if the dead person had been a friend of mine.

"You might want to hold on, because you of all people will know what this means."

"Would you stop babying her and move along?" demanded Warden from below us.

Greave lifted the towel and I saw where Lucy's earlobes had been ripped off. Her lobes and earrings, if she'd worn any, were gone. I gulped and gripped the chair. Greave was right. This was not a good sign.

The towel was from the Host of Kings Hotel; the logo was stitched in one end. Warden noted this in his notebook. Jennings did not. His forensics unit had already recorded all the particulars. Yet if the new gal was to be effective, she had to be shown the ropes. But this new gal was on the ropes, gripping the stand and not giving a damn if she smeared any latent prints.

Greave slid the towel into a paper bag. Paper was preferred to plastic. You never know how evidence will react with polyethylene. "Clean and fresh. I can still smell the softener," he said after a sniff.

Greave handed the bag to Teddy Ingles, who took it, glanced at me, and then trotted over to the forensics people in the mobile crime unit.

Somewhere clean and fresh. That's where I should be, not—

"Chase! I want to talk to you!"

The voice startled me. I teetered, then lost my balance and fell off the four-wheeler. Knowing I was going to hit hard, I threw out an arm to break my fall.

Not good enough. The sand was packed solid from a long winter's night, not like dug-up stuff on volleyball courts. I landed on my side and had the wind knocked out of me. My pack slid off my shoulder and pain shot up my side. I wondered if I'd broken anything and how that might impact my job. Immediately, Jennings was beside me, taking me by the shoulders and righting me.

"Are you okay?" The chief brushed down my very short skirt.

"I . . . think so."

The idiot who had yelled at me was Paul Friddle, huffing and puffing his way across the raised walkway. Lt. Warden stared at Friddle, Chief Jennings held me upright, and Mickey Dee looked over from where he was interviewing the person who had found Lucy Leslie. Retirees stared from the dune, patrolmen's and tech's mouths fell open, and me? I was totally pissed. When I tried to get to my feet, Jennings said he thought I should remain on the ground for a moment. I disagreed and made my position clear, expletives not deleted.

As Friddle came under the crime scene tape, I snatched up my pack, brushed off some sand, and kicked off my flats. "Would you give me a hand back up?"

"Are you sure?"

I slung my pack over my shoulder. "Chief, I'm not your daughter, or anyone else's for that matter."

"Yeah," he said with a reluctant smile. "I guess you're not."

With his help I returned to the seat of the four-wheeler, and that's where I was when Paul Friddle reached the base of the lifeguard stand.

"Chase! Don't go back up there!"

Come up and get me, you fat bastard!

From the other side of Lucy, Albert Greave smiled. "Don't know about you, Susan. One day you're blowing away the bad guys, the next day you're tripping over your own feet."

"Thanks for that vote of confidence, Albert. Now shall we get back to work?"

Friddle stood below me, tie askew, red-faced. "I had an appointment with you." In my peripheral vision I saw his dark-haired partner crossing the walkway.

Greave handed me a clean pair of latex gloves. "Anything else you want to check before we take down the body—say, the mouth?"

I stared at him as I ripped off the soiled gloves and slipped into the new ones. Examine Lucy's mouth?

"Chase? Are you listening to me?"

Once the new gloves were on I squeezed open Lucy's mouth and found . . . a whistle.

Hmm. Right about now I was feeling pretty shitty about some of the things I'd said about the Horry County Police Department. Below us, the conversation continued full tilt.

"Friddle, you'll talk with Chase when she's finished with her examination."

"J.D., don't give me any of your big city lip. I was handling rogue cops before you ever hit the Grand Strand. I can handle Chase."

"If I allow you to do so."

"Are you saying you won't allow me to interview her? Am I going to need more people from internal affairs here?"

"Don't be silly, Paul."

"Then why don't you want me talking to Chase?"

"For cripe's sake, she's working a crime scene. Go get a cup of coffee or something. She'll be in the office later this afternoon."

"I don't have time . . . I need to . . . ."

Something hit the ground behind me.

I turned around to see the female agent bent over her partner, who lay flat on his back.

"Paul?"

The woman shook him, then slapped his face. That didn't bother the fat man. He was out of it.

The woman looked up. "J.D., get the medics! They're on the other side of the dune." She felt Friddle's neck with her fingers and didn't like what she found. "Paul!" The woman grabbed him by the shoulders and shook him. "Paul, stay with me!" She slapped the fat man's face, then thumped his chest. His eyes opened but didn't focus all that well. "Paul, stay with me!"

Jennings ordered Tooney to find the paramedics, and on the double, then knelt beside the unconscious man, loosening his tie, then his belt. I thought I saw Friddle's chest rise and fall. I couldn't be sure. Neither was his partner. She had started mouth-to-mouth.

Ugh!

Rushing across the walkway with a stretcher and a medical bag came the paramedics, one male, the other female. Retirees scattered left and right as the techs broke through the yellow tape, obliterating the footprints inside the crime scene.

"What else you got up there, Chase?" asked my boss.

"A whistle. In Lucy's mouth."

"A whistle?"

"Right," said Jennings, moving out of the way of the techs. "Standard issue lifeguard model. Probably from where it hung around the rearview mirror in the car. There was a worn spot on the top of the mirror stud."

Below us, a stretcher was quickly laid out beside Paul Friddle, and when the techs went to lift him, the female agent snatched a stethoscope off a paramedic's neck and hooked herself up.

"Hey! You can't do that!" But the tech's hands were full with Paul Friddle.

The female agent ripped open her partner's shirt and put the stethoscope to his chest. This was way too much for me. Earl Tackett lay in a hospital close to death. Now this fat guy was on his way, and just yesterday I'd killed two dealers.

"You okay?" asked Greave.

"I'm—I'm okay."

"You're white as a sheet, Susan. Climb down before you fall down."

"I'll be . . . I'll be okay."

Teddy Ingles was staring at me. Hell, Teddy Ingles was always staring at me.

"Susan, if you don't climb down I'm going to come over there and pull you down myself."

Nodding, I let myself down to the seat of the four-wheeler as the female agent told the paramedics to get their asses into gear. DeShields appeared at my side, taking my hands into his black ones. He put an arm around me and held me tight and upright. My ears roared. My stomach was doing flips. If it wasn't for Mickey I might've fallen on my face.

Again.

"What happened?" asked Mickey.

"Delayed reaction I guess . . . to falling off the stand. I shouldn't've rushed back up there."

Mickey asked me to put my head between my legs. When I wouldn't, he forced me.

"What?" Warden asked Greave.

"We need to get the body down. Susan can finish her examination at the hospital."

Don't count on it.

When I looked up I saw the stretcher's wheels stuck in the sand. Somebody hadn't been thinking. Or someone had been pushing too hard. Friddle was strapped down, oxygen mask over his face, eyes closed. The male tech told his partner they would need help moving Friddle. Jennings conscripted Tooney and Ingles, and the four of them each took an end of the stretcher.

"There's a body bag under the stand," said the female tech.

The bag under the stand was open and sand had gotten into it. "I want a new bag."

"Don't know that we got one." The female tech moved away with her end of the load.

"If you don't have a new bag and a sterile sheet, then don't move the body."

"Susan," Jennings said, "you're going to have a problem with you-know-who if you don't get that body off the beach."

I threw off Mickey's hands and sat up. "I don't give a damn what the Chamber thinks. I don't want her contaminated."

The female paramedic groused that she had better things to do than make sure the dead received better treatment than the dying. Over his shoulder Teddy Ingles stared at me as he moved toward the ramp over the dune.

"Miss Chase has made a request of your department," called out Chief Jennings to the paramedics, "and you will cooperate with her."

If the tech heard him, she didn't reply. Gawkers on the walkway scattered as the four of them hustled the stretcher across the walkway and into the parking lot.

Mickey took my arm as I slid off the four-wheeler. The other arm was taken by the female agent from SLED, Friddle's partner.

"I have to go now," said the dark-haired woman, "but I'll make sure you get what you need. I'm sure the forensics lab has a new bag, if the EMS doesn't."

I stared at her. "I know you."

"From the Justice Academy. I'm Theresa Hardy. I lectured you about interrogation techniques."

"Thanks . . . thanks for your help."

The woman glanced at Lucy. "I told Paul not to come here, but we do need to know when we can interview you."

"This afternoon, I guess, like J.D. said."

"And make sure you get something to eat—okay?" She squeezed my arm, then followed the stretcher across the walkway and into the parking lot.

Warden came around the stand to face me. "Chase, will you be able to finish your examination?"

"She needs a moment, J.D.," Mickey said.

"She's got about as long as it takes to get that new bag down here. Why do you want another bag?"

"I don't want Lucy contaminated."

"She's not 'Lucy' any more. You wouldn't happen to want a new bag because she was a friend of yours, would you?"

"At Quantico we were warned about using old bags on high-profile cases."

"And this is a high-profile case because . . . ?"

"Because Lucy, I mean, the victim was posed nude in a public place and her body was mutilated for souvenirs."

Warden nodded to DeShields. "She's okay. Now get back to work."

Mickey glanced at me before returning to his witness. I tried to smile but didn't quite pull it off.

"Take a moment to gather your thoughts, Chase. Make sure you learn whatever the Horry County Police want you to understand about what happened here."

I nodded.

From atop his four-wheeler, Albert Greave asked, "J.D., are you designating this a serial killing?"

"Chase?" asked my boss.

"It has all the signs."

Warden nodded. "Just make sure no one refers to it in those terms."

5

"**A**nything else you need?" asked Eddie Tooney, breaking into my thoughts. "We're closing up here."

I was examining the lifeguard stand. At a normal crime scene, the tape might stay up several days, but this was the beach—the number two moneymaker in the state—and it would have to come down. Besides, how much integrity can evidence retain when weather can get at it?

His two left feet aside, Eddie was a pretty neat guy. He'd survived a broken home and a pair of disinterested parents to make something of himself. He'd been on track to become a Horry County detective before stopping by a girlfriend's house where the single mom was having trouble making her brat go to school. When Eddie arrived, the mother had already left, telling her daughter she'd called the cops. Eddie put the girl in his squad car and took her to school. A few days later, a rape charge was filed against Eddie, the mother backing up the daughter, though there was no sign of forcible entry. Eddie's life was now on hold once again.

"You have anything to add?" I asked.

Tooney shook his head. "Seeing the blue in both legs told me all I needed to know. I called the chief."

"And I told him to stay out of the crime scene," Jennings said, rejoining us. The chief gave Eddie a hard look, then added, "and to keep all civilians away."

Over the chief's shoulder, I saw three reporters on the far side of the tape. I returned my attention to the lifeguard stand. The stand had no markings other than the usual:

"Rent here" and the universal symbol for the Red Cross. The stand was your usual wooden model, painted outdoor latex white, with arms and a tube for an umbrella, if you used one. Most guards don't, until we realize we're darker than anyone on the beach and it's only First Week.

Where'd this thing come from? Someone must've dragged it over from a hotel, but there were no marks in the sand. High tide had obliterated that. Come a storm and out to sea this baby would go.

I scanned the beach again. Maybe the ghost crabs had seen something. They'd been staying out of our way, as we had theirs, while making their pilgrimages to the sea. The ghost crab seems to be going through an evolutionary change from a sea creature to a land one. Several times a day, it has to return to the water to wet its gills.

I looked toward North Myrtle. No motels or hotels in that direction, just houses, and all closed for the winter. One had a plumber's van parked outside, another had a crew laying a new roof. Both groups would have to be interviewed and all houses searched. No problem. Realtors or neighbors would have the keys. People don't like to have a house at the beach if there isn't someone around to occasionally check on it.

"Chief," I asked, "could you have the stand watched until we get the proper equipment to haul it away?"

"There's a truck on the way."

"Excellent."

Jennings knew this could become a possible tourist attraction—of the wrong type. He, too, was staring at the stand. "I always thought they should be marked so we'd know where they belonged. The county commissioners couldn't come up with the money."

Warden joined us, asking the chief if he could furnish some patrolmen for a house-to-house search. It wouldn't be the first time houses along the beach had been broken into and lived in during the off-season. After all, that's where I'd hidden from Social Services until turning sixteen. I suggested we post someone at Lucy's place until we had a chance to search there.

Jennings shook his head. "Dispatch couldn't come up with an address in any of our directories."

"Tell them to drive out the parking lot of the Hudson House and across the Boulevard. Lucy's place is in the attic of the two-story house at the end of the street. They don't have to go upstairs, just keep anyone from using the stairs. It's the only way up."

"Is SLED taking over this investigation?" asked Jennings with a smile.

I looked at Warden, who nodded. I said, "I'm sure forensics has advised you of the possible implications of Lucy's murder."

The chief nodded. "I was there when you presented your material about serial killers to my people." He told Eddie Tooney to gather the manpower needed for the house-to-house.

Mickey DeShields returned. He was told by Warden to coordinate our efforts with Eddie Tooney. Before Mickey left, he glanced at the reporters standing outside the crime scene.

"Show time, Susan."

Warden snorted. "Not likely."

"J.D.," said the chief, "let's see what we can do to keep this thing under control."

I accompanied the two men to the edge of the yellow tape, where recorders, microphones, and cameras were thrust into my face. This was payback for my not being made available after the shooting yesterday. DeShields had hustled me away from the Sunnydale, and today the reporters were armed for bear. A young man from the *Sun News* was there. He wore glasses, a short-sleeved shirt, and clip-on tie, and was flanked by a blonde from the local TV station and her clone from Charlotte. Each female was dressed in a skirt and blouse and looked anorexic. Their cameramen were stubby and scruffy-looking. Neither had shaved in several days.

"Congratulations on your promotion, Susan," said the reporter for the local TV station.

"Er—thank you, Heather."

"Promotion?" asked her clone from Charlotte. "What promotion?"

Color Me A Killer

My boss explained. "Ms. Chase just graduated from the Criminal Justice Academy in Columbia. She'll be handling this investigation, under the supervision of Chief Jennings and myself."

"How can that be?" asked the young man from the *Sun News*. "She shot two people yesterday."

"Are there any other questions?" asked Warden.

"Wasn't Susan responsible for a SLED agent being hospitalized during that shoot-out?" continued the young man.

"Earl Tackett is a sergeant on the Myrtle Beach Police Force, and thank you for asking about his condition."

"I know who he is and what his condition is," chimed in the Wicked Witch from the North, meaning Charlotte, "but I want to know who the EMS hauled away, and I don't mean the dead girl."

Warden filled them in on who Paul Friddle was and why he was at the beach. He spelled the name after the witch mistakenly heard it as "Fiddle."

"Was it something Susan said that set Friddle off?" asked the local blonde.

Jeez, thanks, Heather.

"Lieutenant Friddle was taken to the hospital for observation. Please don't mention this in your stories."

"Lieutenant, are you telling us what to report and what not to report?" asked the young man.

"Actually, I'm hoping someone in your news organization has a father over fifty who is not in very good shape."

"Does Agent Friddle represent the condition of all SLED investigators?" asked the witch.

"Next question, please."

The print reporter thought I might say something for the record and stuck his recorder in my face.

Think again, Bozo. He wanted to know how I felt about blowing away the two bad guys. Was that all that was on anyone's mind? Evidently so. Lights, questions, and cameras bore down on me.

"Please remember Ms. Chase was hired to work undercover. Splashing her face across TV screens or your newspaper could put not only her work but also her life in jeopardy."

"Let's move down here," suggested Jennings, motioning the reporters and cameramen away. "And for those who can't understand how important Ms. Chase might be to the solving of crimes along the Grand Strand, I'll inform your managers."

"Is that a threat?"

"Take it any way you wish, Ms. Jackson."

The Charlotte cameraman had followed Jennings. This sparked a reaction from the Wicked Witch of the North. "What are you doing, Bob?"

"I'm not putting any cop's life in jeopardy."

"You have no right to edit my stories."

The young man shrugged. "You want to interview the cops or what?"

"I may want to interview Ms. Chase."

"And I'd like to get something I can send in before noon. How about giving me some help here."

Heather Jackson stuck her microphone in Warden's face. Not wanting to be left out, the witch stepped over and did the same. Mickey DeShields walked up from behind, giving me something to lean into.

"What do you have here, Chief?" asked Heather.

"A dead woman on a lifeguard stand."

"Was she murdered?"

"We'll have that determination later today."

Which meant after the evening news, maybe tomorrow, as reservations for summer vacations were being made even as we spoke.

"The victim was found naked and on a lifeguard stand. Do you think that's significant?"

"It's against the law to spend the night on the beach," interjected Chief Jennings. "At every access point there's a sign—"

"Do you have a name?"

"Not until the next of kin is notified."

"When will that be?"

Jennings only gave her an icy stare.

"Why was she on the stand?"

"We have no idea."

"Think it was a drug-related death?"

He shrugged.

"Why is Susan back on the street when she should be on administrative leave?" asked Heather.

"Ms. Jackson," said my boss, "as you know we have very few deaths along the Grand Strand so I have to take any opportunity to teach a new person the ropes. That's all that's happening here, and I hope you don't make any more of it than it is."

"Is Susan giving interviews about the men she killed yesterday?" asked the young man from the paper.

"I hope not," I said and shivered.

"And why is that?" asked the witch from Charlotte. Her microphone swung around, but her camera did not.

"That's in the past and I'd rather leave it there."

"Susan," said Heather, stepping toward me, "you're no longer a private eye. You're a public servant and have to answer to the people."

"Only if SLED makes me."

"Once again," chimed in Warden, "I remind you that Ms. Chase works undercover, and pursuing her can only hinder her work. Ms. Chase has abilities SLED would like to capitalize on."

"Which one?" asked the young man from the *Sun News*. "The ability to kill people?"

I glared at the bastard.

"Understand this, people," said Warden. "I'm going to do whatever I can to discourage you from making Ms. Chase a public person. I have a responsibility to my department and her future."

"Then you'll need help from Susan for that."

I started for the bastard, but Mickey held me back.

"What else do you have on the victim?" asked the reporter from Charlotte.

Jennings said, "I can't comment until the coroner's report is filed."

"Lieutenant," asked Heather, "isn't it true you have Susan at this crime scene because she just completed a stint at the FBI Sex Crimes unit in Quantico?"

"Actually," I said, clearing my throat, as Special Agent Jamison Foxx instructs his pupils to say, "it's called the Behavioral Science and Investigative Support Unit."

Everyone looked at me, but only the guy from the *Sun News* wrote down anything, and he asked me to repeat the name of the unit. I did.

My boss tried to spin what I had said. "Which means Ms. Chase studied more than sex crimes at Quantico."

"Why was she picked to go to Quantico in the first place?" asked the male reporter. "Certainly there are others more qualified."

"Please," said Jennings, "that's all we have."

"And keep Ms. Chase out of this," Warden said.

"But she killed two people. How can we do that?"

"By keeping in mind that she's just another investigator in matters pertaining to this case."

Pretty good, I wanted to say. But left unsaid was the fact we might have a serial killer operating along the Grand Strand. And, as Jamison Foxx had also taught me, while it's often a good idea to withhold crucial information about a case, the FBI always favors working with the press when it comes to serial killings.

On our way out of there, Warden stopped by the forensics unit and told them how much he appreciated their assistance. The technicians appeared too stunned to speak. And someone was there who wanted to speak to me, but I brushed him off.

Driving out of the parking lot, Warden asked, "Who was that guy?"

"Bob Yale. He used to work for the *Tribune* in Chicago. Nowadays he writes true crime novels."

From the back seat, DeShields laughed. "Another Yankee retired to the beach, J.D."

Warden grunted. He was turning Bob Yale over in his

mind, a middle-aged guy who'd worn a maroon windbreaker and Cubs baseball cap. Yale's black hair was slicked back and his goatee matched. Neither ever grayed.

"Why'd you want to know?" I asked.

"I remember reading that serial killers occasionally watch law enforcement personnel do their work. Some even try to help with the investigation."

"Bob's no serial killer. That's not his MO." I shifted around in the front seat to face him. "Don't you think we should've alerted the press?"

"Think again, Chase."

"But if we—"

"Will this develop the case or is this more speculation on your part?"

I took a breath and let it out. "If this is a serial killer, he's a pleasure seeker."

"What do you mean by 'pleasure seeker'?" asked Mickey from the back seat.

"It's hard to believe some guy believes he should rid the world of lifeguards, or thinks God gave him such a mission in life."

"They hear voices?"

"Some do."

"But why is this a serial killing?" asked Mickey.

"Because of the mutilation and the towel left over the victim's face. Many serial killers can't look their victims in the eye. And she was stripped naked and a whistle left in her mouth. Possibly the killer's signature."

"Not to mention the shovel."

"I wasn't going to mention the shovel."

"No kidding."

Warden stopped for the light at Kings Highway. "It could be nothing more than an angry boyfriend. Did Horry County have anything?"

"Tooney checked," DeShields said. "No stalkers or peepers on record and Leslie hadn't filed any complaints or asked for any restraining orders."

"NCIC?"

"Nothing there."

The NCIC was for open warrants. "Why should there be?" I asked. "Lucy was no criminal."

Warden was staring at me when the light changed. He turned south on Kings Highway.

Fingering his own earring, DeShields said, "I didn't know earrings could tear the ear like that. You know, when they're jerked out."

"They can't, and since there were no threads around the ears, as there were around the neck, a pair of pliers must've been used."

After expelling a breath, Mickey said, "I'm impressed, Susan. You really learned a lot while you were at Quantico."

"It doesn't take much of this stuff to impress any woman."

A few minutes later we drove into a wide and deep parking lot of a restaurant along Restaurant Row. My stomach tightened as the car crossed the blacktop and parked near a wide, gray-colored clapboard building with an oversized fishing captain perpetually beckoning passersby inside. The oversized captain smiled as if he was sure we'd enjoy ourselves inside. I wasn't so sure.

The Captain's Feast was an all-you-can-eat place with a lunch menu. No more than a dozen cars were in the parking lot, but a month from now you wouldn't be able to get in the joint. By then, the locals would've moved on to out-of-the-way places tourists can only dream about.

Inside, booths lined both walls, picnic benches filled the open space, and halfway down the open space was the seafood bar, currently empty. Against the back wall and between doors leading to the kitchen was the salad bar. Two waitresses moved about the cavernous room taking orders and Lucy's uncle greeted us at the door, menus in his hand.

I bit my lip. Mr. Leslie was a rugged-looking guy in his fifties with very little neck, having once boxed light heavyweight. He served as his own bouncer.

"Good to see you again, Susan. Been a while." He glanced at my companions. "Three for lunch?"

"George, I have some bad—"

Warden's hand clamped down on my arm and I glanced at him.

"Mr. Leslie, you may not know it, but Ms. Chase has recently joined the South Carolina Law Enforcement Division." Warden gestured at Mickey. "Sergeant DeShields is also a SLED investigator."

DeShields shook Leslie's hand. Warden had to release my arm for me to be able to do so.

Trying to regain my professionalism, I asked, "Do you have some place we can talk?"

Leslie glanced at the door. "I am by myself today."

"Perhaps someone in the back could take over the seating—like Kenneth?"

"Kenneth? I had to fire him. He was stealing."

"Just tell me where you want them," said Mickey, taking the menus from the older man's hand. "Every kid growing up along the Grand Strand learns how to seat customers."

"Susan, what's this all about? Are you in trouble with the authorities again? I've warned you about who you hang out with."

"It's not that, George. We just need to ask you a few questions." Without the menus, George was free for me to steer over to the nearest booth.

"Is this a training exercise?" he asked my boss.

"No, sir." Warden took a seat in the booth alongside me. I had to slide over.

"George, I need to ask you a few questions." I took out my pad and opened it.

"Questions about what?"

"Have there been any threats on your family?"

"Threats?" He scanned the empty building. DeShields was showing a couple to a picnic table near the salad bar. "Not during the off-season."

"During the Season?"

"What can I say?" he said with a shrug. "This place seats over five hundred and you can't please everyone. The worst they've done is report me to the Better Business Bureau or throw rocks through the windows."

"Seen anyone hanging around, someone who didn't belong?"

"I would've run them off if I had."

"So, neither you nor Lucy has been pestered?"

"Lucy? I don't think so. My wife neither. She takes a gun everywhere she goes." He glanced at Warden. "She has a permit." He shrugged again. "The children—none of them wanted to be in the business. But you know all this, Susan."

"What I don't know is if anyone was pestering Lucy. Had you heard of anyone bothering her?"

"Lucy? Nah." His face brightened. "Oh, maybe that new boyfriend. I didn't take any lip off him."

"And who would that be?"

"Rex Kilgore."

"The basketball player?" asked Warden.

"Not much of a player since he injured his knee."

"Would Kilgore be the new boyfriend Lucy mentioned on my answering machine?" Out of the corner of my eye, I saw Warden turn his attention to me.

"I guess so." Leslie looked at Warden and back to me again. "What's this all about anyway?"

We told him, and that's why my boss had almost broken my arm upon entering the place. Except for telling us that his niece had last night off and was going shopping, George wasn't much use to us after hearing the news.

As I moved to the other side of the booth to console him, I noticed Eddie Tooney coming through the swinging doors leading from the kitchen. In his hand was an evidence bag. DeShields watched as the patrolman crossed the room and joined us at the booth. Inside the bag was a set of girl's clothing, presumably Lucy's, and presumably from last night. Tooney said he had found them in a dumpster behind the restaurant.

6

At the restaurant, my boss graciously took the evidence bag and asked Tooney to post himself at the rear of the building until the crime lab could check out the dumpster. Driving down Kings Highway, it was another story. Over a cell phone, Warden asked, "Chief, did you assign Eddie Tooney to this case?"

When Warden received a negative reply, he explained the reason for the call. Jennings told Warden he'd have the crime lab people immediately dispatched to the rear of the Captain's Feast and he would speak with Eddie Tooney about overstepping his bounds.

"Chief, I'm not saying I don't appreciate the help, I just want to know when and where it's coming from."

After Warden hung up, he said, "Jennings says he hasn't been able to stop Tooney from pulling stunts like this ever since his name was withdrawn from consideration as a Horry County detective."

"Eddie's had it kind of rough lately, J.D."

Warden dismissed my concerns with a question. "Do you know this basketball player Rex Kilgore?"

"There aren't many along the Grand Strand who don't."

"How well do *you* know him?"

"He's a kid in a man's body."

"Don't shrink him. Just give me facts. From what I read, Kilgore is large enough to fit the profile of our killer."

"He has the hands, too. He can palm the ball easily."

"And if I remember correctly, he was tossed from a couple

of games for losing his temper, right?"

"I was at a party where Rex hit a girl in the face with a beer bottle."

"Jesus," muttered Mickey from the back seat.

"Had to have her jaw wired shut for over a month. She lost four teeth and twenty pounds."

"And Kilgore?"

"Got off scot-free."

Instead of heading for the morgue housed in Grand Strand Regional, we continued toward intensive care.

"Where we going?" Like I didn't know.

"To check on Paul Friddle."

So DeShields and I waited outside intensive care while Warden went inside and spoke with Theresa Hardy.

Nurses hurried by, relatives waited for word on loved ones, and down the hall in my direction came a priest. I shuddered and wrapped my arms around myself.

"You okay?" asked Mickey.

"A little cold. You know how these hospitals are."

"Lucy got to you?"

"Maybe."

"I remember what it was like the first time it was someone I knew. When you're at the academy, you never think it'll be one of your friends lying on that slab."

I acknowledged the approaching priest with a nod.

"And this on the heels of yesterday."

I watched the priest go by. Perhaps, it was time—

"Susan?"

"What?" I asked, startled.

"Sure nothing's bothering you?"

"I'm fine."

"What'd the shrink say?"

"That I was supposed to be upset that I'd blown away those two scumbags."

"Susan, you are supposed to be upset."

"Mickey, it was them or me!"

People stared at us through the open door of the waiting

room: children curiously, adults with frowns. Mickey took my arm and moved me down the hallway.

"You felt nothing?" he asked, lowering his voice.

"I felt a sense of relief, and that's just what I told the shrink."

"Relief?"

"Mickey, I've been through this with the shrink. Do I have to go through it with you?"

"I doubt your shrink's the only one who's asked."

"You're right. Besides you there was Harry and Chad."

"Maybe you'd like to get a cup of coffee?"

Warden came out of intensive care, looked up and down the hall, and started our way.

"Mickey, the last thing I need to do is to rehash this thing again."

"Okay. If you're sure."

"Chase, are you all right?" asked Warden, striding toward us.

"Of course."

"You don't look it."

"I'm—I'm fine."

"Good—because this afternoon you have an appointment with Theresa Hardy. At three. In my office."

I glanced at my watch and saw it was already one. That wasn't all I saw. My hands shook. I whipped them behind my back. "I'll be there."

"See that you are."

We went around the corner to the elevator—where Warden punched the button for the wrong floor.

"Where we headed now?"

"To check on Earl Tackett."

"But I was there this morning."

"So was I, but I'm here again and I might not get back anytime soon."

When the doors opened we stepped on the elevator and rode to the third floor, where the two men preceded me off the elevator and down the hall.

"Er—J.D., I'm not sure I can do this."

They stopped and looked at me.

"I—I mean, I'm not sure I can take it . . . the prognosis isn't good."

"Earl Tackett was your partner. It may've been for only one bust, but you owe it to him."

And with that Warden tromped off, DeShields trailing along behind. When Mickey caught up with Warden, he leaned over and said something I didn't hear. I hurried to catch up with them.

Without turning around, Warden asked, "Anything you want to talk about, Chase?"

"No, no. I'm fine."

"You sure?"

"I'm sure."

Warden glanced at DeShields as they continued down the hall. "What's with her?"

"Yesterday, but she won't admit it."

Doris Tackett sat beside her husband in one of those hospital chairs with a thick-cushioned bottom and back. Her husband lay under a single sheet with an IV plugged into his arm. Earl's head was bound with gauze, his eyes were closed, and his arms lay alongside him outside the sheet. Under the sheet Earl's chest rose and fell, but that was the only movement.

"Mrs. Tackett," asked Warden, through the open door, "may we come in?"

"Please do."

Doris Tackett stood up. She was a thin woman wearing a pale dress covered with small flowers. A gold cross hung around her neck. Her hands were small, her face thin; she had reddish-blond hair, which she pulled back in a long ponytail. At the foot of the bed sat another woman with the same long hair and a similar dress and gold cross. Both women smiled as we filed into the room.

DeShields nodded "Good afternoon" and I mumbled something. I don't remember what.

"How are you holding up?" asked my boss.

"Pretty well. The kids are in school. Ruth is looking after them." She glanced at DeShields and me. "It's so nice of you to stop by again."

"We were in the neighborhood. You never know when we'll get another chance. You know police work."

"I certainly do. Susan, I want you to know our family is beholden to you for saving Earl's life. I didn't get a chance to tell you this morning. There were so many people."

Suddenly, I felt hot in this very cold building. Its walls bore down on me.

Doris took my hands. "You mustn't blame yourself for what happened. Our family believes there should be order in the world." Mrs. Tackett didn't let go of my hands until she'd led all of us into the hallway. There I could breathe again. Even more so when she let go of my hands.

"Good to see him out of intensive care," Mickey said.

"The bad news is he's still in a coma. The doctor says we have to give it time. And pray." She glanced through the door at the woman at the foot of her husband's bed. "The preacher's stopped by. His wife—that's her—said she'd stay a while. She has small children and they're in school."

Through the open door we saw the preacher's wife open her Bible. Her lips began to move, but we couldn't hear what was being said.

"Mrs. Tackett," asked Mickey, "do you need anyone to stay with Earl? Wives of policemen up and down the Grand Strand would be happy to help out, and they, like many of their husbands, work different shifts and can be here anytime you need them."

"I appreciate the offer, but the church has already set up a schedule."

"I'll . . . ." I cleared my throat. "I'll take a shift and let you get away for a while."

"No, no, Susan. My sister's coming this afternoon. She works the third. We're okay for right now."

"All you have to do is ask," Warden said. "Your husband was part of SLED when this happened. That makes him part of our family and we're concerned about him."

"I don't want you worrying about this. Earl would want you to be doing your job. But you could pray for . . . ." She saw someone behind us.

The teenager wore a tank top and you could see her bra straps underneath the yellow top. Black capri pants and sandals. The chain around the girl's neck was one of those "What Would Jesus Do?" You know, initials that look like an East Coast radio station: WWJD. The teenager was a younger version of Doris Tackett, the same narrow face and reddish-blond hair, not clasped like her mother's but scrunched. And too much makeup. Way too much makeup.

"Ruth, is something wrong?" asked her mother.

The girl backed down the hallway, an invitation for her mother to follow. When Doris did, Mickey lowered his voice and asked, "Who's that?"

"Ruth. Earl's oldest."

Mickey glanced in the room where the Bible-reading preacher's wife sat. "Amazing she's dressed that way."

"What's wrong with it? I used to dress like that."

"Yes," said Mickey with a grin and a glance at my schoolmarm outfit, "before we rescued you from that life."

"Are you going to rescue Ruth from lifeguarding? She starts next month."

"She doesn't look old enough."

"Neither was I."

"I'd better see if I can help out." Mickey walked over to where the mother/daughter duo were huddled together, talking. Why he felt he needed to help out, I have no clue, but Mickey's a family man.

Warden looked in the room where the woman read the Bible. "Feel any responsibility for that?"

"You feel responsible, don't you?"

"I'm responsible for everything."

"Then I wouldn't want your job."

"Well, that's something you won't have to worry about until you grow up."

The teenager made it clear she wasn't staying. Her mother tried to convince the girl otherwise but made little headway, then asked where her daughter had gotten those clothes.

Mickey halted their quarreling with, "Why aren't you in school, Ruth?"

"I don't have to be there all the time. I'm a senior." Adding that, she looked right at me before stalking off.

"What was that all about?" asked Warden, catching Ruth's look.

"I have no idea."

"Chase, one of these days you're going to have to learn to tell the truth."

"I do tell the truth."

"Your version, perhaps."

On one side of the narrow room serving as the mini-morgue were three half-doors leading to the refrigerator. On the opposite side was a small lab where a young woman worked as Albert Greave looked over her shoulder. In the middle of the room, on a stainless steel table, lay Lucy Leslie. Naked, and more violated than when she'd been found on the beach.

I followed him over to the stainless steel table. DeShields was in the hallway collecting messages over a pay phone. Lucy lay on her back, arms along her sides. Reddish water ran down troughs on either side, emptying into a drain at her feet. Her pubic hair was black and lightly sown, her eyes closed, and her chest open from an incision from shoulders to sternum to pelvis. Oh, yeah, and there was a toy shovel jammed in her vagina.

Over the surgeon's head hung a sound-activated microphone. Slightly stooped, Benjamin Vickers wore scrubs, a plastic face shield, and latex gloves. The gloves were covered with blood. Behind him stood Teddy Ingles. As I approached the table, Teddy glanced at Lucy, then looked at me. The room reeked of disinfectant, death, and perversion. On the wall hung a clipboard with Lucy's weight and other measurements; on a stainless steel table that swung out within Vickers' reach were hair, samples of anything found under Lucy's nails, and enough bodily fluids to activate a drug panel. I assumed the panel was being studied by the female technician in the smaller room.

Out of the corner of my eye, I realized my boss was staring at me. "Are you going to lead this investigation or not?"

"Who is this?" asked Benjamin Vickers, gesturing at me with a bloody scalpel.

"Generation next," said I, stepping up to the plate.

"Lieutenant, who is this girl?"

My boss sighed. "Susan Chase. The newest member of our team. Ms. Chase is a graduate of the Justice Academy and the Sex Crimes Unit at Quantico."

"Actually, the Behavioral Science and Investigative Support Unit." At the sound of my voice, Teddy Ingles stepped back, and little by little disappeared into the background. Neat trick for a guy the size of Teddy. Or perhaps the trick had been performed by a mere girl.

Coroner Greave strolled out of the lab, Coke in one hand, ham sandwich in the other. "I'll vouch for her, Benjamin. And Lucy was killed shortly after supper. Hamburger and fries. She had a late meal." Behind him, on the other side of the glass wall, the lab tech worked with test tubes, tumblers, and other paraphernalia of death.

Benjamin Vickers was staring at me. "You're the girl who killed those two drug dealers. You shot one through the heart, killed him with a single bullet. Was there good reason to empty your clip into the other man and rip his torso apart?"

"Seemed like the thing to do at the time."

"Do we know anything about the lifeguard stand?" asked Greave.

DeShields came through the door with that answer. "Had a call from a civilian who says we stole his stand. A roofing contractor turned us in."

Everyone stared at the black man.

"Says he bought it from the city and has the receipt to prove it."

"What's a citizen doing owning a lifeguard stand?" asked Warden.

"Sits in it when his kids swim in the ocean."

"Why's that?" asked Greave.

"So he can watch for sharks."

"Have his children been attacked?" asked Warden.

"Has he ever seen a fin?" asked Greave.

"People," asked Vickers from the other side of the table, "can we continue?"

"And the guard who was supposed to be posted at Lucy's apartment?" I asked.

DeShields nodded. "He's there."

"Have the patrolmen been assembled for the house-to-house search?" asked Warden.

"Anslow and Austin are doing that as we speak."

"Stay on it. I want those houses searched before dark, and where they find evidence of someone living where they shouldn't be, post surveillance."

"Will do."

"Anything on Rex Kilgore?" I asked.

"An APB is out on him."

"The basketball player?" asked Greave. "What's he have to do with this?"

"Tell you later," Warden said.

After Mickey disappeared through the double doors, I asked, "Any reason why DeShields is using a land line instead of a cell phone?"

"Figure it out, Chase."

"You know," said the surgeon, "I'm not the ME. I donate my time to the county for the work I do here."

"Shows where your heart is, Doc." I realized my friend no longer had one, nor any lungs. My hand came up. I gulped and turned away.

Vickers sighed, and loud enough to activate the microphone overhead. "When the deceased was placed in the stand she had been dead at least an hour, killed perhaps as early as ten o'clock last night. Time of death is determined by the temperature of the liver, Miss Chase. But this woman was outside, off the ground, and in a breeze from the ocean, so that makes the time of death rather iffy. Still, ten o'clock is my best guess."

Something else rather iffy was whether I could keep down my breakfast. I faced him again. Greave continued to chomp on his sandwich and drink his soft drink. There's one in every morgue.

"But for the torn earlobes there were no postmortem injuries," continued Vickers, "except where the arms and legs were bent to conform to the stand, and no defensive wounds. This girl was asphyxiated, and Nicole found no drugs in her system." He gestured at the stainless steel table which swung out toward him and held all the sample scrapings, strands of hair, etcetera. "All this will be sent to SLED for further examination."

"And the whistle?" I asked.

"Since there was no visible damage to the jaw, that can only mean the whistle was placed in the victim's mouth within minutes following her death, possibly while the killer waited for his chance to dispose of the body."

And people thought I was cold.

"Still, there is little difference in sitting in a car versus a lifeguard stand." Gesturing at the body, Vickers added, "I found nothing unusual in the victim's mouth but threads from a pair of work gloves, which I assume the killer wore when he placed the whistle in her mouth. No threads were found on either side of the victim's head. Something was used to rip the lobes off, pliers, perhaps. Nicole found metal filings in the samples of the ears. She's searching for those same threads in the hair samples I took from the top of the victim's head."

I gripped the edge of the table to stand.

Warden referred to his notes. "Jennings thinks the whistle was the victim's. Footprints found at the scene were size fourteen and army issue. The killer might've been former military or purchased them at an army/navy store. DeShields will check that. He'll also alert Sumter Air Force Base, informing them what size person we're looking for."

Vickers shook his head. "I cannot agree with the size of the man."

We all looked at him, especially Albert Greave.

"He may have large feet," said the doctor, "but he did not have the hands to match."

"He wore gloves." When Vickers looked at me, I released my grip on the table.

"Yes, Miss Chase, but there was an overlap on the thumbs—in the fabric. In other words, the gloves were larger than necessary for the hands that killed this young lady."

"A big man with small hands?"

"Perhaps."

Warden flipped pages in his notebook. "No tools found at the scene, no weapons, no nothing, certainly no pliers. No wallet, purse, or jewelry. ID made from her license plate."

From my pack, I took another paper bag with a soiled Kleenex I'd found while wandering away from the crime scene. For a short while this morning, everyone had given me space, and I was happy they had, until I noticed the laughing gulls picking at something in the sea oats. A soiled tissue.

"This could be anyone's—any guy who jerked off or blew his nose. I found it about twenty yards from the crime scene."

"Give it to Nicole," said Vickers, holding up his blood-stained gloves. "I have my hands full."

"So did this guy—at least one of them for a short while."

In the lab I turned the evidence bag over to a young woman I used to bump into every once in a while growing up along the Grand Strand. Nicole wore a white lab coat over a tee shirt and jeans, and she wrinkled her nose at what I'd found. "They get off on this? You'd think the murder would be enough."

"It's a guy thing."

She placed the bag on a table covered with paperwork, racked test tubes, and specimen jars. "You gonna catch this bastard?"

"If he hangs around—yes."

"That shovel . . . I told Vickers he could have as much of that as he wanted, but I'd be in here." She glanced through the glass at the men standing around Lucy. "I think it's a conspiracy."

"You do? By who?"

"Who you think? All the rapes, muggings, serial killings . . . men letting us know the world still belongs to them. Especially at night." She shook her head. "It's not right what happened to Lucy. I mean, she didn't have much going for her . . . locked into waiting on tables. Some of us can never make the break from all those tax-free tips." And by the way she said it, I knew this woman had once made that break.

I rejoined the enemy—where I noticed the shovel had been removed from my friend's vagina. Thank you, Dr. Vickers. That hadn't been something I'd been looking forward to. The shovel, too, would be forwarded to SLED's forensic lab in the capital, as would the Kleenex I had found. On Lucy's left leg was her only tattoo: a chain looped around her ankle with a dog tag that read "Daddy."

Vickers was bent over Lucy, probing between the legs, using a swab to collect more fluids.

"Was she raped?"

"No," said Vickers without looking up.

"The shovel was just jammed inside her?"

"Yes, but not very far."

"It didn't have to be to make its point. J.D., we need to get moving before this bastard strikes again."

"Again?" asked Vickers, straightening up and staring at me.

"Chase, I'll remind you that it takes more than one dead girl to have a serial killer."

"Yes, but if we work quickly we might stop him before he acquires the proper status."

7

On my way to the Host of Kings Hotel I stopped by a bar and tossed down a couple of quick ones. It was either that or St. Andrews, which served Catholics at the northern end of the Strand. Sitting on a stool, nibbling peanuts, and staring into the mirror, I saw a young woman of the same general age, size, and hair color as Lucy Leslie, but on an entirely different path in life.

Oh really? You were almost killed yesterday in a shoot-out with drug dealers.

I downed the remainder of my drink and used the john. Cardinal rule of detecting: always take advantage of the facilities. You never know what the next facilities will be like or if there'll even be any, especially if you're a gal.

I came out of the rest room straightening my skirt, blouse, and hose—jeez, I hated this outfit!—and the bartender had a question for me.

"Is it true what I heard about Lucy?"

"What's that, Jimmy?"

"That she was found dead. On the beach."

"Where'd you hear that?"

Jimmy was a stocky guy who had worked at this hole-in-the-wall bar since turning twenty-one, even before then. He gestured at a TV mounted on the wall. *Days of Our Lives* was on, which ran after the noon news. "Heather had the story," he explained.

"I'm afraid so."

"Lucy was here last week. Hard to believe she's dead. Never seen you in here this early. Was it Lucy?"

"Nah. Can't get used to working normal hours. Er—who was she with?"

"Lots of people. You know Lucy. Life of the party. Never met a stranger."

"Date and time?"

Jimmy could see I was serious and told me what he remembered.

"I heard she had a new boyfriend."

"Yeah. Rex Kilgore. They got into an argument. After Rex slapped her, I told them to take it outside. Rex gave me some lip, but he finally left." Jimmy pulled a sawed-off baseball bat from under the bar. "I don't put up with any shit." He slid the weapon away. "You think Rex could've killed her?"

"Who said someone killed her?"

He gestured at another TV. "The blonde from Charlotte—the one who reports from here."

Thanks, Wicked Witch of the North. "Jimmy, you don't know if Lucy had gone past using, do you?"

He wiped away an imaginary spot with a handy cloth.

Returning to my stool, I said, "I need your help."

A long silence, then a tight little nod.

"Who?"

He stopped wiping. "Susan, I really don't want to get involved."

"The bastard might've killed her."

"Not this one. He's all talk."

"Who, Jimmy, who?"

"Kenny Mashburn. Comes in here pedaling his shit. I throw his ass out."

I knew Mashburn. Our paths had crossed before. Now they would cross again.

Several princes and one president had actually stayed at the Host of Kings Hotel. They'd been there on deep-sea fishing expeditions. The Host of Kings had been rebuilt twice, once just a few years ago. It was a modern structure with plenty of glass, height, and a humongous parking garage occupying a city block across the street.

To the disdain of the bellboy, I left my jeep at the front entrance and carried the evidence bag containing the towel into the lobby. Greave had okayed me bringing it along. There was a cellophane side to this particular bag. The bag was stapled across the top, and you could see the Host of Kings logo on the towel through the cellophane window. The towel had been the first thing Nicole had gone over with the proverbial fine-toothed comb. Almost brand new, she said, and that meant someone in laundry or receiving might be our man. Or any of the hotel's guests in the past few weeks.

The lobby was an oversized sunroom complete with gold fixtures, a marble floor, and glass elevators climbing the walls. Flora hung from ledges, the lobby was visibly warmer, there was more moisture in the air, and in the rear, an archway led to the pool and beach. To one side of the lobby was a long, highly polished wooden counter, behind which stood three employees wearing the hotel's colors: federal blue with gold trim, matching jacket, tie, and name tags. The nearest one was "Eric," and Eric's hair was parted down the middle and combed to the sides, even over his forehead. He had been staring at me from the moment I'd come through the glass doors.

"You're Susan Chase." Eric spoke with a British accent.

"Yes," I said, pleased to be recognized.

He picked up the phone. "I'll call security."

"Pardon me?"

"Nothing personal. I thought it rather hilarious you chasing that naked girl through the lobby. I was a bellboy at the time."

Reaching over the counter's low wall, I put a finger on the telephone's bar, cutting him off. "That won't be necessary."

"But I've been instructed . . . ."

I flipped open my ID. Up and down the counter, members of the staff stared. One of the gals I knew from long nights at The Attic dancehall turned away, avoiding eye contact.

Behind me a voice asked, "Susan?"

Turning around, I faced Alan Putnam, which meant the

Chamber wasn't standing still with a potential serial killer loose along the Grand Strand.

He glanced around the lobby. "The boss isn't going to like it if she sees you."

"You work here?"

Now I saw the gold-trimmed tag. It said Alan was an assistant manager. Then I noticed he wore the same tie as Eric, but Alan was in short sleeves, with those strong, tanned arms of his.

He took my arm, turning me toward the front door. "You'd better leave."

We moved several steps before I could plant my feet and shake him off. "Alan, I asked you a question." In his free hand was a sheaf of computer printouts.

We had stopped near a pool filled with Christmas, star, and boat orchids growing on flat rocks or from the hollows of a fake stump. Sunlight streamed through the glass walls and struck the strategically placed pool. Around us, the heat and humidity rose considerably.

"Susan, I'm only trying to—"

"Alan, you weren't working here when I chased that girl through the lobby."

He was looking at what I held in my hand. "What do you have in that sack?"

When he reached for the bag, I knocked his hand away. If Alan had any failing, he was totally self-absorbed, and I know a thing or two about self-centeredness.

"One of your towels is inside."

"Where'd you get it?"

A golfing foursome came through the front doors, loud talk and even louder clothes; clothes chosen by their wives, talk generated by being away from said wives.

"Alan, you have somewhere we can talk?" *Who says I can't be discreet?*

"Why?"

I pulled my SLED ID from my pack as the golfers passed by. *And who says I will.*

Alan pushed away the ID. "For God's sake, put that away."

The golfers stared at us, but hey, it could've been the sight of Susan Chase wearing hose.

Alan took my arm and directed me toward the arch leading to the beach. "Call me if you need anything."

"Yes, sir," said Eric from behind the desk.

We went down a hallway that was the backside of a row of shops overlooking the pool. Through the marble arch, I saw the beach and a pool protected by glass walls. A breeze hit us as we passed by.

"When did you start working here?"

"You're the private eye. You figure it out."

"Oh, yeah. I remember. The Chamber didn't offer you the directorship." That had come as a surprise to those of us who knew Alan. When he was on his game, there was no better shill for the Grand Strand than Alan Putnam. "Some guy from Memphis is supposed to know Myrtle Beach better than you—I don't think so."

I've always looked up to Alan, not enough to sleep with him but enough to give it considerable thought. One time Alan talked me into auditioning for Medieval Times. I ended up waiting tables. Alan ended up on horseback and he'd never ridden before in his life.

He ushered me into an office, an improvement over his digs at the Chamber, the old Chamber, that is. This place had wall-to-wall carpet and two chairs with leather bottoms and backs in front of a fancy wooden desk. Behind the desk sat a high-backed chair. The only drawback was the glass wall. Anyone could see what you were up to. On the opposite wall hung photographs of Alan with every famous golfer who'd stroked a ball. Yes, Tiger Woods was there, along with every white guy who'd tried to beat him. Soon Alan would be wheeling and dealing from this office, just as he had at the Chamber, and having his pick of the female guests.

Alan lay the computer printouts on the desk before taking a seat. I placed the evidence bag on top of the stack. He was still drop-dead gorgeous: chiseled features, year-round tan, curly brown hair, and a six-foot frame. Long, delicate fingers, fluid movements, and the boy could dance.

Man oh man, could Alan Putnam dance.

"You and Rivers still an item?"

"Even more so. We're talking marriage."

"You're breaking my heart."

"Yeah, right. Like you ever put a move on me."

"I couldn't and now you're taken."

"What utter bullshit."

"Oh, right, I'm supposed to date the person who's done her best to set back the reputation of the Grand Strand?"

I laughed. "It appears you didn't have much of a career at the Chamber."

His feet went up on a corner of the desk. "Credentials count more than experience."

"Tell me about it," I said, leaning back in my chair. "I had to pass the GED before SLED would allow me to apply to the academy."

"I heard about the shootout yesterday. You're still hot shit."

"Those guys didn't give me any other choice."

"Yeah, right. Maybe it's better I didn't put a move on you. I've still got my balls." Putnam picked up the bag and peered through the cellophane. "What's this?"

"Alan, you know Lucy Leslie?"

"Yeah. Saw her last night."

"You did? Where?"

"At Hard Rock."

"What was she doing there?"

"What anyone does at Broadway—shopping." Broadway at the Beach not only had the shops but featured bridges, paddleboats, and restaurants; planes crashing into restaurants, boats bursting out of buildings, the whole nine yards. Across the road was Planet Hollywood, the NASCAR and All-Star Cafés.

"Did you see who Lucy was with?"

"She wasn't with anyone." His feet came off the desk. "What's with all the questions?"

"Lucy's dead, Alan, and that towel was found at the crime scene."

Putnam looked like he'd been kicked in the chest. The bag slipped out of his hand and landed on the stack of printouts. "That's . . . that's impossible."

I scooted to the edge of my chair. "Why?"

"No—I mean . . . I don't think Lucy was with anyone. I was crossing the parking lot when I saw her." He cleared his throat. "If you want a tee shirt you have to get there early—before the Season starts—or stand in line forever."

"You wanted a tee shirt from Hard Rock Café?"

"My sister . . . in Tennessee. She doesn't want to stand in line."

"So let her kids do the standing."

"Susan, I don't think my sister wants her kids anywhere near Hard Rock or Planet Hollywood. She home-schools."

"And Lucy?"

"What do you mean?"

"What'd you talk about? Anything the two of you said might help us find her killer."

"I can tell you one thing. Lucy wasn't looking forward to the Season. She couldn't lifeguard anymore."

"Marvin Valente said she's on the list."

He shrugged. "Lucy had sun poisoning. Came down with it at the end of last Season."

That was the death sentence for any lifeguard. You can spend your life on the beach, then one day you learn you should've used a higher number sunblock. "What was Lucy planning on doing for money?"

Putnam was staring at the evidence bag as if it held the remains of our mutual friend. "What? Oh, wait tables. She figured she could make a thousand a week during the Season if she didn't report anything, then see if she could go back to lifeguarding the following year. She was only kidding herself. Sun poisoning is forever."

"You two got down to the nitty-gritty in the parking lot of the Hard Rock?"

"You don't believe me?"

"You're a hustler, Alan. I think you talked with her some-where else, had a drink somewhere, might've seen something I need to know."

Putnam tried to say something, but I raised my hand.

"Sorry, Alan. Nothing personal. As mine does me, your reputation precedes you."

"You're damned right. No one else would ask me these questions."

"I guess that's why SLED hired me."

"Oh, I thought it was to wipe out all the drug dealers along the Grand Strand."

For that, he only got daggers.

"Okay, okay. What do you want to know?"

"Did you try to hustle her?"

"Susan, I don't think—"

"Alan, I really don't care what you think. You going to help me or not?"

"I'm . . . going to help."

"Good. So where did you talk?"

"In the parking lot, like I said."

"The whole time?"

"Susan, we weren't there long."

A pair of green cards walked down the hallway and glanced into the office. I sat back in my chair. Alan did the same.

Once the Mexicans disappeared, I asked, "Did you see which way she went when you left?"

"She went into Broadway. I don't know where. Probably a shoe store. You know as well as I do that Lucy had a thing about shoes."

"And you?"

"I was in and out of Hard Rock in a flash."

"Was her car still there when you left?"

"Sure."

"You know her car?"

"It's a gray Nissan. Lucy and I dated a while. What? Am I a suspect?"

"I wouldn't let SLED know you'd been lovers."

He leaned forward on the desk. "But I didn't have any reason to kill her. How was she killed, anyway?"

"SLED hasn't released that information."

"Hey, I'm not likely to tell anyone. Remember who I used to work for?"

I pointed at the paper sack. "All you need to know is one of your towels was found at the crime scene."

He peered through the cellophane window in the paper sack again.

"I'm going to need a list of all your male employees and customers. I'd like the customer list, going back a full month."

"This will not be good for business."

"It has to be done."

"But does it have to be done here?"

"Yes, and I'm starting with you."

"But I wasn't the last one to see her!"

"What do you mean?"

"The person who killed her, that's who saw her last."

Taking out my notebook, I asked, "For the record, when did you see her—before Hard Rock?"

"What?" He waved this off. "Oh, I can't remember."

"Don't worry," I said, leaning back in my chair again. "I've got all day."

"Susan, this isn't fair. You may have all day, but I'm still on probation."

"Your tag says you're assistant manager."

"You're damn right, and if I don't screw up, six months from now they might make it permanent."

"I repeat: Where did you last see Lucy?"

"Oh, hell." He sunk back into his chair. "Let me think . . . ." His face brightened. "I remember! It was at Kroger's."

I looked up from my pad. "When, Alan, when?"

He shifted around in his chair. "This is crazy. What reason would I have for killing Lucy?"

"Alan, could you possibly stop thinking about yourself and consider that what you know might help me find Lucy's killer?" That didn't seem to reach him, so I added, "Come on, help me out here. When did you see her in Kroger's?"

"It was . . . it was last month. She was in the . . . ." He stopped to think. "She was in the wine and beer section."

"The date and time?"

He checked his calendar. "It would've been a Wednesday, and since I pull the late shift Wednesdays, it would've been after midnight." He gave me a date.

"What were you doing at Kroger's?"

"What was I doing at Kroger's? What do you mean 'what was I doing?' Like was I stalking her, is that what you mean?"

"I'm just asking." I tapped my notebook. "To complete my report."

"This isn't right." His chair moved around as if it had a life of its own. "I'd never hurt Lucy."

"What were you doing at Kroger's, Alan?"

"What does anyone do at Kroger's? I was buying groceries. I wasn't buying wine like Lucy. That was why we broke up. Lucy was always meeting guys, having a drink, and listening to their bullshit, being impressed by what they told her, about wines, cars, clothes, anything, then comparing what she'd heard to what I told her. I didn't like it: being compared to college guys. Lucy would . . . ." He gulped. "Oh, shit!"

"What is it?"

He stared at the desktop. When he looked up, his face was strained. "Lucy asked if I had any passes to see Janet Jackson at the Palace. I had to admit I'd lost my job and didn't have any freebies."

"I thought you were passed over."

"I was. 'Lost my job' was how Lucy put it. She said I didn't get the job because I didn't know anything. Can you believe that, and she's buying wine at Kroger's. But I didn't kill her, Susan, you've got to believe me."

"Then why not tell me what you two talked about?"

"Because . . . well, working at the Chamber, the minute there's the hint of smoke, you begin damage control."

"Was she with anyone?"

"No."

"Mention anyone she was currently impressed by."

"Rex Kilgore."

"Uh-huh. Where'd you go after leaving her at the Hard Rock?"

"I went home." His shoulders slumped. "Just home. I bought the tees and went home."

I knew Alan's address. The house fronted the Intracoastal

Waterway. "Anyone go home with you?"

"Susan, I haven't been very good company for the last few months."

I gestured at the room. "This wasn't enough?"

"Not when you wanted to run the Chamber of Commerce." He shrugged again. "At least here there's the chance of advancement. I wasn't going to make that mistake twice. Clarion's looking to pick us up." He glanced at the paper bag again. "What do I do now?"

"Go downtown and see Lieutenant Warden. Tell him what you've told me."

"You're not taking me in?"

"That'd be rather embarrassing, wouldn't it?"

"You're damn right."

"And I'm going to need the names of all your personnel and customers. I want males, Alan, and especially the names of any transients."

"I'll have to clear it with the boss."

I leaned back in my chair. "Give him a ring."

"This is better done in person, and it's a woman."

"Want me to tag along?"

"You'll have to," he said standing up. "No temporary assistant manager is going to be able to give you those names." He took his jacket off a rack built into the wall, and I retrieved the evidence bag. Slipping into the jacket, he asked, "You won't tell her about me having to go downtown?"

"Don't see any reason to."

"'Preciate that."

"Seen Rex Kilgore lately?"

He smiled as he opened the glass door leading into the hall. "If Rex Kilgore or Susan Chase are found on the premises, someone better call security or they'll wish they had."

I couldn't help but smile. "And what did Rex do to become so noteworthy?"

"Punched out Eddie Tooney when Eddie was trying to stop him from raping a guest."

"Eddie works here?"

"Part-time. His wife's trying to move the kids out of state.

Eddie needs money for lawyers."

We headed down the hall, past other offices with glass walls. "Did the woman press charges?"

"It wouldn't've been a good idea."

"Why's that?"

"If she didn't want anything to do with Kilgore, why'd she invite him up to her room?"

"Maybe she didn't."

"Sorry, but the waiter heard her ask Rex if he wanted to go upstairs. I swear sometimes you women ask for it."

We stopped at another glass-walled office where a woman worked at a computer. "Anything missing from the girl's room?" I asked.

"What do you mean?"

I shook the bag in his face. "Like towels, Alan. Towels."

"I'd have to check. But when you're dealing with attempted rape, you don't take a headcount of the towels." Before we went in to see his boss, he asked, "Is there anything you want to tell me about Lucy's death before I go downtown?"

"The less you know, the better."

"I just thought—"

"Alan, I'm not going to coach you."

The woman noticed us outside her door and motioned us inside.

"Susan, I didn't mean—"

"I know what you meant and I'll need the name and phone number of your sister."

"Why?"

"The tee shirts, remember? The tees."

He shook his head. "I can't believe you're doing this, rousting your friends."

"This is business. I'm only sorry private-eyeing didn't pay better so I could've stayed independent."

"Uh-huh. I imagine most of your friends would have preferred that, too."

8

Lucy lived in an A-shaped apartment on the beach, but not overlooking the beach. Her place was the attic of a two-story house her uncle had tried to rent out but never could. A stairway had been slapped on the side of the house and a hole bored through the side, probably violating several building codes. I'd been there. You know, on girls' night out. We'd watch TV, gossip, scream, do each other's nails. Okay, so I'm beyond that, but Lucy was still there. Probably why I hadn't returned her calls.

Parked in the crushed shell area in front of the house was Mickey DeShields' sports car and a sedan from the county police. Mickey was nowhere to be seen, but two homicide detectives were leaning against their cars, smoking cigarettes, and waiting for someone. That someone turned out to be me. Funny. I hadn't told anyone I was coming over here.

"Chase," said the taller of the two, Anslow, "we want inside that apartment."

"Who said you can't go in?"

"Chief Jennings," said the shorter man, Austin. Both men wore suits and had beer guts. "The Season's about to begin and we need to close this case."

"Yeah," said Anslow, "it's just another homicide."

Remembering how Warden had told me to play this, I said, "I'm not so sure."

Austin rolled off the sedan and flipped away his cigarette. "I'm supposed to believe there's a serial killer on the loose so you can be somebody special."

"No," I said, heading for the outside stairway. "You're supposed to take this serious because a young woman was murdered."

"Just another whore, from what I can see."

Austin laughed. "Which one you talking about?"

I faced them again before going up the stairway. "Why don't you guys go get a cup of coffee and come back, say, when your attitude improves about women."

"You can afford to wait that long?"

They both laughed, got into their sedan, and drove away. I shook my head, then climbed the stairs, knowing what I would find, and hoping DeShields hadn't already found it.

The converted attic ran the length of the building, and you had to watch it or you'd hit your head. There were no walls. It was all ceiling, and the triangular living area was filled with odd pieces of furniture scrounged from here and there: sofa, chaise lounge, and card table. In the narrow space on either side of the triangular shaft were rows of shoes. Lucy was into shoes big time.

The only other room, if you want to call it that, was a bedroom at the rear of the triangle shaft. To give the bedroom a bit of privacy, a curtain hung from a wire across a space where Lucy and I had nailed cut sheets of right-angle plywood between four-by-sixes on both sides.

"Susan," Lucy had asked, looking up from the floor where she steadied her end of a four-by-six. "How do you know how to do all this stuff?"

I knelt on top of Lucy's dresser, tapping around with my hammer, trying to locate the joist. Lucy hadn't been happy with where the wall would go. Placing her dresser at the end of the bed pushed the bedroom, if you wanted to call it that, into the party-end of the apartment. I'd had to explain that you couldn't just nail stuff into sheetrock and expect it to hold.

"You pick it up here and there." Sweat ran down my face. A warm spell in late October and all the heat had gathered in this frigging attic.

"Picked it up where?"

"When I thought I wanted to be a carpenter."

"All I've ever wanted to do was lifeguard."

"And all I've wanted was a better-paying job. Now, hold that beam steady. I'm ready to tackle the joist."

"I still don't like how the dresser sticks into the living room."

"We all have our crosses to bear."

"Of course," Lucy had said, wistfully, "it does give me more room for shoes."

Between the bedroom and the door was a fridge, then a card table with a hot plate, microwave, and toaster oven. Pinned to one of the inclined walls was a cluster of photographs, and hanging on posts were pots and pans along with an aluminum popcorn popper, the type that expanded when held over a stove's eye. The popcorn popper had been there for years, gathering dust, purchased before anyone realized the hot plate wasn't intense enough to pop corn.

Under the card table sat a TV, across the triangularly shaped room from a sofa with no legs. I'd knocked off the legs so the sofa could be shoved closer to the angled wall. Sitting that close gave the effect of watching a big screen TV. On one of the sofa's arms lay a portable phone, and on the slanted sheetrock ceiling under that arm, phone numbers had been scribbled.

DeShields noticed me in the doorway. Hard not to. Only one window, and it was behind the headboard of Lucy's bed and filled with a window-unit AC.

"What did you learn at the Host of Kings?"

I let the screened door flop shut behind me. "Alan Putnam gave me a list of employees and recent guests."

"Putnam? I thought he was with the Chamber."

"Passed over for some out-of-towner."

"I know the feeling." DeShields had been passed over in favor of J.D. Warden.

"I figured I'd run them. Might give me an edge."

DeShields had taken off his jacket and wore a pair of latex gloves. "Well, it's your case."

"Then why're you here?"

"If this *does* become a serial killing, you're going to have more people looking over your shoulder than you'd care to think about."

"It'd only take one to do that."

Mickey smiled as he returned to picking up, looking under, and putting down items on the card table: the hot plate, toaster oven, and microwave.

The apartment was pretty much the same as it'd been when I'd gone off to the academy: the curtain separating the bedroom from the living room area was pulled back, the bed unmade as always, and posters taped to the inclined wall. One was James Dean as he appeared on the postage stamp; the other, Kurt Cobain with a wreath around him in black magic marker. Cobain's death had brought me up short. I'd been running with a crowd that used.

"Alan told me he bumped into Lucy near Hard Rock last night." I filled Mickey in on the details.

"You told him to turn himself in?"

"It'll look better for Alan if he does it himself."

"And if he doesn't show?"

"Then we'll have a first-class suspect."

"I don't think J.D.'s going to like that."

"What've you found?" I asked, swinging my pack onto the sofa.

Mickey gestured at the pictures pinned to the inclined wall. "Putnam's in a couple of these. So is Kilgore. I hadn't remembered how huge that kid was."

I, too, was in several shots, and with eyes that come only from a lack of sleep, or too much booze, or something stronger. How in the world had this place held so many people?

"You know any of these?" asked DeShields.

After taking a seat on the sofa's arm, I ticked off names of the young men in the photographs with the use of a ballpoint pen. After that, I crossed off phone numbers I recognized. "This is her uncle's, this is his restaurant, this is Marvin Valente's, this an old boyfriend . . . ." I glanced at Mickey. "Please don't mention my name."

"Don't worry," he said with a laugh. "I don't have time to hear everyone's Susan Chase story."

After sticking out my tongue at him, I ID'd more numbers and DeShields wrote them down. There were three I didn't recognize, but one I did: my boyfriend's at the boat company owned by his father. What was up with that?

"Susan?"

"What?"

"Still with us?"

"Er—just trying to figure out who these last ones are."

"You mean there's someone up there you don't know?"

"Must be new to the area."

"Have to be," said Mickey with another smile.

I took a pair of gloves from my backpack, and Mickey watched as I searched the sofa. It was one of those with cushions you couldn't remove. Instead of running my fingers along the grooves, I used a wooden cooking spoon. No telling what might be in those cracks, ready to stick me. All I found was the remote for the TV. I laid it on the card table.

"You miss living like this?" DeShields had come to rest on the other arm of the sofa, the light through the door making it difficult to see him in the glare.

I returned the spoon to a nail on a load-bearing post. "My life hasn't changed all that much because I came to work with you guys."

"Lucy?"

That wasn't DeShields, but someone who had literally darkened the doorway. We both looked in that direction and saw a skinny kid standing on the landing outside the door. But not for long.

"Fucking cops!"

The thin form disappeared, thumping down the stairs and leaving the screened door open. I picked up my pack and slung it over my shoulder as I ran for the door. •

"Call this in, Mickey!" Outside, I grabbed the railing, taking the stairs two at a time.

"No—you call it in!" He came down beside me, almost knocking me over.

The kid was crossing the crushed shell parking lot. It appeared that he had no ride. It also appeared Anslow and Austin had taken my advice about that cup of coffee. They were long gone.

We tromped down the stairs side by side as the figure ran between Mickey's sports car and my old jeep. The kid was a thin thing, no taller than me, wearing jeans and some kind of hooded jacket, ends flapping in the wind. Mickey and I hit the ground at the same time. I landed on my flats, which caused me to slip, lose my balance, and end up on my ass. My pack stung me as I landed on top of it.

"Damn!"

Kicking off the remaining shoe that hadn't let go when I'd gone down, I leaped to my feet and headed across the parking lot. It wasn't the only thing I stripped off. As crushed shells bit into my stocking feet, I found the Velcroed top of my skirt and ripped it off, tossing the skirt in my jeep as I raced by. Mickey hollered for me to get in his car.

Nope. Wasn't going to do that. When pursuing a suspect, the most important thing was to maintain eye-to-ass contact.

A guy pulling groceries out of the trunk of a red Saturn gawked as I ran by. Under my skirt I wore white bicycle pants, but if my appearance was all that startling, maybe I'd best switch to a color more closely resembling the tear-away skirt.

The kid finished the short road from the beach, then raced across the Boulevard, not looking either way but running straight across, then down the side of the Hudson House. I crossed after him, ripping off the latex gloves when I remembered I still had them on. Ahead of me, the kid disappeared around the corner of the Hudson House where there would be a parking lot, and at this time of the year very few cars. Since I'd given up smoking before entering the justice academy, I felt terrific. I could run for hours, despite stares from a pair of retirees walking their poodle.

Jeez! Haven't you ever seen a gal out for an afternoon jog?

Rounding the corner of the building, I saw the kid

crossing the parking lot. There was an adjoining lot on the other side of a low row of hollies, and a guy in a business suit was right behind the kid. I dodged a woman sitting on the ground, crying. When I sprinted past the suit, he slowed down, thumping to a stop on the asphalt and gasping for breath.

My pack slapped my backside, encouraging me to end this and quick. There were other motivations. A pain in my left foot where I'd picked up a rock or piece of glass. Son of a bitch if I wasn't switching back to running shoes, and I didn't give a damn what SLED thought about it. Having a dress code for women chasing assholes—I don't think so.

Speaking of assholes, the punk had slowed down to twist his body through the hollies separating the two parking lots. When he glanced back, he tripped on a berm held together by railroad ties, then tumbled into the adjoining lot. He was scrambling to his feet when I leaped through the bushes and landed on the other side. Pain bit into my injured foot, but I was on him now. As the punk tried to get to his feet, I kicked him in the butt and sent him sprawling.

That hurt even more!

For sure I was going back to wearing running shoes, and the ones with the steel toes. "Stay down, punk! I've got a gun."

Oops! Hope nobody heard that. I was supposed to alert suspects to the fact that I was a law enforcement officer before threatening him with bodily harm.

He looked up from the asphalt. "You ain't got nothing!" The punk gathered his hands and knees under him for his next run.

I fought with my pack and found it hooked behind my back. As I fumbled for my weapon, the guy in the suit stepped through the hollies and stumbled over to the boy. Seeing the kid trying to get to his feet, he kicked him in the hip with one of his wing tips. The kid howled and went sprawling.

"Knock it off!" I shouted. "He's had enough!"

The kid lay on the asphalt, moaning.

"He's finished when I say he is!" said the suit.

Waving the Smith & Wesson in his face, I stopped him in

mid-kick. "Check on your woman! I'll handle this."

DeShields' sports car roared around the far side of the hotel and raced over to where we were. The man in the suit glanced at DeShields, who climbed out of his car holding his badge in one hand, his gun in the other. Smart move. Whatever else he was, Mickey was still a black man climbing out of a spiffy-looking car, and with a gun.

"You're right," said the man in the suit, catching his breath. "I need to check on my . . . er—wife." He returned through the hollies.

DeShields holstered his weapon. "You could've just as well used my car."

Instead of arguing, I pulled out a pair of cuffs and told the kid to stand up. But for the pain in my foot, I could've run another mile. I might never smoke again.

"Come on, punk, you know the drill. Hands behind your back."

"Why you doing this to me?" he asked as I cuffed him. "I ain't done nothing."

"Then why were you running?"

DeShields was staring at me. "Maybe you should put on the rest of your clothes."

I glanced at my bicycle pants and the ripped and torn panty hose.

"You'd run, too," said the punk, "if a half-naked woman was chasing you down the street." He saw me putting away my Smith & Wesson. "With a gun."

"I didn't have my gun out."

"But you were half naked."

"Your name, scumbag. What's your name?"

"Skip Vaughan. What's it to you?"

I grabbed a handful of tee shirt and pulled him over. "Lose the attitude, kid! I don't have the time and you don't have enough teeth."

"Er—Susan, why don't I take him downtown and you finish searching Lucy's apartment?"

I looked at Mickey and blinked. "Yeah. Okay." I let go of the tee, pushed the kid away, and started walking toward the bushes. Along the way I realized the hollies had scratched me up pretty good. Heat of battle and all that shit. Maybe I should've taken Mickey's car, after all.

"You find some money at Lucy's," shouted the kid, "it's mine."

"And any drugs belong to you, too."

Maids leaned over the railings of the Hudson House. I waved at one who gave me an "attaboy." These were the black women bussed in from adjoining counties who couldn't wait for the Season to begin. Sure, they'd work themselves to death and drag their asses home, but they'd be able to pay off those wintertime bills. I knew the feeling. Come each spring, I couldn't wait for that regular paycheck to begin. But those days were behind me. I was a SLED agent now. Shoeless, limping, and wearing nothing below the waist but bicycle pants and torn panty hose.

Returning to my jeep, I unlocked the footlocker welded to where the backseat should be, took out a pair of running shoes, and slipped them on. But only after ripping off what was left of my hose.

I cleaned the cut with hydrogen peroxide and slapped on a Band-Aid. A tiny piece of rock had found the only spot on my foot that wasn't callused. The scratches from the hollies I treated with Camphophenique. I velcroed the skirt around my waist to the stares of the couple in the ground floor apartment, then found my shoes and tossed them into the locker. No more flats for me. I didn't have a job like Theresa Hardy's.

Glancing at my watch, I saw it was almost three. I was supposed to be downtown. With Theresa Hardy.

From my pack I pulled a phone, hoping the battery was pumped up, and called the front desk of the Myrtle Beach Police Department. I asked the desk sergeant to relay the message to Hardy that I couldn't make our appointment.

"I'm not your secretary, Susan. Tell her yourself."

In the background I heard voices bitching. The Grand Strand was being cleaned up for the Season, and some of those jackasses weren't coming along peacefully.

"I'll put you through."

"No, no, Ernie. Please don't! You'd have to connect me through J.D.'s phone."

"Infighting at SLED? We could use more of that, then you won't be busy embarrassing us."

"I don't want to talk to anyone. I just got rid of DeShields."

"Oh, now I remember. You're the crack investigator who told Alan Putnam to turn himself in."

"Then you understand my problem."

"Yeah, and I'm dying to punch this little button in front of me."

"What you want? I'll do anything. Just don't put me through to J.D."

He thought for a moment. "I want another lesson for Karen. With summer coming on, her mother and I'll feel much better."

"I'll need a pool." I was Red Cross qualified.

"No sweat. All sorts of folks owe me favors."

"I can imagine. It's a deal." And not a bad one. Ernie's daughter was the kind of kid who made you want to have kids of your own. Hmmm. Perhaps I should bring Chad along, and if Chad came along, I'd wear my new bikini.

Inside Lucy's apartment, I switched on the AC, then peeled off my skirt and tossed it on the sofa. After turning on the TV and pulling on a new set of latex gloves, I went about the business of searching the apartment. And I didn't leave any shoe unturned. In a pair under the headboard, and only a reach away, was a cache of cocaine.

Lucy, *puhhhh-lease*. That is so obvious. I took the baggie into the bathroom and emptied it in the toilet. Let the cops think Lucy had a habit and she'd be dismissed as a slut and the investigation would go begging. Anslow and Austin were proof of that.

Coming out of the bathroom, I found Theresa Hardy waiting for me.

9

In one of Hardy's hands was a leather briefcase. In the other the wraparound skirt. "This peels off?"

"Er—yes."

Hardy gave the piece of clothing another look, then tossed it to me. By catching the skirt I was able to hide the crumpled-up baggie behind my back.

"I'd rather you wear it, if you don't mind."

I wrapped the piece of fabric around my waist, but only after shoving the baggie into the rear of my bicycle shorts.

"Ever think of wearing matching shorts?"

"Not until today I didn't."

"Think about it, if you want to continue wearing tear-away skirts."

Hardy noticed *General Hospital* on the screen under the card table, glanced at the legless sofa, and then pulled over a folding chair. At the next commercial break, she muted the sound.

"Do you remember Luke and Laura's wedding?"

"Only from flashbacks."

"What do you think?"

"I was hooked on *G.H.* before Luke told his son about how he was conceived."

She nodded. "That was in the days when rape was considered the culmination of foreplay. Thankfully, we've moved beyond that." She scanned the apartment. "What'd you find?"

"Not what I was looking for."

"And that was?"

Gesturing at the pictures pinned to the inclined wall, I said, "A connection between Lucy and one of the guys in those photographs. DeShields took down the names. He'll run them through the computer."

"But you did have time to go to the bathroom."

"Well, I did have to go."

"And you left the door open. Front door, too."

What did this woman want? Had she seen me flushing Lucy's stash down the toilet?

Hardy continued. "But a young woman who isn't embarrassed about ripping off her skirt in public wouldn't have any trouble using the toilet with the door open, would she?"

"Pardon me, Ms. Hardy, but why are you here?"

"We had an appointment, remember?"

"Didn't you get my message?"

"You didn't expect me to be put off by that?"

One can only hope.

"What was this about you asking a suspect to turn himself in?"

I shrugged. "Alan Putnam used to work for the Chamber. They're awfully sensitive about what people think." I took a seat on an arm of the sofa and tried to keep my knees together. For some reason, I had the urge for a cigarette, but it might've been the crumpled up baggie biting into my ass.

"And if he hadn't?"

"It would've finished me with SLED."

"You want that?"

"DeShields and I've already had this little talk. I was merely jumping ahead to the punch line."

She stared at me for the longest, then shifted around on the folding chair. Hardy wasn't fat, she was, well, built like me, with larger bones than most women care to have. Black hair hung down the sides of her face, cut in bangs across the front. She wore little makeup.

"Susan, nothing you did at the academy prepared us for what happened at the Sunnydale."

"I was told to be on my best behavior while in Columbia."

"Warden told you that?"

"He said I'd be on probation most of my career."

"Did you ask why?"

"Something to do with how I do the job." I patted the tear-away skirt, then raised my feet, showing her the running shoes. "These have steel toes."

Hardy leaned back in her chair and studied me. I gestured at the TV. *G.H.* had returned.

We watched until the next commercial break. Then she said, "I reviewed your record on the way down. Excellent class work for someone with only a GED. You also have above-average upper body strength, which is to be expected from a former lifeguard, but only an average rating on the firing range."

"I'm a snap shooter."

"Pardon?"

"Just fire and shoot. Aiming makes it hard to hit anything."

"And your explanation for such excellent classroom work?"

"Study, study, and more study."

"This was more than study. You displayed a grasp of law enforcement techniques someone with your background wouldn't generally have."

"I used to be a private eye."

She shook her head. "Private eyes usually cut corners and know only what'll keep *them* out of jail. Granted what Paul did was dumb, but I want some straight answers or my report will say that you're unreliable."

"You mean how I know stuff is important?"

"Everything is important when you're trying to build trust."

She stared at me until I finally admitted, "It was on the web."

"The web?"

"Cops-on-line. They told me what to expect. The games teachers played, what they were really trying to get at, you know, to make you think."

"That may be so, but you couldn't've been prepared for the sexual harassment. You *were* harassed at the academy, weren't you?"

Now I really did need a smoke. "Not that I remember."

From her briefcase Hardy pulled a folder. "By someone who did not work for SLED, who groped you in an elevator."

"Sure you've got the right gal?"

"That man is no longer an independent contractor with SLED."

I wanted to tell her how nice all this was, but I'd run off this morning without setting up my VCR and *GH* had returned. That didn't seem to matter. Hardy smelled blood in the water. Well, being a woman, maybe I should've come up with a better metaphor.

"Susan, why didn't you report this incident?"

"Nothing happened. Honest injun."

Hardy sighed. "Susan, you're part of a team. I'm part of that team. I'm also part of a generation who insisted certain changes be made. I'm not saying the changes made the men happy, but I don't generally worry about what men think. I wanted to be in law enforcement and I had little interest in moving around the country with the FBI." She glanced at the folder again. "The man who groped you had to be taken to the infirmary. Why is that?"

"He fell down."

Hardy leaned back in her chair and regarded me. With a finger, I gestured at the television screen.

"Susan," said Hardy, tapping the folder with the remote—after she'd turned off the TV—"this report says when the two of you were on an elevator, the outside expert patted you on the behind. During the follow-up investigation into his injuries, he said you asked him if you'd passed, as if being patted on the behind was part of SLED's selection process."

"I was only kidding."

"You were told to report any incident of harassment to the captain in charge. We have an open door policy at the academy. The captain's secretary isn't even allowed to ask what a young woman wants to talk about when she reports to that office."

"I imagine she can guess."

Hardy shook her head. "All female trainees are required

to visit his office weekly, whether they have a problem or not. The secretary doesn't have a clue as to what goes on in there, even though the door remains open. This incident in the elevator was never reported."

"I guess I forgot."

"I imagine you've also forgotten that when the elevator stopped and the doors opened, you exited, leaving this so-called expert lying on the floor."

Again I shrugged. "I guess it wasn't his floor."

Hardy studied me. "I'm not going to get anywhere with you on this, am I?"

"You mean me admitting that I broke your rules? I don't think so."

"Susan," said the woman, shifting around on the metal chair, "these are your rules, too. They were established long ago for your protection."

Straightening up on the sofa arm, I felt the baggie scratch my ass. "I don't need to be protected, Ms. Hardy. I've taken care of myself since I was fifteen."

"And I'm here to tell you that SLED has had rogue agents in the past and they always disgrace themselves and the State Law Enforcement Division."

"Then I'll try not to do anything real stupid."

"That's why I'm here."

"Oh, you're not the 'good cop.'"

"You'll have to forgive Paul. He hasn't been feeling well lately."

"He should lose some weight and exercise."

"I think he has problems at home."

"His problems, not mine."

Hardy let out a sigh. "After suffering through more sexism and racism than SLED would care to admit, we've finally become a family. Paul Friddle is as much a part of that family as you are."

"Agent Hardy, what's your point? Boys will be boys and I'm a girl."

"But you could be a tremendous role model. SLED needs tough young women who haven't allowed life to run them over." She shifted around on the chair again. "I also want to talk to you about what happened at the Sunnydale, but could we possibly talk somewhere a little more comfortable?"

"Sure," I said with a smile, "if you can wait until *General Hospital* is over."

Given enough time even I can figure out when to back off. Or make an overture. In the parking lot of T.G.I. Friday's, I asked Hardy if she'd like to have a home-cooked meal instead of something out of franchise heaven. She said she'd love to, and we drove to her motel where she changed into slacks and a blouse while I disposed of the baggie, instead of allowing it to carve me a new asshole.

I asked if she'd like to ride along, but she said "no," that she always liked to have a set of wheels at her disposal and not to take offense, that riding in a jeep looked like a lot of fun. So off we went down the bypass toward Murrells Inlet, then toward the Waterway to follow a sandy road to Wacca Wache Landing. Wacca Wache is Indian for "friendly waters." Maybe the Landing would work its magic on Theresa Hardy. I called Harry and gave him the skinny on who I was bringing home for dinner.

"What about Chad?"

"Haven't heard from him."

"Well, I'll certainly be pleased to meet your friend, Princess. There's more than enough food. Was Hardy the one sent from Columbia to question you?"

"Yes. I think she needs some home cooking."

"I understand."

"Good. We'll be there in a few minutes. While I change, you can entertain her."

"How'd it go today? You didn't look all that well when I saw you at McDonald's."

"It didn't get any better. Lucy Leslie was found dead on the beach between Myrtle and North Myrtle."

"My God! What happened?"

"Can't tell you over an unsecured line, but it wasn't pretty."

"I'm sorry to hear that. What are the funeral arrangements?"

"I suppose you could call Lucy's uncle."

"Perhaps Lucy's uncle thought this was bound to happen to someone—"

"Don't go there, Dads! Don't even think about it."

"Very well, my dear. I'll take care of the flowers and let you know the details of the funeral."

"It may be a week or so before they can release the body."

"That long?"

"I'll explain when I see you. Hardy knows all about Lucy's death. We can discuss it over dinner."

"Not at my table, you won't."

But dinner wasn't where the action was. That happened while I was showing Hardy around my father's former shrimp boat. Inside the pilothouse was a busy Pick. Dads had sent him over to make sure everything was shipshape. I appreciated that. Making up my bed has never been my strong suit.

Pick's a good-looking kid, blond hair, six feet tall. Mildly retarded, he earns a living picking up odd jobs around the marina; hence the name. Abused at home, Pick finally ran away. Evidently, there's a limit to the number of cigarettes you can snub out on someone's body. Cigarettes so turn off Pick, you either stop smoking while Pick does your odd job or find someone else. These days Pick lives in a shed off the landing where the boats are stored.

Hardy made the same complimentary noises anyone does about folks who live on the water: like it's totally awesome. I'm not so sure. Most of those people live in houses that don't leak, and they don't have to deal with scum in the shower, and other places.

The paneling was new, as was the flooring, so the interior didn't look so bad, but the same tired furniture sat in what used to be the boat's pilothouse, which I'd converted into a living room/bedroom. The galley and head were to the rear, and over the couch hung *Day's End*, a surrealistic painting marking the end of a relationship with a runaway who didn't want to be found, but desperately needed to be.

As I was ushering Hardy off the boat, Pick returned with

a clump of clothing, a pantsuit and top in a smear of colors: red and blue with a streak of yellow. The suit looked relatively new, but the label had been cut out. Having the label removed wasn't all that big a deal considering the Grand Strand is where many designers dump their overruns and irregulars. It's one thing to meet yourself coming down the street, another to learn the person paid one fourth—sometimes less!—what you paid for the same outfit.

Scratching Max the Wonder Dog behind the ear, I asked, "These are for me?" Evidently cleaning up my mess had reminded Pick that he had these clothes on hand.

"Yes, Susan."

"Where'd you find them?"

"Floating in the water."

We went on deck so I could hang them out. The clothes weren't wet, but they did smell. Even Max turned up his nose. Over the years the Intracoastal Waterway has become a home to folks who don't want to ride out the weather along the coast or pay the price of beachfront property. You can find homes that could grace the cover of *Southern Living*, even buildings that were part of the Old South. Back here, the water's calm, averages about nine feet in depth, and if you're of a mind, you can travel all the way to New York or as far south as Miami. All you need is a decent boat.

Pick didn't have such a boat, but he did spend a good bit of time in a skiff. He spent lots of time girl-watching. Actually, Pick didn't watch girls so much as he watched what boys did with those girls. That's what really interested him. At one time Pick asked me about my relationship with Chad, and soon I noticed him hanging around. I told him this wasn't going to cut it and for him to keep his distance.

After that, Pick spent a lot of time pretending to fish along the Waterway while guys and gals horsed around or became even more serious. One time he followed a couple into the woods and the guy beat the hell out of him. Another time, Pick was caught peeping and I had to cajole the powers-that-be to get the charges dropped.

You shouldn't be prosecuted for being retarded, I told

Warden. The man, not my boss at the time, said, "Ignorance of the law is no excuse."

Still, Warden spoke with the county police, who released Pick into my custody. I was told if he was ever caught peeping again, he'd do hard time. I passed the message along to Pick, who remained fascinated by the thing between his legs and what to do with it. I was afraid some girl was going to show him and that would really open a can of worms. So I taught him to whack off. Better than going to jail. Lots better.

As casually as possible, I asked, "Where'd you find the outfit, Pick, I mean where in the water?"

"Under the bridge."

"A girl hadn't just gotten out of them"—I glanced at Hardy—"swimming with her boyfriend like I sometimes do with Chad?" I felt a bit warm around the ears.

Pick's hands came up. "No, no, Susan, I didn't do that."

"Which bridge, Pick?"

"501." US 501 was the main drag into Myrtle and ran past the Pottery Warehouse, a notorious tourist trap.

Turning the clothing over in my hands, I said, "I guess it could've come from anywhere, the hotel along the waterway, off someone's clothesline. Thanks, Pick. I'll see if I can use them."

Hardy cleared her throat. "If you don't mind me asking, when did you find them?"

I stared at Hardy.

"Out fishing." Pick's face brightened. "Has Susan told you what a good fisherman I am?"

"Yes, she has." Hardy watched Pick return to his shed as I hung the clothes on a line running from the pilothouse to the stern. "Strange fellow," she said.

"Mildly retarded."

"Does he often bring you clothing?"

"No," I said, finding a bra and underpants in the stinky stuff. I tossed them over the side. "This is a first."

Max thought it was a game and went in after them. Now, if those obedience classes paid off, Max would shake himself off before returning to the boat.

Hardy glanced at the clothing pinned to the line. "Think those would fit the dead girl?"

"Not a chance. Eddie Tooney found Lucy's clothes in a dumpster behind her uncle's restaurant."

"Is he a suspect for Leslie's murder?"

"The uncle—nah."

"I meant Eddie Tooney."

Dinner should've been terrific, and it usually is at Dads', but Chad showed up and you could tell he was still ticked about the Sunnydale. Once my boyfriend learned Theresa Hardy had been a SLED agent for more than twenty years—and here I use the term "boyfriend" lightly—he pelted her with questions, finally taking her topside and leaving me to do the dishes.

Harry brought over more dishes to rinse and stack in the dishwasher. If we were aboard *Daddy's Girl*, Max would've taken care of the rinsing. "Seems like you solved your problem, Princess."

"That depends on what Hardy's telling him."

"I'm sure it's nothing but good."

"Yeah. Right."

"The only way to make someone trustworthy is to trust them."

I shook a wet finger at him. "You dare quote something like that to me?"

"Come on, Susan, it's impossible to go through life without trusting others. That's to imprison yourself in the worst cell—oneself."

"And who said that?"

"Graham Greene."

I gave him a blank look.

"He's one of the authors I've asked you to read."

"Are any of his books on DVD?"

A half hour later, the dishes were in the machine and Dads and I were fighting over the remote. I wanted to watch *Real World*, but Harry had a book for himself and, sad to say, one for me.

Color Me A Killer

Mine was by Graham Greene. The guy was a frigging novelist. In other words, what he wrote had nothing to do with real life, or everything, as Harry says. Some of my friends were ape-shit over romance novels, but I wasn't into that, and certainly nothing by Graham Greene. Still, I didn't want to go topside and check on Chad and Hardy, so I stuck my nose into the book.

Twenty-six minutes later, Hardy preceded Chad down the gangway. Well, the boy had always been a gentleman. He smiled, bent down, and gave me a peck on the cheek. "Dishes already done?"

"Chad, it's almost ten o'clock."

With a stretch, he said, "Guess I'd better be going. Big day tomorrow. Someone's coming to look at a new design."

"Me, too," said Hardy, yawning.

"Chad, you *are* going to walk me home, aren't you?"

"Sure, Suze. Just let me see Theresa to her car."

Theresa?

Hardy told Dads it had been a wonderful meal. Moments later, the bitch disappeared up the ladder with *my* boyfriend.

"What do you make of that?"

Harry had returned to his seat, book in hand. "What do you mean?"

Gesturing toward the ladder, I said, "What you think I'm talking about?"

"I thought they got along rather nicely."

All I could do was stare at the man. And fume.

"I'd think you'd be rather pleased to see Chad taking such an interest in your work."

"I'd rather him take an interest in me."

"Don't be silly. Chad only has eyes for you."

"And what table were you sitting at tonight?"

Dads closed his book, some tome about the intellectual history of the world. It would end up on my nightstand, if I didn't use it for ballast. He said, "I wouldn't be surprised if Ms. Hardy hasn't spent the night reassuring Chad about your job."

"If I appeared on his scope."

"All Chad thinks about is you. Can't you see that?"

I stood up, leaving Graham Greene behind. Someone had a gun for sale, but the people in the novel were so damn dense, especially the cops. The girl in the story was pretty sharp but about to take a fall. For her guy. Some stories never change.

"All I saw was my boyfriend taking an interest in someone sent here to interrogate me, then disappearing topside with her for the whole frigging evening."

Harry sighed long and hard. "And I thought after the academy, things would be different."

"Different? Different how?"

Chad returned, hair kicked up by the evening breeze. At least I hoped that's what'd mussed up his damned hair. He clapped his hands, then rubbed them together and smiled. "Well, Suze, ready to be walked home? The few steps that it is."

"Don't bother," I said, rushing past him up the gangway. "I need to get to bed early. Your new friend's going to grill hell out of me tomorrow."

10

When Max and I left for work the following morning, Lt. Warden was sitting in his sedan in the gravel parking lot of the landing. He was reading the *Sun News*. That reminded me I should subscribe to the paper—because of my job, not for the sales. You can't miss sales along the Grand Strand with all the billboards, radio ads, and banners. Not to mention stores using windows to an advantage probably unseen anywhere except in other beach towns.

"Have you eaten breakfast?" Warden glanced at the dog trailing along behind me as he folded his paper and laid it across the passenger seat.

"I don't eat breakfast."

"Today you do. Follow me."

I did, to a local pancake house on Kings Highway, where we received prompt, courteous service because the Season had yet to begin. Max the Wonder Dog was left in the jeep, looking rather forlorn.

The restaurant was an airy place, tables covered with red-and-white checked cloths, and its windows painted with a guarantee that this place offered the best pancakes along the Grand Strand. Warden ordered buckwheat cakes, sausage, and coffee. I hesitated. I really shouldn't be eating this close to the Season.

"Eggs and bacon for the young lady. Coffee. Black."

"How do you like your eggs?" asked the waitress.

"Actually, I don't—"

"Scramble them," ordered my boss.

So Warden had his pancakes and I got my eggs, and when they arrived, I stared at them. I couldn't remember the last time I'd eaten eggs.

"Eat up, Chase. I don't want you running out of energy today, especially when you're chasing perps without any clothes on."

"I have an explanation for that."

"I'm sure you do, but is that the way you want to build your reputation with SLED?"

"Did this come from Columbia? Theresa Hardy, perhaps?"

His answer was to take another bite of pancakes. He ate them like they *were* the best pancakes along the Grand Strand.

"Look, J.D., I can't catch bad guys if I have to wear a skirt and you don't want me in pants."

"Perhaps we should rethink the pants."

"Plenty of women wore pants at the academy."

"Eat your breakfast, Chase."

I picked up a piece of toast and nibbled it, then discovered the jam and fixed the toast properly. My stomach could tell the difference between toast and jelly and a Pop-Tart.

"I'm simply concerned with the image you project. That's why I asked you to wear skirts and blouses. I didn't ask you to wear a dress because—"

"As damn well you shouldn't've."

He put down his cup. "What was with this skirt you ripped off yesterday?"

"Wanna see?" I asked, scooting back from the table.

"Not particularly."

"Don't worry." I stood up. "I changed from white to blue." And with that I snatched off the tear-away skirt and did a pirouette that proved, indeed, I wore bicycle pants matching the skirt.

Warden's face turned beet red but his voice remained calm. "Would you put your clothes back on and sit down?"

I did, to the stares of customers and waitresses alike. Behind the register, an old guy took off his glasses and wiped them with the tail of his shirt.

"The navy blue was Hardy's suggestion," I said, scooting my chair under the table again.

"Let's skip the skirt for a moment—"

"Because I caught the perp."

"Don't let success go to your head."

"You'd rather me look ladylike than catch bad guys?"

"That question doesn't deserve an answer." He returned to his hotcakes. "Did you tell Alan Putnam to turn himself in?"

"I did."

"You didn't think it was necessary to accompany him to the law enforcement center?"

"I thought my time best utilized searching Lucy's apartment, and it was. I caught that kid."

"DeShields could've done that."

"Maybe."

"What'd you find?"

"No sign that Lucy had anything going with Putnam, that it was probably as Alan said. He'd run into her, chatted her up, and probably hit on her."

"Any sign of drugs?"

"Not that I saw."

"Then someone was there before DeShields."

I went rigid. "How do you know?"

"Leslie's rap sheet is filled with drug busts. We might get a lead from her supplier."

"But I . . . I found no drugs."

Now it was his turn to eye me. "Are you sure?"

"Check the place yourself."

"I did and found traces of cocaine in the toilet."

"What are you getting at, J.D.?"

"That's why the kid you ran down was at the apartment. Leslie was his supplier."

My arms folded across my chest. "Does this mean Lucy's death won't get the proper attention it deserves?"

He appeared puzzled. "What are you talking about?"

"Because Lucy was a slut and got what she deserved. The coke only proves it."

"I never said such a thing."

"That's okay," I said, leaning back in my chair. "I can read minds."

"Reading minds can get you into trouble. Stick to the facts." After a bite of his sausage, he asked, "She wasn't your supplier—when you two ran together?"

"I passed the drug test. I'm clean."

"Answer the question."

I sat up and pushed my chair away. "You think I ripped off Lucy's stash? Want to search my boat? Is that why you're here?"

"Calm down, Chase, and lower your voice. I'm not accusing you of anything."

"And I think you are."

"Pull your chair over here and listen to what I have to say."

I didn't move.

"Chase, that's an order!"

Reluctantly, I returned to the table but recrossed my arms as I faced him.

"If a young person doesn't receive the proper guidance while growing up, that person can end up taking a walk on the wild side."

"Meaning me?"

"I was speaking of myself."

"You were a bad guy?"

"I was in a gang before I straightened out. Nothing like what they have today, more like in *West Side Story*."

"What story?"

"Forget it."

Actually, the food didn't look all that bad. And the eggs were getting cold. Maybe I should eat a bite or two.

"You're a bright girl, certainly bright enough to do this job, but only if you learn to work within the system."

"I don't do drugs, and I didn't steal from Lucy so I could deal in my off-hours."

"But you agree that Leslie could've been this boy's supplier?"

I shrugged, then picked up my fork.

Warden pushed his plate out of the way and leaned on the table. "It only took a few hours in a jail cell with guys a lot tougher than Skip Vaughn before that kid was giving up everything and everybody he knew. Lucy Leslie was his supplier."

"I just can't believe it."

"I've done this longer than you and met all kinds of sleazeballs. Now my question is, and because of your reaction I think it's relevant, are you going to let your feelings impede this investigation?"

"They never have before."

Warden looked like he'd choked. He sat up quickly, face flushed, snatched his napkin, and coughed into it. After clearing his throat, he sipped from his coffee. Slowly, his face returned to normal.

"You okay?" I asked.

"Fine."

Looking from under my eyebrows, I asked, "You really think I get emotional about my cases?"

"As a private investigator those were the only cases you took."

I shrugged. "Maybe."

"I have the bodies to prove it. Now eat."

I forced down some eggs, then bacon. While I ate, Warden read my crime scene report.

"You need to be more specific in your measurements."

"I saw DeShields using the Rollatape and figured I'd cadge his numbers." The Rollatape looks like a golf club with a wheel and measures from Point A to Point B.

The look on my boss's face told me that was not the answer he expected. "Okay, okay, I'll go out there and measure again."

"Measure what? The stand is at forensics and the nearest fixed point is the wooden walkway over the dune, though how you can say you have a fixed point along any shoreline is beyond me."

"Then what do you want?"

Warden stared at me, silent.

"Okay, okay, I'll be more careful in the future."

"See?" he said, with absolutely no smile. "I said you were a bright girl."

The waitress was there to take away our plates and pour more coffee. She took Warden's, left mine.

"I had Putnam's place checked out."

"You did?"

"Some rich guy willed him a house along the Waterway because of all the work he did at the Chamber."

"And if that guy was still on the board, Alan might've been made director."

"Please don't speculate. Stick to the facts. Putnam has a boat, an outboard."

"As do lots of people along the Grand Strand."

"A boat that could've been used to reach the crime scene."

"But Lucy's car was there."

"Chase, are you going to let me finish?"

I went back to my eggs and bacon. As a matter of fact, they weren't so bad.

"The car was there, but how did the killer leave the scene? We found no prints like the ones on the beach, none in the parking lot or on the street, and there's plenty of sand on that street, especially after the number of winter storms we've had. Why were there no boot prints?"

I drank my coffee and listened.

"What if Putnam left his boat at the crime scene, below the tide line, after moving the lifeguard stand? The stand is from three houses down the beach, and there are few people on the beach this time of year, especially in out-of-the-way places. You, yourself, pointed out a cold front came through, which kept people, who are mostly retirees, off the beach."

"For Alan Putnam to have done what you suggest, he would've had to go all the way up to Little River to reach the ocean, then down the coast the same distance. If you ask me, that's a stretch."

"Maybe his boat was already full. Leslie's uncle's restaurant butts up to The Ditch."

The Ditch runs from Little River to where the Waterway hits the Waccamaw. It's just that: a ditch dug by the Army Corps of Engineers to create the northern section of the inland waterway. It runs behind Barefoot Landing and Restaurant Row.

"Horry County police found traces of a footprint the size we're looking for on a piece of cardboard that had been slid in one of those dumpsters used for corrugated boxes."

"Want me to check out his boat?"

Warden shook his head. "I had the wildlife people stop by and look it over, to see if we might need a warrant. No reason to take up a judge's time if we couldn't find probable cause. The boat was moored in plain sight and washed down. Did you check Putnam's car before you sent him downtown?"

"Looked through the window. Alan's a neat freak. The one time he came over to my place—"

"Chase, please."

I shrugged. "He simply doesn't fit the profile of a serial killer."

"Why not?" Warden drank from his coffee again. "He's a white male between twenty and thirty-five and from a middle-class family. By the way, did you call his sister in Knoxville?"

"Yes."

"Were you going to share that information with us?"

"She asked him to buy the tee shirts, J.D."

"How did you phrase the question?"

"I know how to phrase a question."

"Just tell me how you did it."

After letting out a sigh, I said, "While Alan gathered the names of his male employees, I called his sister on my cell."

"She was home?"

"She homeschools her kids."

"And the question?"

"She knows me. We've met before."

"Go on."

"After assuring her that Alan wasn't in trouble or in the hospital, I asked her if she had spoken to Alan recently. She laughed. She said she hadn't asked Alan for any money lately but had asked him to purchase a couple of tees from Hard Rock Café."

"She brought up borrowing money from him on her own?"

"My impression was that it wasn't the standing in line that worried Nancy, but that she couldn't afford the tees. Alan puts the family up whenever they come to the beach."

"It's a free trip if he puts them up. Don't they have gas money?"

"Nothing's free at the beach. Just ask any tourist with kids. I don't think Nancy wanted to disappoint her kids by bringing them here and not being able to do anything more than take them to the beach."

He sat there, thinking.

"Putnam doesn't drive the right car," I went on. "He has one of those new VW bugs. Serial killers generally use vans, nowadays even SUVs, so the guy could be anyone."

"Not important if he's using a boat. And Putnam's affable, another characteristic of serial killers."

"He worked at the Chamber, for Christ's sake."

"I talked with several members of the board. Putnam's considered selfish, ambitious, and does things on impulse."

"Don't we all."

"And he comes from a broken home."

I sat back in my chair. "You really like him for this?"

"I'm just pointing out the traits Alan Putnam shares with serial killers."

"Yes. Surprising how many males share those same characteristics: selfishness, ambition, acting impulsively."

Warden stared through the window at Kings Highway. Traffic was light. First Week would soon be here and most adults would postpone their vacations until the college kids and high school grads finished tearing up and down the Strand, literally tearing up the Grand Strand. I used to look forward to First Week. Guess I'm getting old.

"Still," said Warden, breaking into my thoughts, "you don't have a serial killer until we have more than one body."

I almost laughed. "You can't have it both ways, J.D. It's either a serial killing or it's not."

"It has to be considered both ways."

"And unnecessarily alarm the Chamber?"

"The Chamber was on his mind when Putnam came to see me. He gave me the names of board members who would vouch for him."

"I'd think that'd be the last thing he'd want to talk about."

"Putnam didn't sound like he'd been cut loose but made this move on his own."

"You're not close to him like I am."

"And perhaps you're too close, or perhaps you absorbed too much information at Quantico."

I felt my mouth wrinkle. What was this jumping from one side of this argument to the other? J.D. Warden wore dark business suits, white-on-white shirts, wing tips, and club ties. He was not the type to be fickle. "And the conclusion you drew talking with Alan?"

"That everyone connected with this case should keep their opinions to themselves until we learn what really happened to Lucy Leslie."

"Oh, right. We can't let another young woman's death get in the way of having a decent Season."

"Chase, I want your word you won't talk your idea up."

"I'm still on the case?"

Our waitress returned, refilling coffee cups and asking if there was anything else she could get for us. Warden asked for the check and a receipt. The young woman produced both from a pad in the back pocket of her jeans. She was someone I didn't know, which meant it was the beginning of another Season. The waitress asked if she could take my plate. I said "yes" and snatched the bacon, rolling it into a napkin for Max.

Warden was checking the bill and checking it twice. "You're still on the case. I'm simply telling you not to make an issue of what we're not sure of until we have more proof."

"You mean, another dead girl?"

He glanced at me, then the waitress. "Chase, please don't attempt to read my mind or I'll read yours."

I leaned back in my chair and smiled. "Now that's something I'd like to see."

He took out his wallet. As he placed bills on the table, he

said, "You didn't want to eat breakfast this morning because this time of year you girls want to be able to fit into your newest bathing suit."

My face heated up. The waitress laughed, took Warden's money, and left with my plate.

"Remember, all we have is a young woman who might have a boyfriend who killed her, then decided to humiliate her for some imagined grievance."

"Like Rex Kilgore?"

"That's a possible MO. So is Kilgore's size, and from what you've said, his temper."

"Any sign of Rex?"

"Nothing yet. The APB is still out."

"I'm sure he knows all about it."

"What do you mean?"

"Jocks and cops. They go together."

Warden considered this.

I asked, "What did the police find in the houses along the beach near the crime scene?"

"A former felon by the name of Carlos Rodgers. Looks like he's lived there all winter. He used blackout curtains in a bedroom, hot-wired the electricity, and turned on the cable. The place is a real mess, according to DeShields."

"How'd you ID him—prints?"

Warden nodded. "We've got an APB out and Jennings has someone baby-sitting the house."

"What's his record?"

"Burglary and rape, but the women dropped the charges."

"There was more than one?"

"A mother and daughter. Rodgers moved in with the mother, then took up with the daughter. His attorney played the two against each other. The burglary was a prior offense."

"Sounds like an economic predator more than a sexual one. And the kid I ran down yesterday?"

"Skip Vaughn's gay and gave us the name of his lover, who verified his alibi. Vaughn said his father would beat the hell out of him for having sex with guys."

"That'd be enough to confuse me about my sexuality."

The waitress returned with the change, but Warden shook his head. The young woman smiled and left us to ourselves.

"Vaughn was at Leslie's to buy drugs, so there's always the possibility of a disgruntled customer."

"I don't think so. Druggies don't get mad, they find another source. Addicts are notoriously lazy."

Warden leaned back in his chair. "That's why something this elaborate, meaning how Leslie was posed in the stand, probably means it wasn't some coke-head. A competitor, yes, but not some user. I'd really like to locate Leslie's supplier and find out what he knows. Leslie might've given him a short count."

"It's Kenny Mashburn."

He gestured at my notebook lying on the table between us. "There's nothing in there about Mashburn."

I didn't know what to say.

"Chase, it's going to take a lot longer to teach you the ropes if you constantly resist."

"I'm not resisting."

"Don't argue with me. If I say you're resisting, you're resisting."

I gritted my teeth, then asked, "Did Vickers find anything else in the autopsy?"

"No one had sex with Leslie before she was killed, nor did they ejaculate on her body after she'd been murdered."

"What about that Kleenex I brought in?"

"We'll keep it for any suspects we develop, but otherwise Vickers found nothing." He looked out the window again. "Catching criminals at the beach is like catching fish with your hands. This place is always in flux. People come and go, and here I'm not talking about the summer trade. The Grand Strand has more unsolved crimes than any area in the state." He returned his gaze to me. "I want that trend reversed or at least slowed down."

"That's why you hired me."

"But if it becomes a zero sum game, the folks in the capital aren't going to allow you to remain on my staff. Chase, I want you to follow up on this as you would any other case, but remember, you're not working alone."

"You're right," I said, sitting up. "There's no way I could've learned all this alone."

"Are you patronizing me?"

"Not at all. Just stating the facts."

"And you have our total support. Do you understand what I'm saying?"

"I do."

"You don't act like it, keeping information to yourself. That's why there will always be questions about what happened at the Sunnydale."

"Ask Earl."

"Tackett has problems he doesn't even know about. His daughter was picked up last night. She tried to make a buy from an undercover officer."

"Aw, shit."

"You know her?"

"I know her type."

"Probably from looking in the mirror."

"Is Ruth out on bail?"

"Someone in the department fixed it."

"Good. Ruth doesn't need a record. She's only eighteen."

"That's one year older than you were when you were picked up the first time."

"Wait a minute," I said, leaning forward. "I thought juve records were sealed."

"Not for those recommended to the academy."

"You . . . you know everything about me, don't you?"

"Even what you tell your shrink."

"I'm not sure I like all this belonging."

"Then stick to the facts. Find Kenny Mashburn. He might be Leslie's killer."

"I don't think so . . . ."

"Don't think so much. Just follow orders for a change."

"What are you doing with the list of suspects the Host of Kings gave us?"

"Anslow and Austin are interviewing them today."

"That won't work. They don't believe we're tracking a serial killer."

"Jennings read them the riot act about some girl chasing down a perp they should've caught in the parking lot. More will come out of those interviews than you think."

"Has the Chamber asked about Lucy?"

"The director has—the new guy—as soon as her death was reported. They learn quick when they hit the beach." He stood up, then maneuvered his chair under the table. "If I remember Alan Putnam, he was everywhere: parties, grand openings, schmoozing with the chiefs of police, not to mention the powers-that-be. But killing people because you don't get a job . . . ." Warden shook his head. "I think that MO is taking an automatic weapon into the workplace."

I got to my feet. "Speaking of that, you'd better have some hard evidence on Rex Kilgore if you bring charges. Lawyers will line up to represent that jerk."

"Why? His basketball career is over."

"So is Michael Jordan's."

"You don't think Horry County will bring him in?"

"A white boy who could play round ball and blew out his knee before he had the chance to show up all those colored kids? All cops will remember is being introduced to plenty of Division I coaches at ball games where they were pulling security to make a few extra bucks."

"Then," said Warden, coming around the table, "maybe SLED should look into Mister Kilgore."

"If I see him, I'll pick him up."

"You'll call for backup, that's what you'll do." He put his hand in the small of my back and directed me toward the door. "Don't forget, you have an appointment with Theresa Hardy this morning."

"We had dinner last night."

He smiled. "You see, I told you you were a bright girl. How'd it go?"

"Hardy showed more interest in my boyfriend than she did in me."

"I'm not surprised. We all wonder what Rivers sees in you."

"J.D!"

"And get rid of the dog. The jeep works but not the dog."

Looking through the door at an eager pooch waiting for his snack, I said, "But Max goes everywhere with me."

Warden reached for the metal bar across the glass door of the restaurant. "It's not professional."

Max, who had left the footlocker, now leaped into the front seat in anticipation of a treat.

"That's what puzzles me," I said. "Serial killers don't fit in. It doesn't mean they can't con us or make us get in their car, but there's usually something disturbing in their background. Alan Putnam doesn't even have a record."

When Warden pulled back on the bar, the glass door closed in my face. "How do you know he doesn't have a record?"

"I checked."

"You didn't bring him in. You sent him in. How'd you know Putnam doesn't have a record?"

"Er—I guess I looked . . . sometime."

"Those records are confidential."

I glanced through the glass. Max was seconds from barking his head off. So much for obedience classes.

"Chase?"

"Er—I ran all my friends, that included Alan, to see what you had on them. When I go down, it's not going to be for them running a game on *me*."

"Then why didn't you find Leslie's record?" When I didn't answer, he said, "But you did, didn't you? You knew all about her record. That's why you hustled over there and dumped the cocaine down the toilet." He let go of the metal bar. "Let's see what we have." Warden began to tick off a list of my sins using his fingers.

"You have enough," I cut in, "if you want me gone."

"But I don't want you gone, and I don't know why you would say something like that. I have a lot invested in you."

"That's your problem, not mine."

"No, Chase, it's *our* problem."

11

Rex Kilgore was staying with a friend. That's what the phone logs said. Using a program downloaded from the Internet and "brute force"—a geek term for the hours it takes to crack a system—I'd been able to hack into the phone system's records.

A few years ago, I'd been recruited as a member of a "tiger team." That's hackers hired to bust into someone's supposedly secure system. If you truly want to keep people out of your files, it's as easy as having an odd password, but people won't do it, and in we hackers go. As for going through channels and pulling the lugs on Kilgore's phone, well, that wasn't going to happen anytime soon. Call it a guy thing.

Rex's mom's number had received several calls from Daniel Potter, a resident of a mobile home park off the bypass. Daniel Potter was the uncle of Terry Manning, and Terry Manning had played ball with Rex Kilgore in high school.

Ignoring the pain in my foot from yesterday's cut and run, I left my jeep on the road and walked into the park, down a gravel road separating two rows of trailers. To my left and right, the same depressing scene was repeated over and over: single-wides, with weeds and a muddy parking place for the cars, usually American; not many foreign jobs here. Nor pick-ups. This time of day most pickups would be hard at work in the Grand Strand's support system, if the man of the house had a job. If there was a man of the house.

Teenagers smoked cigarettes, more than one baby was slung

over a young mom's shoulder, and quite a few senior citizens sat on tiny wooden porches, looking genuinely puzzled about the way their lives had turned out. Rex Kilgore belonged here.

As there are no provisions for the discarded athlete in our society, Rex had returned to the Grand Strand and taken a job in a lumber yard. The work did not suit him. Neither did pickup games at the Y. So Rex joy rode in cars he thought were his due, and after being busted for that and possession of marijuana, he was finally thrown out of the house by his mother. It's called tough love. Tough love is where Baby Boomers don't have to take shit off anyone, including their own kids. You know, the same kids they sent off to school with the key to the house tied around their necks.

I found the trailer, stepped up on the cinder blocks used for steps, and hammered on the door. No car in the driveway. If Kilgore's wheels were around, he'd parked them elsewhere. To make this scam work, I wore different clothing: a red wig, too much makeup, a cropped top, mini-skirt, and boots reaching for my ass.

"Come on, Mitchell!" I hollered. "Let me in!"

No answer from inside, so I went at the door again.

"Mitchell, you gonna let me in?" As far as I knew nobody named "Mitchell" lived there, but the idea was to get Kilgore to open the door.

"Mitchell! Open up!"

"Nobody here by that name!" That was Rex's voice.

"Mitchell, I ain't gonna take no shit off you. Open the fucking door and open it now!"

"Go away before I come out there and pop you."

I laughed. Well, actually, it was more of a shriek. "Yeah, right, Mitchell—you and whose army?"

"I'm telling you there's no one in here by that name, so get lost." The voice was behind me now, at the window. Rex was scoping me out.

"I fucking recognize your voice. You can't fool me."

Someone thumped across the trailer's unstable floor and the door was jerked open. Rex Kilgore stood there, dark hair down in his face, eyes bloodshot, and skin a splotchy white.

Unshaven for days, he was barefoot and wearing a dirty tan tee with jeans. Given his height, Rex had to bend down to come through the door and get at me.

When he did, I stepped back and flipped my badge out of my cropped top. Now it hung across my chest on a lanyard. My pistol came out from behind my leg.

"Just keep coming!" I two-handed the grip and pointed the Smith & Wesson at him. "Right down here."

"Susan?" Rex was almost a full foot taller than me and a hundred pounds heavier.

"Come out—now!"

"What are you doing?" Rex gripped the frame, leaned out, and scanned the trailer park. "What's going on?"

"Rex Kilgore, you are under arrest for the murder of Lucy Leslie. You have the right to remain silent. Anything you say, can, and will be used against you."

"But I didn't do it!"

"You have the right to legal counsel. If you're so fucking broke you can't afford an attorney, one will be provided for you. Come out of the trailer and do it now!"

Still, he did not move.

Lowering the Smith & Wesson, I asked, "Which one's the bad knee, Rex?"

"What?"

"I asked which one's your bad knee, from playing ball."

"Er—the left one."

"Okay. I'll shoot you in the right one. Doesn't seem right shooting you in the bad knee. Might not be enough cartilage to put it back together."

Rex's hands shot up, thumping into the ceiling. "Don't shoot! I'm coming out."

"Then do it!" And I continued reading him his rights, the one you never hear on TV. "If you decide to answer questions without a lawyer present, you can stop anytime you realize you're a real weenie."

Kilgore hit his head on the trailer door, and I had to wait until he righted himself and eased himself down the cinder block steps.

"Up against the wall!"

"Susan, why are you doing this?"

Lowering the Smith & Wesson again, I said, "Rex, I'm going to shoot you in the knee for resisting arrest if you don't assume the fucking position!"

He faced the trailer and put his hands over his head on the metal wall. I kicked his feet farther apart, patted him down, then cuffed his hands behind his back and took him into the office.

My boss looked up from my desk as I pushed Rex into the squad room ahead of me. In Warden's office, Theresa Hardy was on the phone. Trying to scare up someone to scare, I suppose. This morning she wore a comfortable-looking pair of slacks. Like, figure it out, J.D.

"Rex Kilgore. J.D. Warden."

Rex nodded and began to charm his way out of custody. "Pleased to meet you, Lieutenant."

"Where'd you find him?" asked Warden.

"I was hanging at a friend's," explained Rex. "Didn't know you were looking for me or I would've turned myself in."

"You understand the charge?"

"Yes, sir, but I think Susan's mistaken." He smiled down at me. "Don't worry, I don't intend to press charges. She gets in enough trouble on her own."

"Do you have an attorney?" asked Warden.

"Several."

I'd had enough of this entitlement-ballplayer attitude. Grabbing an arm, I twisted Kilgore around. "Remember the girl you hit in the face with the beer bottle?"

"Refresh my memory," he said with another easy smile.

"You know who I'm talking about, you dick. You left her on her parents' porch, buck naked and bleeding."

"Sorry, but I don't remember it that way."

"She wouldn't sleep with you, would she?"

"Really," he said, smiling and glancing around at the men in the squad room, "that would be telling."

When I tried to slap the bastard, Warden grabbed my arm.

"That's not how we do things, Chase."

Stepping back, Rex bumped into my desk, then righted himself. Didn't he always?

"That girl had to have surgery and wasn't able to eat for a month, except through a tube."

"It was a simple misunderstanding. She fell down." He looked around at his adoring public. Officers had filled the squad room to stare at their fallen hero.

Warden had to restrain me as I went after him. "You're not a hotshot ballplayer anymore, Rex! You're just another loser I'll have to scrape off the highway someday."

"Chase," asked Warden, pushing me back, "have you informed Chief Jennings that you've located Kilgore?"

I stopped struggling. "I got him, didn't I? I brought him in, didn't I?" I couldn't see clearly. The room had a red hue to it.

"You can't use your badge to right past wrongs."

"Past wrongs?" Now I could make out Warden just fine. "What in the hell are you talking about?"

"That party where Kilgore hit the girl with the beer bottle. You were there that night, and before Kilgore assaulted the girl, you'd already passed out, hadn't you?"

I stared at the floor.

"Otherwise, Kilgore's basketball career would've ended earlier, wouldn't it?"

My head jerked up. "Fucking A!"

"Chase, if you don't do something about your mouth, you're going to pull desk duty. Understand?"

After swallowing hard, I said, "I understand."

He led Kilgore away.

"Think he did it?" asked Hardy from the doorway of Warden's office.

It was a moment before I could speak. "It's—it's possible. Rex doesn't think his shit stinks."

Hardy looked me over from head to toe. "That's quite an outfit." She meant the red wig, cropped top, miniskirt, and boots reaching for my ass.

"I can change if you'd like."

She shook her head. "It's not necessary. I've posed as a hooker before."

I glanced down at my outfit. "You think this makes me look like a hooker?"

Hardy had been to the hospital. She told me her partner was out of intensive care and that Earl Tackett had come out of his coma but didn't remember anything. Good. When he did, Earl would have to deal with his fellow officers ribbing him about having his ass saved by some girl. All in all, Earl might not want to recover.

On Hardy's side of Warden's desk lay a legal pad and a fountain pen. Lying on my side was a handheld tape recorder. This wouldn't be anything like the interview conducted at Lucy's place. Lucy's former place, that is.

"Tell the truth, Lucy. You tried to flush a tampon down the toilet, didn't you?"

"Susan, I don't know what that blood's doing there. Anyway, it's supposed to flush."

We stood at the door of the bathroom in her triangularly-shaped apartment. The bathroom was little more than three rectangular pieces of metal, two of them attached to the corner wall, the third between the apartment and the shower wall, then a plastic curtain which could be pulled back to give you some privacy. The metal base of the narrow room, which had a two-inch lip, also had a tube allowing excess water to exit to the outside—which meant you could shower in the tiny room, but Lucy said she'd merely taken a dump.

I turned away. "I'll get a snake."

"A snake! Oh, my God, I hate snakes."

"Don't worry. This won't be a real one, like that isn't real blood in the toilet."

Hardy brought me back to the here and now with, "SLED doesn't care how many county solicitors have cleared you of any wrongdoing in the shooting at the Sunnydale Motel. You *should* be on administrative leave. People can make serious errors in judgment after undergoing the stress you've undergone."

I waved this off. "I brought in Rex Kilgore when nobody else would."

"Nobody else would? What do you mean?"

"It's a guy thing."

"You could've called for backup."

"My last backup was a fuck-up." *Oops!* I glanced at the recorder in front of me. Hardy hadn't turned it on, but still, I should watch my mouth.

"I don't think that's going to fly with SLED."

"You're saying I don't have a legitimate bitch?"

"I'm telling you that's not the way things are done."

"'The way things are done?'" I could hear my voice rise. "Or are you telling me SLED girls don't whine?"

"Susan, can we stick to the subject?"

"Which one?"

"Your picking up Rex Kilgore. I would be derelict in my duty if I didn't point out the stress you've been under when you undertook—"

"Look, Ms. Hardy, it would have only pissed . . . it would've only made Rex mad if I'd taken a bunch of cops along. Daniel Potter gives marksmanship lessons for the NRA. There're all kinds of guns in that trailer. A girl had a better chance of drawing Rex out."

She gestured at the squad room behind me. "Then what was that outburst?"

I could only shrug. "I have history with Rex." Right about now I could use a cigarette.

"Or maybe it's the residual from the shoot-out, and the reason you *should* be on administrative leave. Did you ever consider that?"

I fell back in my chair. "Could we get this over with?"

"I've read your therapist's reports. Have you considered that you might be in denial?"

"She never uses that word with me."

"I don't think a therapist would. At this stage she's letting you talk yourself out."

"I don't have anything to talk about. I face the world on its own terms, not mine, not yours, not SLED's."

"And I disagree. I think you have a lot to talk about, but that's not why I'm here." She reached over and turned on the recorder. "Today, I want you to tell me what happened when you and Sergeant Tackett tried to make the drug buy at the Sunnydale Motel."

I did, leaving out nothing but the possible rape. Hardy regarded me as others have when I've told them some guy didn't want to lay me. Hell, if I took up all the offers I'd never get any work done.

Hardy concluded with: "There was something muffled on the tape, one of the men asking you to take off your clothes."

"We didn't get that far . . . because I killed them." How many times would I have to admit I'd killed those two scumbags and didn't feel the least bit sorry.

"You feel you had to kill those men because your backup was late?"

To this I nodded.

"Susan, please speak up for the recorder."

Glancing at the machine, I said, "Our backup was late."

"Are you aware the wire was smashed when Sergeant Tackett was kicked in the back, and that's the explanation your backup is using for being tardy?"

Again I nodded, then said, "Yes."

"You were very, very lucky."

"Maybe. Maybe I was very, very good. Can I go now?"

She regarded me. "You think Earl Tackett brought this on himself, don't you?"

"I didn't say that."

"No, but he did put himself in harm's way to protect you. An examination of the crime scene and what we have on tape support such a hypothesis."

Sitting up, I asked, "What is it you want to hear?"

"I want to hear your side."

I really needed a cigarette, but if I could hold out here . . . . Leaning forward, I said, "Look, Ms. Hardy, you may've blazed a trail at SLED, but men have to get over the fact that I might take a bullet and lie there bleeding to death while they're trying to save our lives. Bottom line is: will my partner take out the bad guys or will he hesitate—because of me bleeding out? Our society may value women more than it does men, but at that particular moment, I hope he's taking care of business and not worrying about me. What I did at the Sunnydale is the example I set for the women coming along behind me."

Hardy leaned back in Warden's chair. "You've given this considerable thought, haven't you?"

"It's the real world, like the bad guys wanting to 'do' me. What's the big deal?"

"You know what the big deal is. Those men wanted to take you along, and they couldn't do that unless they removed your partner from the equation."

"Oh, give it a rest. You know very well why I was chosen for this bust."

"I concede the point that you were chosen because you are a woman. It has been done thousands of times in the past and will be used thousands of times in the future. Still, you have no compassion for Earl Tackett?"

"I've learned to take responsibility for my own mistakes."

Hardy inclined her head in the direction of the squad room, where Rex Kilgore and I had gone toe to toe. "Then J.D. was right when he said you tried to use your badge to right a past wrong."

I glanced at the recorder. "Sorry, but that's not relevant to this investigation."

She reached across the desk and turned off the machine.

When she did that, I nodded. "Yes. He was correct."

"So what would you've done if the drug dealers had taken you along?"

"But they didn't."

"But what if they had?"

"And what if Luke Perry shows up on my doorstep? I really don't see the benefit of playing 'what if .'"

"Susan, SLED wants to know their agents are safe."

"Then they shouldn't employ women. That way they

wouldn't have to spend so much time polishing their armor."

"That's not going to happen."

"Because your generation insisted on the opportunity to be shot in the line of duty."

"I wouldn't put it that way."

"What other way is there to put it?"

She sighed. "You certainly have an odd way of reaching the bottom line."

"What other line is there?"

"Susan, I wasn't sent here to give you a hard time. I'm a woman, too."

"Then may I go?" •

"Of course. The formal part of the inquiry is over."

I stood up to leave, then picked up the recorder and turned it back on. "Of course, none of this would've happened if there had been drugs there for us to buy."

Hardy glanced at the machine. "What do you mean by that?"

"Since our backup wasn't there, it doesn't surprise me there were no drugs to buy."

"What are you saying, Susan?" She was well aware that the machine was still running.

"I'm saying we didn't have good intelligence, but SLED's chosen to investigate me, and they're using the dead drug dealers as an excuse." I gave her a sly smile. "Probably intending to set back some of the progress *your* generation made."

Snapping off the recorder, I tossed the machine at Hardy and left. There was a note on my desk from Warden asking me to see him when I finished, but since he was interrogating Rex Kilgore I left the building and headed for a street off the Boulevard. Despite everyone's irrelevant concerns, I still had a job to do.

The Artists' House is across the street from where a couple of dudes hang out, shucking and jiving, smoking and joking, catcalling the ladies, and dealing dope to all comers. Both wore shirts unbuttoned to their waists, tight-fitting pants, plenty of jewelry, and cell phones on their belts. I stopped my jeep beside one of them, a kid of mixed race who wore a black shirt and red slacks. His dusty-looking chest was rather hairy for the son of a Latina, his hair slicked back and oily.

"Come over here, Kenny. I want to talk to you."

Mashburn didn't move. "You got no right hassling me, Chase. I'm liable to call the cops on *you.*"

"Before you do, look where you're about to plunk down your worthless black ass."

He stepped down from the curb. From there he could see the ID in the passenger seat. When he reached for it, I slapped his hand away.

His eyes lit up. "Where'd you get that? Want to sell it? That why you're here?"

"Kenny, don't waste my time."

"Come on, girl, what you saying—that you're with SLED now?"

"What's the matter—not keeping up with the news?"

"What the news got . . . . Oh, Lordy, you the one smoked those two dealers."

"Get in the jeep. You and I are going to have a little talk." A vehicle passed behind me, but I gave it little attention. I had eyes only for Kenny Mashburn, wondering if I'd need the pistol in my backpack between the front seats.

"What you want with me?"

"Information."

He looked down the street. His companion was moving in our direction. "You got no right doing this to me."

"That badge says I do." I watched Kenny's eyes. If any trouble started, it would begin there. "Now get in the jeep."

His companion sauntered over, a black-skinned, scrawny young man. "What's happening, man?"

"Tell him, Kenny."

Mashburn scowled. "This here's Susan Chase."

The young black man stared at me. "This the bitch wasted the dealers at the Sunnydale?"

I reached for my pack. "Wanna see my gun?"

His hands came up. "Hey, I don't wants no trouble." He backed away, then turned and walked away. Very quickly.

Mashburn started after him. "Where you going, Roscoe? She ain't after us." But his companion was gone, practically running down the street. "Roscoe, you get your black ass back here! You got a shift to pull."

"Get in the jeep, Kenny."

When his buddy disappeared around a corner, Mashburn returned his attention to me. "This ain't right."

"Kenny, get in the fucking jeep!"

He did, and I didn't have any trouble until I turned into an alleyway where we could be alone. By then, my pistol lay in my lap.

Mashburn's head swiveled around like it was on a stick. "Why we going back here? You got no right doing this to me, even if 'n you're with SLED."

I stopped midway down the alley and parked beside a set of air conditioners that threw up a wall of noise separating us from the street. Sitting with my back to the units, I could see up and down the alley in both directions. The place reeked of grease and some god-awful smell from a set of dumpsters. A black kid wearing kitchen whites came out the back door of a restaurant and hung out a mop to dry. He glanced at us, then returned to the restaurant.

I slid a photo out of my pack, one taken from the wall at Lucy's place. "Know the girl in this photo?"

Mashburn shook his head without looking at it. "Don't know her, babe."

"Kenny, remember the scumbags I blew away?"

He shrugged. "Musta been trying to rape you or something—that's why you're still on the street."

I held the photo where he couldn't miss it. "Kenny, you know this girl. Someone's already ratted you out. I want to know what you know about her. Tell me here or tell me downtown, one's the same as the other to me, and there's people downtown that'd really like a heart-to-heart with you about unrelated matters."

"You'd do that to me? A brother that's been of assistance

to you in the past? You'd do that to ole Kenny?"

I nodded. It was either that or burst out laughing. Holding up the photo again, I said, "Lucy was a friend of mine."

"Not a good idea to take things personal, babe."

I cranked the engine.

"Hey, I didn't do her and you can take that to the bank."

"That's not what I'm asking."

He looked down the alley. "That's all I'm saying."

I looked in the opposite direction, toward what Kenny considered his turf. "You know, I think I'll post myself on this street for a while." Slipping my SLED ID on the lanyard again, I added, "You know, hang this around my neck to let everyone know I'm official."

"I use a cell phone for most of my business."

"Whose number I can trap and fuck up your business but good. You'll never leave this street. You like screwing those long-haired white girls who shop back there." Meaning the Artists' House where wannabe artists bought their art supplies.

Mashburn shifted around in his seat. "Look, babe, helping you, how's that help me?"

I let out the clutch.

He touched my hand on the four-on-the-floor. "Wait a second."

I took my feet off the gas and clutch and reestablished contact with the brake.

"Folks like me might need a little help from the authorities from time to time."

"I only help those who help me."

"Yeah, well, I'm not sure you've been with SLED long enough to help your friends."

You could get a serious case of whiplash trying to follow this conversation. "I can do all kinds of things for my buds. You know me, I'm not afraid to bend the rules."

"I knows that, babe, and that's why I'm gonna take a chance on you."

"Gee, Kenny, that's mighty white of you."

"Hey!" he said, sitting up. "Don't be using them racial

epitaphs. They lower my self-esteem."

My only answer was to race the engine.

"Okay, okay. The bitch had lots of contacts with college boys. They always knew where to find her and always knew she had the good shit."

I turned off the engine. "Anybody pissed at her?"

"Nah. The girl loved those college boys, and they loved her back." He smiled. "How you doing for boyfriends?"

"Already have one."

"White boy, I would imagine."

"Matter of fact he is."

Sunlight flashed off the chains around Mashburn's neck as his chest swelled up. "There's a big difference between me and them white boys you're fucking."

"I want to talk about a girlfriend, not my current boy-friend, and you were her supplier."

He straightened up in the seat. "Who's saying?"

"I'm saying."

"No way you can pin that on me."

"Depends on who you give me—whether I can pin some-thing on you or not."

"I don'ts have to give you nobody."

I glanced down the alley. "Kenny, we come back here for a little chat and the next thing I know you're all over me, trying to rape me."

He raised up, gripping the dashboard and the back of his seat. "I didn't do no such thing!"

I cranked the engine again.

"Hey, don't be so hasty. You white girls, always in such a rush." When I cut the engine, he said, "You know, your friend was okay, but she did something real stupid."

"What's that?"

"I tried to warn her—"

"Kenny!"

"Okay, okay. She pissed off Nelson Obie."

Nelson Obie ran one of the lifeguard services along the Grand Strand and he was considered one of the major drug traffickers. But no one had been able to pin anything on *him.* There were too many cutouts.

"Come on, Kenny. Lucy worked for Marvin, same guy I used to work for."

"Old news, babe."

"Meaning?"

"Meaning she's working for Nelson."

"Dealing? That doesn't make sense. You were her supplier for the college boys."

"Like I said, babe, old news." He shifted around in the passenger seat. "Got a cigarette?"

If I couldn't smoke, neither could he. "Didn't it bother you that Lucy would go to work for one of your competitors?"

"Nelson and I not in competition, babe."

"He supplies you?"

Mashburn held a hand to his mouth and stifled a fake yawn. "You got anymore questions, make them quick. I got a business to run."

"I've asked one."

Mashburn continued looking over the hood. Evidently, there were some things the asshole wouldn't talk about. Down the alley the black kid came out of the restaurant and dumped trash into a dumpster. I'd heard Kenny's pitch to young black men—you know, how the white man's always screwing you, and you might as well make some money off Whitey. And the dealer was right—to a point. Eighty percent of users were white, but eighty percent of those in prison were black. I don't think people like Kenny Mashburn ever told black kids about *that* eighty percent.

"I won't be needing any friends if'n I'm dead, babe."

That might be true. Along with Nelson Obie controlling the drug trade along the Grand Strand went a reputation that anyone who screwed with him was dead. Once when Nelson and I'd been tight, I thought I saw a guy go flying off Nelson's balcony. But when the body didn't show up, or any cops at Nelson's door, I blew it off as a bad trip.

"What is it you want, Kenny?"

He looked me over. "I can see by the way you're dressed that you're serious about this SLED shit."

"I am." He meant the skirt and blouse I had changed into at the law enforcement center.

"I'm serious about my business, too, and I don't need some cop coming around saying we got to get down. You've messed up Roscoe but good. There's gots to be better ways to meet. If you and I are gonna do business."

"What do you suggest?"

"All you gots to do is cruise by in this raggedy-ass jeep of yours—nobody can miss it—and that means we're gonna meet somewhere in an hour."

"If *I* want to do business that way."

"You want me to cooperate or what?"

"How would I recognize this so-called cooperating? All your radio's playing is static."

"Nelson's the one you want to see about your dead friend. Now, you want to talk to me, drive by and I'll meet you, say, at one of the sports bars an hour later. Your pick."

"Make it Barnes and Noble on the bypass. You won't be seen there by anyone who knows you."

"And neither will you, babe."

12

After the hassle of dragging anything out of Kenny Mashburn, I wanted to go home and take a nap. But since Kenny had fingered Nelson Obie for Lucy's murder, I stopped by a brokerage firm where Nelson can be found before the Season began. Unfortunately I had to pass St. Michael's, but instead of stopping and talking with a priest, I tried to use my cell phone and found the battery dead, probably from posting too many "1-2-3s" on Chad's beeper.

Leaving the phone to pump itself up, I charged into the brokerage house to see Nelson. He didn't recognize me, nor did a bodyguard asleep in the front seat of a Caddy parked outside. Still, I had to elude a secretary inside the door.

"May I help you? *Miss!* May I help you?" She hustled to her feet as I rushed by, a willowy brunette wearing an outfit I'd seen in Casual Corner last time I'd been in the mall.

Two geezers watched me hustle by. They'd been staring at the ticker like it was the most important thing in the world. It might've been. The market had been awfully choppy of late and bonds were paying diddly-shit. Who has time for all this? Invest in a couple of decent index funds and get on with your life.

Nelson sat at the far end of a double row of leather-backed chairs. He was thick through the middle but had powerful arms and legs from racing a schooner up and down the coast. Drunk, Nelson was practically unbeatable, taking chances no one in their right mind would take. I speak from experience. I'd crewed for him and I could still remember the day he'd gotten in my face and told me we would press on, despite the fact all was lost. At the moment, it sounded rather cheesy, but we did win the damned race.

To make up for the loss of most of his hair, the middle-aged Nelson wore a beard. The beard was as brown as the thatch of hair sticking out the top of his shirt. The tail of the shirt fell over a pair of white jeans. Loafers but no socks. Like Alan Putnam, Nelson Obie thought he was a rather slick fella. At one time I'd thought so, too.

I took a seat beside him.

"Susan, is that you?"

"'Tis me."

"Long time, no see."

"Probably good for both of us."

He nodded as he checked my outfit. My backpack lay in my lap. "Now I remember. You went to the academy. The Grand Strand's own Susan Chase is now a member of the State Law Enforcement Division. Imagine that."

"Yeah. I'm pretty fucking important these days."

"I knew you could do it. Why you'd want to, I have no idea."

"Private-eyeing doesn't pay like a regular job."

"But you have to put up with a good amount of bullshit."

"I can get that anywhere. Matter of fact, I might even get a little of that from you."

His attention returned to the numbers running across the far side of the room. Most brokerage houses had removed their electronic tickers, but this is Myrtle Beach, and there are one hell of a lot of old folks with little to do.

"I heard Lucy Leslie ditched Marvin Valente and was coming to work for you."

"That is correct. Though, in your present position, why that might interest you I have no idea."

"Despite her having a case of sun poisoning."

Now he looked at me. "I didn't know that."

"I think you knew about her condition and planned on employing her in another way."

"What in the world are you talking about?"

"You know why SLED hired me. I'm a local."

"And that means?"

"Nelson, I'm not wearing a wire. This is just between you and me."

He glanced at my chest, for the wire, that is. Well, maybe.

"Look, Susan, I just got back into town. I don't have a clue as to what you're talking about. Last I heard Lucy was waitressing at her uncle's place."

"And she had something going on the side. Something she was doing for you, and I've verified that from more than one source."

He looked at the ticker. "I wouldn't know anything about what you're talking about."

"Lucy was found dead yesterday morning on the beach near North Myrtle."

"And that's supposed to surprise me, the trouble you girls get into?"

I turned on him so quickly my backpack slid off my lap and clunked to the floor. The two geezers looked our way. From a glass cubicle a hefty sales rep stared at us. Nelson looked at the geezers long enough to make them return their attention to the electronic ticker. But the sales rep continued to stare at us. He wore a white shirt with a red tie and matching suspenders. The secretary had long ago returned to her desk near the front door.

My hand was on his arm. "Nelson, I want to know if you did it or had it done."

"Oh, now I'm responsible for every dead girl found along the Grand Strand?"

"The ones who work for you, maybe so, and there have been quite a few."

"Show me the bodies."

"I wish to hell I could."

"Susan, I think you're allowing your personal feelings to cloud the issue."

"You're damn right I am!"

He glanced at my hand on his shoulder. After I removed it, he said, "For the record I don't know anything about Lucy's death. All I know is, if you're telling the truth, I have to find another lifeguard."

"Or someone else to do your dirty work."

Nelson finally stopped denying he didn't know what I was talking about. Now he said nothing at all.

I recovered my backpack from the floor. "Okay, who do I need to see to check your alibi?"

"I was at Charley O's," he said, returning his attention to the ticker. "Shooting pool."

"I thought you were out of town."

"After I returned."

"What time?"

"Close to midnight."

"Who can vouch for you?"

"Marcel and Huey. I don't remember who else was there, but there were plenty of others watching the game."

"Which ball game, Nelson?"

"Susan," he said, looking at me once again, "I'm here to conduct business, not to be interrogated."

"The game, Nelson, the game."

He sighed. "The Braves and the Padres from the West Coast. Braves lost two to one. Susan, I haven't had any contact with Lucy Leslie since she applied for employment back in . . . April. Now, am I going to have any more trouble with this?"

"Nelson, I'm going to find out who killed her."

"You do that. Just keep it away from me."

"Generally speaking, I've been pretty good at keeping my distance, but in this case—"

"And all this time I thought it was your loyalty to Marvin Valente that kept us from doing business."

"That and my sense of moral outrage."

"Don't point fingers. You've been there."

"But I left, and while I was there I never dealt and you damn well know it."

"You're still crabby as ever." He shook his head. "How your boyfriend can stand you, I don't know . . . ."

When the Smith & Wesson slid out of my backpack, Nelson

stopped sneering, the geezers at the other end of the row stopped yammering, and behind the glass, the hefty sales rep's mouth formed a small round *O*.

Nelson leaned back in his chair. "For Christ's sake, Susan. Put that away."

"Take it back, Nelson," I said, leaning toward him, my pistol at my side. "Take it back."

"Look, it doesn't help when you pull a gun."

"I said take it back!"

The sales rep picked up his phone while the geezers hobbled out of the building, and me, I leaned into Nelson, jamming the pistol into his midriff, daring him to try something. My finger was hard against the trigger guard.

"Take it back or be taken downtown." I liked this new power of mine, threatening to ruin everyone's day.

He eyed the pistol. "And the charge?"

"If I can't trump up something, who can?"

"Susan, I don't think—"

"I don't give a damn what you think. Now are you going to take it back or go downtown?"

He glanced at the pistol again. "I take it back."

"You can do better than that."

"Okay, okay, I apologize for mentioning your boyfriend. Honestly, Susan, I wasn't making a threat."

I got in his face. "Never, Nelson, do you understand, never ever hint you'll harm my family."

"You don't have a family, Susan. You're an orphan."

" . . . because I will dedicate my life to ruining yours, SLED or no SLED."

"Okay, okay, just put away the gun."

As the pistol went back into my pack, an old fella in a pinstriped suit approached us. He was accompanied by the hefty sales rep. I didn't see any "S" on the sales rep's chest, and that meant no matter how good a salesman he was, he was still a frigging idiot. Any one of them should be on the horn to the cops, not facing down some fool who'd drawn a handgun.

The older man cleared his throat. "Young lady, I was told

you have a pistol in that handbag."

"It's a Lady Smith & Wesson Model 36. Wanna see it?" My hand went into the pack.

"No, no!" said the older gent, throwing his hands at me. "I don't want to see it! I just wanted to . . . ." He cleared his throat again. "It's against state law to bring a concealed weapon into this building. There's a sign on the door."

Sure there was. I'd seen it on my way in.

When I stood up, the old man stepped back, but the sales rep stood his ground. Well, we'd already determined this particular Superman was an idiot. My hand came out of my pack, this time with my ID.

The old fart was so relieved I thought he might faint. He glanced at the badge and the dreadful photo taken at the academy. "You're with SLED?"

"Yes, sir, and I knew Nelson was here so I stopped by to show him my gun."

"You stopped by . . . to show him your gun?"

"And my new ID. Mister Obie has always taken an interest in my career. Isn't that right, Nelson?"

"Whatever," said Nelson, staring at the ticker.

"Miss Chase, I'm sorry to've bothered you, but you have to understand that Mister Obie is one of our most valued customers."

"Oh, yes," I said, glancing at my former lover. "Mister Obie can help you make lots of money if you're crazy enough to listen to him."

I left the brokerage house and drove to Charley O's, the sports bar where I had a sandwich and a beer and confirmed that Nelson had indeed been shooting pool there the night Lucy had been killed. That's how I confirmed Nelson had been there—when Marcel arrived and started bitching, not wanting to tell me anything.

But what did that prove? Nelson never soiled his hands but employed mugs like Marcel and Huey to do his bidding. Marcel was Huey's alibi and Huey was Marcel's. And there were others, like the bartender who gave me the evil eye, wondering if I was going to be bad for business. I don't know. Give me a minute.

During a commercial break in *General Hospital,* I called Marvin Valente. Did he know for sure that Lucy Leslie would be lifeguarding for him this season?

"She's on the books, kiddo. More than I can say for others."

"You're cracking on me? You're one of the few who wished me well."

"My telling you not to quit would've changed your mind?"

"Marvin!"

"You asked."

"I didn't ask for this grief."

"Force a man to take on second-raters and you don't expect some grief? The pickup still doesn't run right."

"What's the problem?"

"Stalls out when it rains, and I just had it tuned up. Runs fine once you get going."

"Belts?"

"I had them replaced."

"Check the coil tower. There must be a crack."

"I'll have it looked at."

"Marvin, did you hear anything about Lucy having sun poisoning?"

"If I had, I would've hired someone else."

"Rumor has it Lucy was going to work for the competition, you know, where the pay's better because of the fringe benefits."

"Don't know anything about that, but I'd better plan on hiring more people. I can't compete with Nelson and his fringe benefits, or SLED's either, it would appear."

"Look on the bright side, Marvin. Without me around you have a reason to buy a new truck."

I was finishing another beer and watching my soap when Earl Tackett's daughter strutted through the door. Ruthie wore cut-offs, and because it was kind of breezy, a sleeveless blouse overlaid with a long-sleeved shirt open to the waist and tied off there. On her hip was a fanny pack, on her feet sandals.

With her scrunched reddish-blond hair, too much makeup, and cute little figure, she drew every man's eye.

I patted the stool beside me. "Hop up here and have a seat, Ruthie." The TV was set for the drunk-impaired so you could read what was being said on *G.H.* over the noise of other sets.

"I'll take a Bud," she said to the bartender.

"So, how's your dad?"

The bartender was studying the ID she had given him.

"He's out of the coma, but for some reason my mother insists on staying with him."

"He's her husband."

"But it means I have to take care of my brother and sister."

"Of course."

"I want to be independent. Like you."

"You can't. You have kids you're responsible for."

"They're not mine."

"But they *are* your responsibility."

She noticed her Bud had not arrived. "What's the problem?" she asked the bartender.

"I don't think you're old enough to be in here." He placed the ID on the bar in front of her.

"Tell him I'm old enough, Susan."

"Shut up, Ruth, and watch *G.H.* before I arrest you."

"But I thought we were friends."

"I'm trying to be your friend. You just won't let me."

"I don't need friends if this is how you're going to act."

"Ruth, your father's in the hospital, you haven't been to school today"—with my beer, I gestured at the ID—"and you're way too young to be in here. You need someone to talk some sense into you."

She returned the ID to her fanny pack. "I don't know why I can't drink. I have all these responsibilities."

"When you need one, that's the worst time to drink."

"Like you never used alcohol to drown your sorrows."

"You have sorrows?"

"Living with my father, I sure as hell do."

"I'd take your life any day."

Her face twisted up into something robbing her of all her attractiveness. "A father hassling you—you miss that?"

That didn't require an answer, so I returned my attention to the screen. When *G.H.* stopped for another break, I asked, "Why aren't you in school?"

"I have a pass."

"To hang out at sports bars?"

"You had a phony license when you were my age."

"I don't think that's relevant."

"Oh, yeah, it's relevant." She slid off her stool and her hands went to her hips. "It's relevant as hell. You don't want anyone having fun after you've had a ton." Ruth looked at the men staring at her, some making plans for the remainder of the day, some of those plans including this young girl.

Over Ruth's shoulder, I saw Nelson Obie come through the door. He saw us and walked over to the bar.

"Find out what you needed, Chase?"

I nodded, wondering how to get rid of this creep.

"Can I buy you lunch, Ruth?" he asked.

"Sure," she said, visibly brightening. "Susan told me I wasn't old enough to be in here."

"Yeah. She's become a real prig in her old age."

That night Chad took me to the China House restaurant. I had to admit he looked terrific, though I didn't say so. He wore dark whipcord slacks with a cream-colored, long-sleeved shirt, sleeves folded a couple of turns to the elbow. I wore a jacket. It was rather chilly with the Vette's top down.

"Is this to make up for last night?" I asked as we rolled down Ocean Boulevard. We held hands across the console.

Though I was still pissed, I didn't want to be alone. You can't live by yourself and not have the occasional bad night. A couple of nights ago, Lucy Leslie had had one that'd been absolutely the pits. Sometimes you wonder if that's how you'll end up. The thought usually passes, but it's always there, lurking in the shadows, out of sight of any number of lights that can be strung up along Ocean Boulevard.

He gave my hand a small squeeze. "You know I love you, Suze."

When he let go, I brushed back the hair that had fallen across his forehead. Wasted effort. The top was down. "I love you, too, my man."

"Then let's get married. What do you say?"

"I'm not sure your mother's ready for that."

"She's like any other mom. She doesn't want me marrying anyone who carries a gun."

"If it wasn't that, it'd be something else." I stared down the highway. Nighttime came later and later these days. The Season was almost here, but not for Lucy Leslie. Why hadn't I returned her calls?

The voice on the answering machine had said, "Susan, are you there? If you're there, please pick up."

I didn't. At the moment Chad had his hands where they didn't belong and I was loving it!

"This is Lucy. Look, I don't know why you haven't returned my calls, but if it's something I did, I'm sorry. I didn't mean to."

My eyes popped open and I pushed Chad away. What had the girl done now?

"Susan, I was thinking maybe you and I could get together. Maybe you could drop by the restaurant. You could eat for free."

I had tried to get out of bed, but those hands pulled me down. "Chad, let me get this."

"No way. You just got back from Quantico and I want to see what those Marines taught you." He goosed me and I let out a little shriek.

"Chad!"

The voice on the machine continued, ". . . got something I need repaired. It's the—er . . . it's the . . . I could really use your help."

"I was with the FBI, not the Marines. Now let me go!" I fought to get away. Okay, okay, I didn't fight very hard.

"Give me a call sometime, Susan. I've got a machine, you know."

Chad let go just in time to hear Lucy hang up. "She's

been calling me at the office."

Standing naked beside the bed, I asked, "What's she want?"

"She wanted to know where you were."

"And what did you tell her?"

"That you were out of town."

"I think you could've told her where."

"Uh-huh." He slipped his arms around me and pulled me down on the bed again. "Why didn't you tell her where you were going?" Something hard bumped into my leg.

"Chad, please stop! I need to call her back."

But he wouldn't let go, and it'd been an awfully long time since we'd been together. And what he was doing felt *sooo* damn good.

"We don't ever have to see them again, you know."

"Huh?" I blinked as I realized I was in Chad's Vette rolling down Ocean Boulevard.

"My parents. We don't ever have to see them."

"Uh-huh. And where were you planning on working to keep me in the style to which I've become accustomed?"

"I have offers, one in Savannah. People like my designs. Some say they're better than my dad's." He pulled into the parking lot of the China House. After turning off the engine, he took my hands in his. "Look, you want to get married. Let's do it. We can drive over to Wedding Chapel by the Sea."

I shook my head. "A year of SLED under my belt. That's what we agreed."

"I'm ready now." Chad held my hands tightly. "I'll buy the ring tomorrow. I have all the money saved up."

"No, Chad. Christmas, like we decided."

"You sure?"

"Chad, it won't be me changing my mind. It's your mom who has to do that."

"At least we agree about that." He took me into his arms and held me close. It was a long time before I was ready for Chinese.

144

Steve Brown

During dinner, he said, "I understand I deserve the Great Wall of China but not this Sphinx."

That drew my attention away from the couple across the room. Behind a stylized drawing on a paper wall sat someone who, from the rear, looked a lot like Alan Putnam. "Sorry. What did you say?"

"Chinese is the kind of food people like to talk about, you know, make comparisons as to where they've eaten the best egg roll, noodles, etcetera."

"Chad, what in the world are you talking about?"

"You haven't heard a thing since I mentioned marriage. Am I putting too much pressure on you?"

"No."

He gestured at the room with his chopsticks. "Tonight's an apology, but I can't compete with your job. The rush you get . . . don't you think I can see the way your eyes light up when you talk about SLED?"

"Chad, what the hell—what are you talking about?"

"You remember the time I spent topside with Theresa Hardy?"

"How can I forget."

"She's quite a woman, isn't she?"

I picked up my chopsticks. "I couldn't care less."

"Oh, goody, you're jealous."

My head jerked up. "I am not!"

"Theresa was brought in to nail you, wasn't she?"

"You know she was."

"She's not going to do it." He picked up a piece of pork with his chopsticks. "She thinks too much of you."

"And how would you know?"

"Because of tonight."

"Now you're the one not making sense."

He gestured at the meal with his chopsticks. "This is my apology for not understanding what happened in that motel."

"I thought you knew. I killed a couple of bad guys." For some reason I shuddered.

He finished chewing his bite. "I was angry that you'd placed yourself in such danger, but Theresa says it's unusual that any agent would ever find themselves in such a situation. Very atypical."

I didn't know which shocked me more: Hardy's feeding Chad this line of bull or his believing it.

"You know I love you, Suze. Twenty-four seven."

Oh, shit. Chad looked so sweet when he smiled. It's quite a delicious feeling to be devoured by someone's eyes.

So we finished the evening in bed, and I can guarantee he didn't leave the following morning thinking about my job. Though he would've if he'd been there when my boss called. A second dead girl had been found on the beach, and right about now I wasn't so sure I wanted to be the expert on sex crimes. I'd known this girl, too.

13

Before I left my boat I called Heather Jackson, one of the two blond reporters at the crime scene the day we'd found Lucy. Heather became instantly awake when she heard who was calling.

"Susan! What can I do for you?"

"I need a favor."

"Shoot!"

"You filmed the crowd at the beach, didn't you, the day Lucy's body was found?"

"Yes?"

"I need to see the tape."

"Is that why you called? Good lord! It's just past seven and I had to fill in at eleven last night."

"Can I see the tape?"

"Yes. Now can I go back to sleep?"

"Er—can you do the same thing this morning?"

"Film at the place where—Susan, what are you saying? Has there been another murder?"

I didn't reply.

"Where?"

Again I said nothing.

"Susan, what is it you want? You were in such a snit the other day—"

"Heather, I'm not going to say anymore until you promise."

"Absolutely. I can have the crime scene filmed."

"And the crowd?"

"Of course."

"Promise?"

"Susan, I've never broken a promise to you yet."

"I can get my ass in a sling if they ever find out I called you."

"They'll never hear it from me. Why do you want people filmed at the scene—you think the killer will be there?"

"I have no idea. I just want you to film the crowd."

I could hear her fumbling out of bed. "Just tell me when and where to meet you."

The dead girl was another blonde, and she'd been found by morning beach walkers at Garden City, a town on the Southern Strand. Garden City is a big hit with families. It sports its own pier and mini-arcade, which means it's just a notch above being as boring as Pawleys Island. Of course, there had been the time they'd had to shoot an alligator that'd come ashore, but that incident doesn't get much play in Garden City's brochures.

The young woman had been found in the water, and by the time I arrived her body had been moved above the high-tide line and covered with a sterile sheet at the request of Albert Greave. He was kneeling beside her, his remaining hair blowing around and camera hanging around his neck. Teddy Ingles was staring at me once again. The couple who'd found the body had been detained: two retirees wearing caps and windbreakers that displayed their undying devotion to the Carolina Gamecocks.

Though it was early, people hung over the railing of the six-hundred-foot pier and stared the fifty or so yards separating us from them. Another group had collected next to the restaurant and arcade. Below that was the parking area. Jennings was there with his forensics unit. Yellow tape stopped anyone trying to enter the crime scene, which included me, even after flashing my ID. *When would people start thinking of me as a real law enforcement officer!*

Garden City has no police department—because Garden City is not a city—go figure!—and the Horry County Police Department has jurisdiction. When I was finally allowed into the crime scene, I passed the female retiree pointing at the base of the pier. She was talking to a sleepy-looking Mickey DeShields.

She said: "The poor dear was hooked to the piling and it took forever for the EMS to drag her out of the water. She must've gotten caught on the barnacles after hitting her head on the pier."

"Morning, Susan."

"Morning, Mickey."

I left the retirees with DeShields and walked over to where the dead girl lay face down on a surfboard and covered by a blanket. People in California would laugh at our puny waves, but kids still make the effort, usually during stormy weather. Hurricanes make the best surfing and kids have been known to follow storms up the East Coast, chasing waves like people pursue tornadoes across the Midwest.

A glance under the sheet confirmed what the retiree had said. What the woman hadn't noticed was that the naked victim was fastened to the board by a piece of clear nylon rope strapped around her waist and across her shoulders. Tricky, keeping her weight on top of the surfboard. But the girl's hands had hung down, giving the board stability. The surfboard was manufactured by Perfection, a local board shaper. The whole scene nauseated me.

My boss stood with Jennings. The chief had a stunned look on his face. Reality had finally sunk in. The Grand Strand had its first serial killer.

"You're late, Chase." Warden wore his usual suit and tie; Jennings in his uniform and black Stetson. "I called you an hour ago."

I knelt on the other side of the surfboard across from Albert Greave. The coroner inclined his head in the direction of the pier. "It's the same as at the other crime scene. The footprints suggest the killer weighs two-fifty or more, and the stride makes him over six feet tall."

"Alan Putnam is over six feet tall but he doesn't carry the weight."

"Then," said Jennings from above us, "he'll have to do as

Color Me A Killer

the primary suspect because Anslow and Austin turned up nothing at the Host of Kings Hotel. Putnam's already called and complained. He's lost a couple of employees because of the interviews. They must've thought my men were from the INS."

Lifting the sheet, Greave pointed at a six-pointed star on the victim's shoulder. If the star had been inside a circle, it would've meant the victim had been a devil worshiper, but there was no circle.

"Could this be gang-related?" asked Greave. "Some kind of ritual killing?"

"Don't you wish."

The earlobes were ripped away again, but the young woman's nails were intact and painted a dark purple. The body had been in the water long enough to be bloated, and some creature had gotten to her fingertips, nose, and nipples. Her eyes were closed and she had eyebrows that would have demanded a good deal of work.

Greave re-covered the body as Eddie Tooney joined us. The forensics unit continued to walk on line down the beach, paying special attention to the area under the pier. A technician dusted the railing of the stairs leading to the beach, where I'd been detained. North of us were all hotels, motels, and condotels. Below us, houses once again. A couple of the houses were open, and on their porches people stared in our direction. One even used binoculars. Plainclothes detectives Anslow and Austin were questioning them, along with those who continued fishing in the surf.

Tooney brought along one of the techs. "It's the same funny sort of walk again."

"What's this?" I asked, getting to my feet.

"Read what's in your 'in' box sometimes, Chase."

Warden was right. I hadn't glanced at my mail after the grilling by Theresa Hardy. And I was going to have to do something about the time it took to reach a crime scene. Damn pantyhose!

"Our guy has a funny walk," explained Tooney, shifting around with all that gear he wore on his equipment belt.

150

"It's not pigeon-toed, but it's a different gait."

"How's that?"

"He doesn't come down on his feet properly. More on his heels."

"Could it have to do with how the body was carried?"

Tooney shook his head. "The pattern continues after the body is dumped."

Warden grunted. Evidently that had been in the report, too.

"Where was Rex Kilgore last night?" I asked.

"Out on bail," said my boss, glancing at Jennings.

"A murder suspect out on bail?"

"He knows a good lawyer," said the chief. "You had to expect that."

Pointing at the dead woman, I said to Warden, "Remember the girl I told you about, the one Rex Kilgore hit in the face with the beer bottle when they were much younger? This is the girl."

"I remember that," said Tooney, nodding. "I'll pick him up."

"Do it," said Jennings. He was watching Heather Jackson and her cameraman tromping through the sand toward us. The chief shook his head. "I don't know where they heard it. I told everyone to keep it off the air."

"Susan," asked Albert Greave, "since the body was moved from the water, you don't have any problem with Teddy and me taking it off the beach, do you?"

I wanted to tell him we should worry less about the approaching Season and focus more on the number of young women dying at the hands of a serial killer. But what can you do with a body found at sea?

I told Greave to go ahead. Besides, I was supposed to be more mature, at least in my relationship with the Chamber. Like that was going to ever happen. Teddy Ingles stared at me as he shook out a body bag. He and Greave fitted the bag around the surfboard and the dead girl's feet.

"Who is she, Chase?" asked my boss.

"Kitty Flanagan. She works for Nelson Obie." My voice

sounded flat as I looked out to sea. "Kitty's almost thirty, married, and makes her living house-sitting and selling cosmetics at the Inlet Square Mall when she's not guarding the beach." I knelt beside her and pried open her mouth. Since Kitty was facedown, once her jaw was pried open, the lifeguard whistle easily tumbled into my hand.

Greave looked at Warden. "At least we can stop deluding ourselves."

Jennings frowned at a tech who walked over with Eddie Tooney.

The tech shrugged. "We planned on letting Doc Vickers examine her at the hospital. We just wanted to get her off the beach."

This did not please Jennings. SLED had trumped him again. Worse, it had been done by a woman.

I dropped the whistle into a sack held out by the tech. The tech did not smile, nor did he give me an "attaboy."

Heather Jackson was ready for a standup. She hadn't spoken to anyone while her cameraman went about filming those leaning over the railing or those watching from down the beach. Clumping through the sand behind them came the reporter from the *Sun News*, tie askew, shirt hanging out one side of his pants.

"Is this a serial killing, Lieutenant Warden?" asked Heather when the camera swung around on her. Heather was dressed as I was: skirt, blouse, and flats for negotiating the sand. "Two girls in three days—"

"Sorry, Miss Jackson, but I won't speculate."

"What can you tell us about the dead girl?"

"We'll have something for you before noon," Jennings said. Meaning the noon broadcast.

"But if there's a serial killer working the beach, shouldn't people be warned?"

Way to go, Heather. Beside her the *Sun News* reporter thudded to a stop in the sand. He adjusted his glasses and tried to ask a question.

"That's all we've got." Warden looked toward the restaurant on the pier. "Chief, are they serving breakfast up there?"

Jennings glanced at the crowd lining the pier. "They'd be fools not to."

"I wouldn't mind a bite. Can you do something about moving those people along?"

"J.D., I don't think this is the time—"

"Chase, will you be joining us for breakfast?"

I glanced at the body bag containing Kitty Flanagan. "If I have the stomach for it."

The print reporter glanced at the pier as the cameraman began filming in that direction again. There was a face up there that I recognized: Bob Yale, former reporter for the *Chicago Tribune*. Yale leaned on the railing and stared down at us.

"What's he doing?" Warden asked Heather, referring to the cameraman.

"Serial killers sometimes return to the scene of the crime. What do you say, Lieutenant, why don't you let us help you catch this guy?"

"You have the tape from yesterday?"

"Of course."

"Can you make a copy?"

"If you'll cooperate."

"I'll think about it, after I see what you have."

She gestured at me with her microphone. "May I talk with Susan?"

"I think you already have."

We adjourned to the outdoor restaurant. Two girls had been killed in the last three days, but we were enjoying coffee and Danish on a breezy pier overlooking the ocean. Mickey bought mine, then went to work in his notebook. Jennings joined us once his patrolmen had moved those along who had been standing on the other side of a latticework wall.

"What do you know about the victim?" asked my boss.

"Kitty's married to a wife beater who drives a cement truck. And Luther's large enough to throw girls over his shoulder." I told them the name of the company. It was an out-of-town outfit, as were most who plundered the Grand Strand. Words tumbled out of me. "Luther beats Kitty when he's drunk. He could've done this. Tying her to the surfboard, I don't think so."

"Think it was smart to let Kilgore out on bail?" asked Mickey Dee.

Jennings shrugged. "There's a good bit of sympathy for Rex. Things have been pretty tough for him lately."

Sitting up, I hit the table, causing coffee to slop over the edges of our cups. "I don't want him walking the fucking streets!"

"Don't make this personal, Chase."

"Personal? This case is downright sexist, if you haven't noticed."

Mickey asked me, "Have any idea where we can find this Luther Flanagan?"

I sat back in my chair and took a breath. "They usually house-sit in Surfside. There's a realtor over there related to Kitty. I don't know her name."

Jennings stood. "I'll get on that."

"DeShields, why don't you go with the chief. I want a better timeline than we have for Leslie. And have everyone check the shoe stores. Shoe outlets, too." When we looked at him, Warden explained, "Leslie liked shoes. Her apartment was full of them."

Warden's remark reminded me to ask, "The phone numbers on the wall?"

DeShields referred to his notes. "Most were friends who hadn't seen Lucy for several days, even weeks. One number was disconnected. Another was an off-and-on boyfriend by the name of Greg Sitton. The disconnected number belonged to a Jan Pacewic, who has returned to Cleveland and was in Cleveland when Lucy was killed. Pacewic hadn't spoken to Lucy since last summer. The off-and-on boyfriend is a married guy she broke up with a couple of weeks ago. He was stealing her stash."

"How'd you get that?"

"Lucy's uncle. In a second interview."

"Does Sitton have an alibi for last night?"

"It's on my list to check out."

After they left, Warden asked, "You say both girls worked for Nelson Obie?"

"Yes, dammit."

"Then perhaps, if you can control yourself, we should have a talk with him."

I brought him up to speed as to what I'd done, leaving out the part about showing Nelson my gun. "Anything on Alan Putnam?" I was having trouble controlling my breathing. There was a serial killer out there and I was helpless to stop him— as long as I sat here pretending to be in control of my rage.

"DeShields pulled half the night watching his place. Anslow and Austin took the other half. Putnam never went out after he got home."

Now wait a minute. Didn't I see him at the China House Restaurant last night? "He could've used his boat."

"We had someone covering that."

"And the drainage ditch that runs by his neighbor's house?"

Warden glanced in the direction DeShields and Jennings had taken. "I was told that Putnam arrived home after dark and Jennings' people took over in the dark."

"I'd put both Nelson and Alan under the fucking jail!"

"Chase, watch your language."

Leaning into the table, I asked, "Then tell me when we're going to start treating this like a serial killing? People should be warned."

Warden looked through the latticework. On the beach below, Heather and her cameraman were putting away their gear. The guy from the *Sun News* stared up at us.

"J.D., I'm asking you: When do we go public?"

"After you and Greave report to me on the Flanagan autopsy and no sooner."

"What about Carlos Rodgers, the guy living in the beach house? Did he show?"

"He's dead."

"Dead?" And I'm sure the surprise showed on my face.

"When Eddie Tooney confronted him, Rodgers leaped out a window. Tooney said Rodgers' foot must've caught on the windowsill because he landed hard. Dead on impact."

"Tooney was pulling an extra shift?"

"Being disciplined after I complained to the chief about

Tooney digging Leslie's clothing out of the dumpster behind her uncle's restaurant."

"Discipline usually takes the form of admin leave."

"We need everyone for this. That's why you're still on the street and threatening people with handguns."

I said nothing. Evidently, J.D. had spies everywhere.

He gazed out over the beach again. "Tell me, Chase, what's the attraction of being a lifeguard? Hundreds of kids come here each summer, get a job, stay in guardhouses, proving it's a dead-end job." Guardhouses were where out-of-town lifeguards stayed while working at the beach.

"The dead girls were people, too, J.D."

"Who were mixed up in drugs."

"If you believe that, then let's bust Nelson Obie."

"We need proof."

"Everybody and their brother knows Nelson deals."

"Then," said Warden, getting to his feet, "it'd be nice if one of those brothers squealed on him."

"Kenny Mashburn did."

Warden stared at me as I stood. "And?"

"I don't believe anything Mashburn says, even if it's the truth."

Heading for our vehicles under the pier, we ran into Bob Yale.

"Looks like you've got a serial killer on your hands, Susan." Yale wore a pair of chino slacks with a navy blue pullover. As usual his black hair was slicked back and his goatee neatly trimmed.

I introduced my boss.

"Good to meet you, Lieutenant." Yale stuck out a hand that Warden did not shake. "Susan and I go back a ways."

"Er—he wanted information about locating runaways for one of his books."

Yale withdrew the hand. "Anyway, I hope you'll let Susan tell me all about it when you solve this case. I've covered serial killings before—"

"And the way you cover them," said my boss, "is why you lost your job in Chicago."

Yale was taken aback, and me, I was shocked.

"I can explain—"

"Mister Yale, we don't know that this is the work of a serial killer, and I'd appreciate you staying away from this investigation"—Warden glanced at me—"and my investigators."

"Okay, okay," said Yale, nodding rapidly, "I know how the Chamber works." He backed away. "I can't say I blame them. This *is* a tourist town."

As Yale returned to his ride, Warden asked, "How well do you know that guy?"

"Not as well as you do, it would appear."

"All it took was a phone call."

"Why even call?"

"Because he showed up at the previous crime scene."

"A lot of people did."

"But Yale doesn't live anywhere near North Myrtle. That was easy to check, too."

"He could've been in the area, seen all the activity, and stopped by out of curiosity. He was once a reporter."

Yale's ride was a Harley-Davidson. As he put the machine into gear, he glanced in our direction, nodded, and roared out from under the arcade.

Watching him go, Warden changed directions again. "Or Yale could've heard it on a scanner. They have scanners on bikes these days, and there was a Harley at the crime scene like the one he's driving."

"Just whose side are you on, J.D.?"

"As I told you at breakfast yesterday, Chase, I don't take sides. I check facts."

"And the facts surrounding Bob's losing his job, what were they?"

"Somehow Yale gained access to the Cook County coroner's computer. The Chicago police had Yale on their list of suspects because of the characteristics of evidence reported in his newspaper, which hadn't been released to the general public."

I watched the Harley disappear down the street. Many a time I'd seen young women on that bike, gripping the sissy bar, as Bob whipped around the Grand Strand.

"Chase, what do you have planned today?"

"I'll drop by the morgue."

"That's later. What now?"

"I want to stop by the Tacketts' and make sure the kids got off to school. Their mom has lots on her mind."

"So you've nominated yourself to make sure Ruth Tackett stays on the straight and narrow?"

"It's more than that. She's scheduled to work for Nelson Obie this summer."

"I don't buy Obie doing this thing."

"It's the off-season and he might want to send a message to his dealers."

"You're reaching again. This isn't private-eyeing where you work your own hours and agenda. What about stopping by to see Paul Friddle while you're in this do-gooder mode?"

"I'd planned to. What did Hardy tell you?"

"I won't know anything until the report comes down."

"Come on, she must've given you a hint. Friddle knows you personally."

"That only works when you aren't dumb enough to keep an agent on the street who's killed two drug dealers. What about those clothes your friend gave you? Did you bring them in to see if we can match them to Leslie's wardrobe?"

"Clothes? What clothes?" Now I wanted to find Theresa Hardy and choke her. *Damn that bitch!* While she'd been sweet-talking my boyfriend, she'd been squealing on another of my friends. "You can't actually believe Pick's involved in these murders just because he came across some clothing discarded along the Waterway?"

Warden flashed his first and possibly only smile for the day. "I may have to, if you insist on calling these serial killings."

14

The Tacketts lived in a duplex several streets off the beach. The rent Earl's tenant paid made the payments on both sides of the building. Everything in its place and a place for everything. Perhaps it was Earl's sense of orderliness that irritated me, not his devotion to his family and his church.

The duplex sat on a flat piece of ground with loblolly pines in both the front and rear. The yard was well-trimmed and maintained—azaleas pruned back to a manageable size and a sidewalk that split off and ran to both front porches, which were slabs of concrete. Storm doors protected wooden ones. There was no bell, so I opened the door on Earl's side, matching the name on a corresponding mailbox at the street, and knocked on the interior door.

No answer.

I knocked again.

No answer again, but there was the sound of machinery being operated in the backyard. The kids were supposed to be in school, and Earl and his wife were at the hospital. I really needed to get by the hospital.

Walking around the side of the house, I saw no one on the Tacketts' side of the yard. The sound came from the other side of a yard split down the middle by trimmed ligustrums, the bush that's supposed to replace the redtips when they finally become extinct. Finding room to pass between the end of the row and the rear of the house, I saw Earl's tenant was a man about my age with rippling muscles across his back. On a screened-in back porch sat a baby in

159

a playpen, watching daddy plow up the backyard. The baby wore a pink top with a matching bow in her curly black hair.

Giving her father a wide berth so he wouldn't be startled, I stood to one side, waiting for him to notice me. His hair was black and curly, his skin pink, and he had the pecs to operate any piece of equipment. Sweat ran through stubble on his face and dripped to the broken-up ground. Not much sand where he was digging, so the garden might have a chance.

He noticed me, stopped the machine, and grinned. "Here to help?"

"I'm not dressed for the job." I still wore my schoolteacher attire.

The young man continued to smile. "I think we can scare up an old pair of jeans for you."

"And whose would those be, yours or the baby's mother's?"

He glanced at the porch where his daughter chewed on a rubber toy. "What can I do for you?" Sweat dripped from the strong line of his chin onto his hairy chest.

All of a sudden it felt rather warm for a spring morning. "I dropped by to see if the Tackett kids got off to school."

He glanced at his neighbor's back porch. "I don't know, but I've been kind of busy. I want to get this plowing finished before going in to work."

"I'll bang on the door again. I don't think their teenager showed up for school, and it might take that to wake her up."

"That'd be Ruthie."

"I saw her yesterday and I didn't like who she was hanging with."

"And you'd be who, in relation to the family?"

"I was partnered with Earl when he was injured."

He gawked. "That was you . . . you're the one who shot those two dope dealers?"

"I'm afraid so."

"No apologies necessary. Drugs killed my brother." He wiped his hand on his jeans and extended it. "Billy Joe Randall."

"Susan Chase."

We shook hands. His was damp, as were parts of me.

Randall pulled a bandanna from the back pocket of his jeans and wiped the sweat from his face, then ran it over that gorgeous chest.

"Er—who told you about the shoot-out?"

"Ruthie, of course."

Of course?

"Miss Chase, since you're a friend of the family, can I speak to you frankly?"

Friend of the family? I wouldn't go that far.

"Ruthie looks up to you."

To this I said nothing.

"I'm not sure her parents like it, but she does."

"Pardon me, Mister Randall, but is there something you wanted to tell me, before I break into your neighbor's house and make sure the girl isn't there?"

"Oh, no, I didn't mean . . . . Miss Chase, don't take this wrong, but if Ruthie was home today, she'd be out here with me." Randall glanced at his back porch. "And I'd be wearing a shirt."

"Ruth has a crush on you?" *The little twit.*

His face went from pink to red. "I know, I know, I'm old enough to be her—"

"Brother?"

His was a nervous smile. Certainly the temptation had been there while his old lady had been bloated and more demanding than any admiring teen. "So you don't think Ruth's inside?"

"I don't think Ruth came home last night and her mother doesn't know it."

"But the younger kids—"

"Would cover for her. Ruthie gives them money."

"Where would she get that money?"

He cleared his throat. "I'm sure she has a job."

"Not until summer when she guards the beach. Earl said his kids' grades were too important to be doing more than odd jobs around the house."

Randall glanced at his porch again. Standing there was a young woman wearing a sundress. The fabric clung to her curves, such as they were. She could've used more of a chest.

"Mister Randall, did Ruth ever try to sell you drugs?"

"I really think I've said more than I should." He reached for the cord to crank the tiller. "Now, if you don't mind, I need to get back to work." He pulled the cord and the engine caught.

Reaching down, I jerked the wire off the plug, then straightened up. "Billy Joe, Ruth was busted two nights ago for trying to make a buy. Cops won't cover for her forever. If it's true Ruth looks up to me, I still might have a chance to turn her around."

Randall glanced at his wife, who now held the baby. Jeez. First the fuck-me dress, now Madonna and child.

"Miss Chase, I didn't want to say anything, but the truth is Ruth said . . . that we might take off one afternoon and smoke up—is how she put it." His face colored before he bent over and reconnected the spark plug. "Now if you don't mind, I'd like to get this done before going in to work. There's a key over the back door if you have to get inside the Tacketts'."

I left him, looping around the ligustrums and giving the wife a little wave. She did not return the gesture.

Was that what I'd be like someday: spying on Chad while he planted our garden, after he'd plowed my furrow and planted his seed?

The key was where Randall had said it would be, and when I let myself in, once again I saw the Tackett house had everything in its place and a place for everything.

"Anyone home?"

No answer.

"Ruth, are you here? It's Susan."

The breakfast dishes stood in a plastic drainer, water gleaming on their surfaces, and the beds were made. That made it easy to tell Ruth's room from the rest. It was an orderly mess, with the usual teenage paraphernalia across dresser, nightstand, and desk. On a corner of a neatly made bed lay a note.

> *Mom,*
> *Have an early meeting at school.*
> *Danny and Rebecca have a ride with the*
> *Arnolds.*
>
> > *Love,*
> > *Ruth*
>
> *P.S. After school I'll bring Danny and Rebecca*
> *by the hospital to see Dad.*

Nice touch, Ruth. You sound as straight as your parents hope you'll turn out to be. Now it's time someone bent you back into shape.

Nelson Obie lived in a high-rise condo along the beach. It was built after Hurricane Hugo blew everything into the second row. Second row is anything off the beach. The condo was six stories tall with a beige stucco finish and individual balconies overlooking the beach. An elevator led to the penthouse where Nelson lived, the envy of every guy along the Grand Strand: unlimited money, girls, and dope.

A security guard sat on a stool in the hallway housing the elevator. A phone hung on the wall near his shoulder but no cameras. Weird. Nelson was known to be a stickler for security. In the rear of the narrow hallway was the elevator, but you had to get past the guard, and that didn't look easy. He looked like a pro football player who had let himself go. His gut poured over his belt as he leaned on a lectern, reading the sports page.

"Need to see Nelson."

The guard looked up. "Don't do the hiring here."

"I'm not here for a job."

"What's your name?"

"Chase. Susan Chase."

Lifting the paper, he glanced at a calendar. *SI's* swimsuit calendar. Didn't guys realize those girls were touched up in Photoshop? Did they really care?

"Sorry. You ain't on the schedule."

"Nelson'll want to see me. I'm an old friend."

"Nelson don't see nobody before noon, old friend or not." He returned to the sports section, leaning on the lectern. I didn't see how the skinny piece of furniture held him up.

Whipping out my ID, I held it where the lug could see it. "This help?"

He looked at the ID, then sat up. I'm sure the lectern probably appreciated that. "You with SLED?"

I returned my ID to my backpack. "Yeah. Let's go."

"I have to call upstairs."

"Nah. Let's surprise him."

"Nelson's got rules. Nobody goes upstairs unless they're announced first."

"I don't want to be announced."

"Sorry, them's Nelson's rules."

"Even though I'm from SLED?"

"Even if you got a search warrant, I'd have to let Nelson know you were coming." He reached for the phone mounted on the wall.

My hand was still inside my pack, putting away my ID. "Look, you're bigger than me, so let's do it this way." I pulled out the Smith & Wesson and stuck it in his face.

His hands went up, including the one holding the phone. "What's this?"

"My ticket to ride."

"Look, Hon, you'd better put that away. Somebody's liable to get hurt."

"How about you just shut up and take me upstairs?"

He hung up the phone. "You ain't gonna get upstairs without Nelson knowing you're coming."

Now that didn't make sense. I was the one with the pistol. I motioned the fat guy off his stool and toward the elevator.

"Watch where you're pointing that thing, Hon. We don't want it accidentally going off."

"Believe me, Hon, it's never gone off accidentally."

I followed him into the elevator and took a position in the far corner, pistol jammed into my side, making it harder to grab. He hit the button for the penthouse, then another beside it, jury-rigged into the panel.

"What's that?" I asked.

The guard only smiled as the doors closed. Once the elevator started upward a hissing sound began and a mist began to fall from the ceiling. Well, hell, Nelson hadn't gotten where he was today by being a fool, but you, Susan, now that's another story.

The guard used his hands to lower his huge frame and belly to the floor. "You best settle in, Hon. We're all gonna take a little nap." He was still smiling when his eyes closed and his head clunked into the corner.

15

As the fat man slumped to the floor with that stupid grin on his face, I grabbed a breath, let most of it out, and then hunkered down as the elevator rose. Dropping my gun to the floor, I ripped off the skirt, hoisted it overhead, and fell to my knees.

Under my impromptu shelter I pulled out my cigarettes. After breaking off the tips of two of them, I jammed a filter into each nostril, then pulled my skirt tight around my head and waited, holding my breath as long as I could. Usually three minutes since giving up smoking. There was an irony there, using filters from the smokes, but I didn't have time to consider it. After a short lift the elevator had stopped.

The filters didn't work so good, and just as I was becoming groggy, I pulled out a stick of smelling salts. Believe me, I've considered what a scumbag can do with you once you're unconscious. Okay, okay, actually I've learned from past mistakes.

Snapping the smelling salts, my head jerked back, but I couldn't curse until I caught my breath. By then the elevator had begun to move toward the penthouse once again. When we finally stopped, the doors still didn't open, but through the fabric of my skirt I heard a fan exhausting the gas. It seemed to take forever and I had to use the salts again. Really, it was no fun. I remained on my knees, skirt over my head, until someone entered the elevator and grabbed my shoulder, turning me around.

I looked up as the skirt came off. "Morning, Nelson."

"Chase, what the hell are you doing here?"

He stepped back. In his hand was a .38 special. In mine was my Smith & Wesson, and when he stepped back it was easier for me to jam my gun into his privates than for him to raise his weapon. I told the bastard to toss the .38 into the room behind him. I had to repeat myself before he obeyed me, and all the time my pistol hovered near his privates.

Never taking my eyes off him, I picked up my pack and skirt and followed him. As I left the elevator, I hit the "down" button and the doors closed, taking the fat man away. Nelson had on blue pajama bottoms and nothing more, and since the pj's were made of silk, I could see the impression his equipment made on the fabric. Less intimidating to look in his eyes, which were crusty with sleep. Dropping my pack and skirt to the floor, I scanned the penthouse. No one in the kitchen, which had a serving window opening on the living room, and no one in the hallway to my left.

"Just what the hell do you think you're doing? You can't break into someone's home without a warrant."

"I'm not here on official SLED business. Your name, however, did come up when another dead girl was found on the beach this morning."

"Who is it this time?"

"Kitty Flanagan."

"I didn't have anything to do with that."

"Horry County still wants to talk to you. They'll be here soon."

"And SLED?"

"SLED is watching and waiting, but that's not my style." Moving toward the hallway, I ignored the view of the ocean and the sky framing Nelson in his silk pajama bottoms. I was more interested in the .38. It lay near a scooped-out piece of furniture, which looked as if any occupant would be lying in the bottom of an oversized spoon. Backing Nelson toward the balcony, I snatched up the pistol and took it with me when I moved toward the hallway.

A door shut. I glanced in that direction. No one there. Smears of paint across pieces of canvas passed for artwork in the hallway leading to a pair of bedrooms. No one in the spare and the bed made. Behind me were the stairs to the ground floor, but I'd hear an audible "click" if someone came in that way.

"What're you looking for?" Nelson followed me around the wall separating the hall from the living room.

I was halfway down the hallway, his .38 tucked in my bicycle pants, and looking in both directions. "Ruth Tackett."

"God, but you are one serious pain in the ass."

"So I've been told." Staying close to the wall, I knocked a painting cockeyed. Nelson winced.

Without looking I found the master bedroom door with my free hand and passed across to its opposite side. The knob turned, but the door would not open.

I tapped on the door with the barrel of my pistol. "Open the door, Ruth."

"Go away, Susan!"

"Not without you."

"I'm eighteen. I have a right to be here."

"Not unless I say so."

"You don't run my life!"

"Then you haven't been paying attention."

"Susan, get out of here and leave us alone!"

"Not unless you say it to my face. Then I'll leave."

Down the hall Nelson snorted.

When the door opened, I stepped inside, pushing the door back and the girl into the bedroom. Quickly I shut the door, then locked it.

"Susan, you promised!"

From the other side of the door, Nelson shouted, "You dumb bitch! All you had to do was keep the door closed." There was a pause, then "Damn!" and Nelson moved down the hallway. At least that's what it sounded like.

In the middle of the room stood a circular bed, beige covers and sheets on the floor. Matching curtains kept out any light, and the carpet was plush enough to hide my running shoes. Scattered around the place were men's clothes and those of a teenaged girl. More clothing lay across a chaise lounge, and on a dresser, chains hung from a jewelry tower.

Pocket change and other items lay in a shallow clay bowl. The walk-in closet was open, but not the bathroom door. I checked both and found them empty. I broke the action of Nelson's .38, dropping its rounds in the tub, then tossing the pistol in the closet among numerous pairs of shoes.

Ruth wore an off-white robe too large for her, and where it touched the floor, the fabric piled up around her. Hair a disaster, makeup a mess, being angry didn't make her look any more attractive.

"Susan, you have no right busting in on us like this."

"You're supposed to be in school."

She tossed her head. "I made it further than you did. I'm a senior."

"And you're going to graduate. Get dressed. I'm taking you to school."

"You can't make me go!"

"I can't make you stay, but I can make your life miserable if you don't."

The girl wrung her hands. "Why are you doing this?"

"Because I didn't have anyone to warn me not to come up here when I was your age."

"But don't you see? You're doing it again. You don't want me having fun when you've had plenty."

"Ruth, get your clothes on before I call the cops."

"Sorry," she said, straightening her shoulders, "but this is out of my father's jurisdiction."

I stepped over to the nightstand and lifted the portable phone from its cradle. The surface of the nightstand was shiny and reflected something overhead.

Something that moved!

Startled, I dropped the phone, stepped back, and looked up, then relaxed when I saw the mirror. Well, kind of relaxed. And no, I didn't revisit the times I had enjoyed how I appeared in that glass over the oval bed.

"Ruth, you may make friends by sleeping with guys, but one of them is not going to be Nelson Obie."

"But I love him."

"You don't know what love is."

"And you do?"

"I don't date men old enough to be my father."

"You used to date Nelson."

"Ruth, don't try reasoning with me. I have too much on my mind."

"This is so unfair!"

"Cops' daughters don't get to date whoever they want to, especially drug dealers."

"You don't know that about Nelson."

"Don't piss me off by proving the depth of your ignorance. Just get your clothes on."

She had a few more choice words for me, nothing she'd learned in Sunday School. Finally, she took off the robe, put on her clothes, and left with me.

We found Nelson making coffee in the kitchen, and man oh man, did it smell good. I had my pistol out, but it wasn't necessary, until I asked for a cup to go.

"Don't push it, Chase."

Ah, Nelson, but that's just what I intend to do. I've seen what happens when you lose your cool. More than once all that's stood between you and a prison term was a lawyer who told you to keep your big mouth shut.

"Black," I said with a smile. "To go."

When he saw I wasn't leaving without my java, Nelson opened cabinets until he found a mug he knew he'd never see again. He poured the coffee into the cup and passed it through the serving window.

After a sip, I said, "You still make a mean cup of coffee, Nelson."

"Get out here, Chase, and next time you come back, make sure you're wearing some clothes."

As I retreated down the wall to retrieve my pack and paste my skirt back on, Ruth asked if she could have a moment alone with Nelson.

"Sure. But it won't do you any good."

She faced the serving window. "I'll be back, Nelson."

"No, you won't."

"I promise."

"Chase, get her out of here!"

"What about your friend downstairs?"

"Ernie won't bother you. I sent him to the store for some Egg Beaters."

Tears ran down Ruth's cheeks. "Nelson, you don't want me to come back?"

The drug dealer put his hands on the counter and leaned down to where he could see through the window. "Tell her, Chase. If she'll listen. She's not much better at listening than you were at her age."

"I was much younger, Nelson."

He shook his head. "You were never that young."

"Now you've gone and done it," said my passenger as we rolled down the Boulevard in my jeep. The wind whipped Ruth's hair around as she applied her makeup. But I had this delicious cup of coffee and I was feeling pretty good. And I don't think it had anything to do with the coffee.

"If Nelson doesn't want to see me again, it's all your fault."

"I can live with that."

"Oh, you are *sooo* hateful!"

"I'd be interested to know what you told Nelson your father did for a living."

"I said he worked for the city."

"Well, you probably won't go to hell for that."

She whipped around and jabbed the lipstick at me. "Don't preach to me! I know more than you'll ever know about piety. I get it all the time. If I don't attend a prayer group before school, my car's taken away. It's enough to make a person sick. My mother even has us praying for you."

Surprisingly, I didn't run off the road. Still, coffee spilled from my cup and ran down my hand, which I wiped off on my skirt. Well, coffee was going to get there sooner or later.

We picked up Ruth's Chevette at Charley O's, which was not open. Good. I might go in and toss down a few. I don't ever remember anyone praying for my soul, except a priest and that's his job. And quite a job at that.

Color Me A Killer

I followed Ruth to school, where we had to park across the street. Student parking had a fence around it and the gate was locked for the day. Ruth jerked her pack out of the back of her car.

When I joined her, she said, "You don't have to come inside."

"Then how will I know you signed in?"

"You don't trust me?"

"Not in the least."

As we went up the steps, she said, "My mother says you have to trust people to get them to trust you back."

"And look where that got her."

Ruth made a growling sound as we went through the doors, then the metal detectors. Knowing the detectors would be there, I had left my weapon in the jeep.

A teacher stood at the entrance of one of the classrooms. Around the woman's neck was a lanyard with a photo ID. "Good to see you this morning, Ruth."

The teenager didn't reply but did speak to a couple of students on our way to the office. Those kids also wore photo IDs. Posters on the wall touted a spring fling, one supported the soccer team in the playoffs, and there was a professionally produced "Today in History."

I felt no nostalgia for this place, as Boomers often do, waxing poetically about their high school daze. My memories of those years were from the street, and of the occasional encounter a lot more serious than any damn soccer match.

In the office I gave my card to a black woman on the other side of the counter and asked her to give me a call if Ruth didn't show up for school again. To give my request emphasis, I flashed my SLED ID.

"She has no right doing this to me!" whined Ruth.

The woman studied my card, then nodded. "I'll make sure this information is placed in Ruth's permanent file."

"Shit!" muttered my ward.

"Ruth! Apologize to the lady for such language."

"You're not my mother!"

"Since your mother prays for me, it's the least I can do."

"Susan, you really are mean!"

"Do it, Ruth! Now!"

The girl looked at the floor. "I'm sorry, Mrs. Andrews. I didn't mean to be vulgar."

Andrews said, "I'm sure Miss Chase is only interested in making sure you graduate."

Her head jerked up. "She didn't—why should I?"

The black woman regarded me. "And I'll bet Miss Chase regrets it."

"But not when I was eighteen."

"Ruth, your mother's so active in our school, especially at a time when most mothers work; if you didn't graduate, we'd feel like we'd failed your family. You've only got a few weeks to go, why not finish?"

Ruth was hanging her head and the black woman was chatting her up when I left. But it did appear she'd be there the remainder of the day.

With the battery of my cell phone pumped up, I could call the office—where I got the best possible news. There was to be a meeting at the Myrtle Beach Convention Center later in the day, and most every businessman had been asked to attend. I tried to keep the excitement out of my voice when I thanked Warden for doing this. After Hurricane Hugo had blown through, a procedure had been put in effect in which people who wanted to save their collective asses could get together and chat.

"Don't thank me, Chase, thank Rex Kilgore."

"Kilgore? Why's that?"

"He was injured in a shoot-out with Eddie Tooney not a half hour ago. With two girls dead and Kilgore wounded, it's time to bring this thing to a close. Where are you headed?"

"To see Doc Vickers. What's the status of Rex Kilgore?"

"Both were taken to Grand Strand Regional."

"Eddie, too?" My foot slipped off the accelerator, causing the jeep to slow down and someone behind me to honk.

"Did you finish your personal business?"

"Ruth's back at school."

"Where'd you find her?"

"With Nelson Obie."

"Are you serious? He's old enough to be that girl's father."

I didn't want to go there.

"Maybe someone should stop by and have a talk with Mister Obie. There's quite a number of young women under his supervision each summer."

"You won't get any complaint from me."

"You'll be at the convention center at four?"

"I'll be there."

"Make sure you are, and make sure you know what you're talking about."

Eddie Tooney sat in the waiting room of the emergency room. He appeared to be stunned. Next to him sat his partner, the young woman who hadn't taken my credentials seriously the day Lucy's body had been found. At the moment, they were the only ones there, but when the Season began every day would be like Saturday night. And when the bikers arrived . . . oh, why even think about it.

Taking a seat beside him, I took Eddie's hands in mine. "Are you all right?"

It was a moment before he could focus on me. "I—I shot him, Susan."

"You had to do it," Vance said. "He came at you with a carving knife."

"What happened?"

Eddie shook his head. "I can't believe it. I shot Rex."

"He came at you with a knife," repeated his partner.

"You were there?" I asked.

Vance shook her head. "I had the back door."

"Where was this?"

"At the Kilgore home. It was a condition of his release. He had to remain at home at all times."

"His mother, does she know?"

"I don't know," Vance said, "and I don't care."

I glanced at the pay phones on the wall. "You should notify his mother."

"I'm here for my partner, not some scumbag."

"Eddie, does Rex's mother still work at the county courthouse over in Conway?"

Tooney came out of his trance long enough to say, "I don't know. I stopped running with that crowd years ago." Eddie had played on the same team as Rex but was too mechanical in his movements to go to the next level.

"I'll make the call."

"Thank you . . . ." Tooney looked as if he was about to cry. "And tell his mom I'm sorry."

"No problem," I said, standing up.

The nurse at the desk was a Latina with a big butt.

"Could you tell me the status of Rex Kilgore? He was brought in with a gunshot wound."

After racking a chart, the woman faced me. "You next of kin?"

"No," I said, pulling out my ID, "but I need to tell his mother something when I make the call."

She glanced at the ID. "We don't have anything to tell her."

"Don't or won't?"

She leaned over the counter and lowered her voice. "Honey, if that boy makes it, he's living a charmed life. He took a bullet in the gut."

"That bad?"

"I'm no doctor, but if it were me, I'd have a priest in there. The bullet hit his spleen."

"I think Rex was a Christian."

"Whatever. A preacher, somebody. That kid don't have long to live."

"How about rustling up someone while I call his mother?"

"Can do," said the woman and she picked up a phone.

Leaving the counter, I glanced at Eddie, who was bent over and staring at the floor. His partner had an arm around his shoulder, and when Vance saw me staring at them, she flashed a look that told me she didn't care to hear anything about Rex Kilgore's condition.

I had to cross in front of the emergency room to reach the

phone. When I did someone barged through the double doors behind me.

"Chase, get in here!" It was Benjamin Vickers, and he wore scrubs and a pair of bloody latex gloves. "Kilgore wants to talk to you."

Reaching for the phone, I said, "I was about to call his mother."

"He may not last that long."

"Are you sure?"

"Chase, are you going to let this young man die before speaking to you?"

"Rex . . . Rex wants to talk to me?"

Vickers used an elbow on one of the doors. "Make your damn phone call then."

"No, no. I'm coming."

Vickers held back a door with his backside, and I dodged his blood-stained hands going through. "I thought I might find you here," he said.

"Really?" I scanned the ER. Each gurney was marked by curtains that could be pulled away from the wall. All were empty save one.

A nurse behind a small desk had a phone in her hand. "You found her."

"Of course," said Vickers with the arrogance of the typical surgeon. He pulled off his gloves and tossed them into a trash can marked *Biohazard*. "You're here about the second dead girl. Greave has all the particulars. I finished her a few minutes ago. This is more immediate." Vickers gestured me ahead of him, toward the single curtained-off area in the ER.

"What's this all about?"

"Kilgore has something to tell you."

Inside the curtained-off area a doctor hovered over Kilgore who had a patch across his stomach and was coughing up black blood. Jeez, I never wanted to take one in the gut. Then I remembered that's where I'd shot a drug dealer a couple of days ago. A couple of days ago? It felt like a lifetime ago.

Rex's eyes were closed, his shirt cut away, and his pants loosened. His shoes were still on, size fourteens hanging off the end of the gurney.

"Is he still with us?" asked Vickers.

The other doctor, already in scrubs, said, "We've got to get him into surgery."

Rex's eyes opened. He looked around wildly. "I'm waiting for Susan."

Taking his hand, I said, "I'm here, Rex."

His head turned toward me. "Susan . . . you came."

"Let them get you upstairs. I'll see you after they fix you up."

"No!" He gripped my hand. "There's something I have to tell you."

I looked at the doctors. No encouragement there. The nurse had pulled the curtain back for a quick getaway.

"Okay, Rex, but make it quick. Your mom's on the way and you need to get fixed up."

"Not . . . going to make it."

"You'll make it."

"Why? To fuck up . . . someone else's life?"

"Rex, I don't think this is the time or place—"

"I didn't kill them." He gripped my hand. "You've got to believe me."

I squeezed back. "I understand. You didn't kill anyone."

"Doctor Vickers," said the doctor in scrubs, "if this boy's to have any chance, we need to get him to surgery."

"Chase, do you have everything you need?"

"Everything I need?" I stared at Vickers.

"Don't you get it? Kilgore's making a deathbed confession. He's saying he didn't kill those two girls."

I looked at Rex, who nodded.

"Okay," said the other doctor, "time to go."

The nurse grasped the railing of the gurney and pulled Rex away, causing our hands to separate.

"Good luck, Rex!" I called after him, not knowing what else to say.

16

.

I found a pay phone and made the call to Rex's mother, but when the Horry County Courthouse put me on hold I drifted off, or froze up. That's where Albert Greave found me. He took the phone from my hand and I leaned into him.

"She's on her way, Susan," he said, hanging up the phone.

"She'll never make it." The county seat was at least twenty minutes away, even with me doing the driving, and right now I wasn't doing much of anything, not without a good deal of support.

Greave escorted me down the hall. He was saying something. ". . . seen a boy fall so far so fast. Why is it athletes always take up with the worst element when their careers are over?"

The next thing I knew I was in Greave's office while Nicole cleaned up what was left of Kitty Flanagan. From the desk Greave took a bottle of bourbon and poured a drink I gulped down, then asked for more.

"Sorry, but you have a meeting this afternoon and need to have a clear head."

My stomach turned over and I don't think it was from the liquor. "Rest room . . . ."

Nicole showed me the way.

Once she was gone, I threw up anything I'd eaten. Actually, I didn't remember eating. After washing my face, I gripped the counter and stared in the mirror at a person who had a reputation for being so damn tough. And smart.

Smarter than most, and gaining on the rest.

Yeah. Right. If I hadn't brought Rex to the attention of SLED . . . . I knew what a hothead he was.

Nicole returned with my pack. Not that I use much makeup, but I needed to do something about the splotches on—

"Susan, there's a gun in here."

"I'm sorry. I left the pack upstairs, didn't I?"

"Do you think I should get one?"

I stared at her.

"Do you think I should carry a gun?"

"I don't leave home without it."

Nicole left me to myself. A few minutes later I was ready for Albert Greave. Or so I thought.

"Did he make it?" I asked, taking a seat again.

Greave shook his head.

"Oh, Jesus!" And I broke down again.

This time Nicole stayed with me in the rest room until I fully recovered. Fully recovered. Yeah. Right.

After wiping away my tears, I asked, "Did his mother get here in time?"

"No, but a priest gave him last rites."

"Rex was Catholic?"

"I think a priest was all they could find."

I crossed myself.

"Are you Catholic, Susan?"

"Only when I need to be."

"This might be one of those times."

"No shit."

Greave and I talked in his office as Nicole worked in the morgue, occasionally glancing in my direction. Nicole had to be wondering when it would be safe again to walk the streets of the Grand Strand. I couldn't say. With a serial killer on the loose, it was best that women stay worried and alert.

Greave put his hands behind his head, leaned back in his chair, and sighed. Usually the coroner didn't get this involved, but this was different. We were finally mobilizing.

I should've been pleased, but I was nervous. Rex Kilgore had been our prime suspect. Now he was dead and everyone would accept his deathbed utterances. Just how smart was this FBI-trained Susan Chase?

But Warden *had* asked for a meeting, and the meeting was being held. That meant the powers-that-be thought something should be done to stop this monster.

"Er—what you got for me, Albert?"

"The Kleenex you brought in . . . it was nothing more than snot."

"Okay."

"SLED is moving on this faster than I've ever seen." His hands came down from behind his head and he sat up. "Sure you want to do this?"

"People will have questions."

He nodded. "It's the same as Lucy. Choked to death, but this time, tied to a surfboard instead of placed in a lifeguard stand. We're just missing the shovel."

"The surfboard was the shovel."

He stared at me.

"If we're tying the murders together."

"We are tying them together, aren't we?"

"Uh-huh." In my lap I fiddled with my hands.

"Susan, are you all right?"

"Sure."

"Susan Chase rattled." Greave shook his head. "I remember how Jenny talked about you. She said there wasn't anything you wouldn't try."

"I was young and foolish, Albert."

"I forbade her to hang out with you, you know."

"She told me."

"But I couldn't stop her."

"Like I said, Albert, I was a fool."

"No. You're a survivor."

"You can't beat yourself up about that."

"Parents aren't supposed to outlive their children. The pain dulls with time, but there's no such thing as closure."

"Closure's for Baby Boomers. They want everything in neat

little packages." Perhaps that was why I was trying so hard with Ruth Tackett. The old Susan Chase would've called Ruth Tackett a "sucker!" and been out of her life, but this new and improved model . . . hell, what was new and improved? Three people dead and I was on the job. Three people were dead *because* I was on the job.

Greave was talking. ". . . leave the van for Teddy. Can I catch a ride with you?"

"Sure."

"Do you have any suspects?"

"The only person who works at the Host of Kings Hotel who might be a suspect, besides Alan Putnam, hit the road. An illegal from Mexico."

"Think he could've been our man?"

"Serial killers don't generally operate outside their own race." Straightening up in my chair, I asked, "Albert, would you listen in on a conference call? I want to talk with someone I know at Quantico."

"Set it up." He picked up the phone and turned it around to face me.

While I contacted Special Agent Jamison Foxx, Greave told Nicole that she was to catch the calls and tell folks he'd get back to them. By the time he'd closed the door and returned to his seat—clipboard in hand—I was being connected to Agent Foxx.

"Jamie, this is Susan Chase."

"Susan! How are you?"

"Putting your expertise to work sooner than I expected. Jamie, I'm putting you on the speakerphone." Greave took the receiver, stuck it in the cradle, and pushed a button. "I'm here with Albert Greave, coroner for Horry County."

"And," Albert said, leaning toward the phone, "I have to tell you, Agent Foxx, I'm too close to retirement to become involved with a serial killer."

"Aren't we all, Doctor?"

"I'm not a licensed physician but an elected official. 'Albert' is just fine with me."

"Yes, sir, I understand."

Referring to his clipboard, Greave went through his findings, giving me more information than I cared to know about the human body after it gives up its ghost. He also threw in that both victims had been lifeguards and had whistles stuffed in their mouths. A shovel and surfboard were also mentioned. I gritted my teeth at the rumblings of my stomach and glanced in the direction of the rest room.

"Are you sure they were back-to-back kills?" asked Jamie. "One couldn't've been earlier, say a week or even longer?"

"The condition of the bodies rules out that possibility. There could be someone in-between we haven't found yet." Greave stopped for a moment, then added, "God, but I hate this."

"We all do," said the voice on the speakerphone.

"Albert's . . . ." I cleared my throat to start again. "Albert's daughter was murdered in—"

"I get the picture, and I'm sure there's nothing I can say—"

Albert slapped his clipboard down on his desk. "Can we just get this over with?"

"That's fairly quick to kill again. Serial killers usually have a hard time letting go of their last kill. Are these the only two you know about? Any other missing girls down there?"

"This is the Grand Strand, Jamie. Girls go missing all the time."

"So you have no idea if this is the first and second or fifth and sixth?"

"It has to be the first and second."

"Why's that?"

"They were posed."

"So being a lifeguard has a bearing on this."

"Look what we have: two blond lifeguards with whistles stuffed in their mouths, ears ripped off to disfigure them, and left in public access areas where they're sure to be found. Found, I might add, involved in activities people participate in at the beach."

Silence from the other end of the line. In my mind's eye I could picture Jamie sucking on a pipe he was forbidden to smoke in what the media called "the profiling unit." Sixty feet below ground, and surrounded by horrors no one should ever see, Jamie Foxx and his team worked in what had once been J. Edgar Hoover's bomb shelter. The shelter had been constructed on the off chance the Soviets might target old fags who wore dresses.

"Jamie, I think someone has a case of the ass for lifeguards."

"How about the entire Grand Strand?"

Greave and I looked at each other.

"Anyone there?" asked the voice on the speakerphone.

"You're serious?" I asked.

"You have to consider the possibility that this person is very angry with the Grand Strand."

"Would that possibly include someone who didn't get the job they wanted?"

"Turned down for a job?"

"Passed over."

"Perhaps, but most serial killings are about sex and power."

"I don't see this guy being full of hate or contempt for women. Pulling earrings off, that's small potatoes compared to the stuff I was shown at Quantico."

"Then fall back on what I taught you. You might not be able to determine motive, but you can always examine the behavioral aspects of any case."

That made me think. Jamie went silent, and across the desk, Albert Greave stared at me. It was a moment before I blurted out, "A spree killer—like Andrew Cunanan."

"Very good. A young man who got very angry and killed his victims over a short period of time. Serial killers usually stretch out their kills—"

"Because they like to relive them." Everybody and their sister had talked me into a serial killer and I had gone along for the ride. Dammit! I was the one who'd started this ride. Wasn't there anything I could do right?

"But the disfigurement by ripping off the earlobes?"

"That's what doesn't fit. Still, this man has to be stopped or tourists have to be warned about the dangers of coming to the Grand Strand. He isn't moving on. Anyone could be next if the killer thinks he doesn't have access to another lifeguard. Susan, I'm going to be out of town the next few days, but if you need me don't hesitate to call. They'll know how to reach me."

After disconnecting the phone, Greave asked, "Could it be as simple as someone who feels they received a raw deal on their accommodations?"

"Sweet Jesus, I hope not. Think of the numbers."

"If it's someone working along the Grand Strand, what's to be gained by ruining the Season? It'll hurt his business, too, or where he works, one would imagine."

"Tell me about it." This was way weird.

I glanced at my watch. It was after three. As I stood up the phone rang. Mickey Dee reporting that Greg Sitton's alibi had checked out. I was surprised Mickey knew where to find me.

"You know about the meeting at four?" he asked me.

"Yes."

"It's going to get busy fast, so I wanted to bring you up to date. First, is it true Rex Kilgore was killed by Eddie Tooney this afternoon?"

"Er—yes."

"Never would've thought. I don't think Eddie's ever drawn his gun. To update you, Kitty Flanagan's husband has disappeared. Neighbors say he's been gone over a week."

"So Luther didn't kill Kitty." That put Alan Putnam at the top of my list again. Yeah, but when was the last time I was right about something?

"But Luther *did* piss off Nelson. Flanagan spent what he owed Nelson on a trip to the Bahamas. Gambled it away."

"No one could be that stupid."

"Susan, Luther's done drugs so long you're not dealing with someone with much gray matter, and that job driving a cement truck, that was over two years ago. Luther's been reduced to day labor."

"What did you find in the house?"

"Only dust." Meaning you could tell the place was used for dealing, but there wasn't enough to make a case. Mickey went on, "The way I see it, Luther's still responsible for his wife's death. He left her without any wheels. Kitty probably caught a ride with her killer when she left the mall last night. It was her night to close."

"And the timeline?"

"Susan, beyond that, we don't have anything. Anslow and Austin are combing the neighborhood. People saw Kitty come and go, you know, when she'd be walking toward the mall. Some of the neighbors gave her rides to the Food Lion, but you try to form a timeline for a person who lives alone and doesn't have wheels. They don't go out much and people simply don't see them. Susan, when I was with Anslow and Austin, they received a call from Jennings to drop by and have a talk with Nelson Obie about sleeping with underage girls. Was that your idea?"

"Warden's."

"Well, for your sake I hope Nelson knows that. Are you ready for this afternoon?"

"I'll be at the meeting, Mickey."

"Susan, you *are* the meeting."

Needless to say, the Myrtle Beach Convention Center was packed. First up was Albert Greave, but when the grilling became too intense, and in some sense many of the questions premature, Warden took over and addressed the group. Everyone was there, not only from Myrtle Beach but smaller towns up and down the Strand. This was worse than any shark attack.

Greave didn't return to his chair on the platform but took a seat in the front row. With me on stage was the new head of the Chamber of Commerce, the mayor of Myrtle Beach, and its chief of police, along with the sheriff and my boss. The press huddled outside, wondering why they were barred from a public forum. Unbeknownst to the reporters, their bosses were inside, and after our meeting broke up, they'd speak to their employees and make their reporters and editors even more unhappy.

The Chamber was trying to keep a lid on things. That was

their game plan, not an alert. The meeting had been called to identify possible suspects and sweep the Grand Strand clean on the QT. To accomplish that, carts with stacks of brochures from the Chamber were rolled up the aisles. The brochures said nothing new but did give the audience something to take away, if anyone needed a prop after hearing such news and orders to keep their mouths shut.

I sat and fumed while, of all people, Alan Putnam tried to cheer me up. At least that's what it looked like he was doing. Alan stood behind the last row of chairs and smiled at me. He wore a gray business suit and a Cheshire cat grin.

Alan Putnam was the serial killer.

Standing beside Putnam was Bob Yale. How'd Yale gotten in here? He was closer to being a member of the press than any businessman. When I was introduced there were groans from the audience. Greave looked up at me sympathetically, and for the first time, I felt vulnerable. Who was I to tell these people, who had their life's work at risk, what was up?

Very quickly, the director was at my side. That rattled me even more. The new leader of the Grand Strand's Chamber of Commerce was a tanned, middle-aged guy wearing a pinstriped suit. His hair was styled and, admittedly, he was attractive enough to be on TV. Which he was, instead of Alan Putnam. Bolstered by his support, I gave "Smiling Al" a big wave.

The crowd thought I was taunting and booed me. Still, the smile vanished from Putnam's face. Bob Yale, however, smiled. Smiles of encouragement? Grins from a lech, more likely.

The director leaned over to the microphone. "If Lieutenant Warden vouches for Ms. Chase, I'm sure she'll do an excellent job." He flashed a radiant smile, then said, "Ms. Chase, the microphone is all yours."

"Thank you . . . sir."

I ignored the chatter sweeping the crowd and plunged into impressing these bastards that they should take what was being said seriously, that we indeed did have a killer on our hands: a spree killer, which meant this guy was out of his frigging mind.

From the last row, Alan Putnam stared daggers, but Yale only nodded and took notes. And me? I'd hit my stride, explaining the thinking of a serial killer versus a spree killer, and what type of person we were looking for. When I told the crowd this was economic payback for an imagined grievance, the concept rocked the room. From his seat Albert Greave shook his head. Greave liked to think of himself as a small-town coroner and the Grand Strand had just gone big-time.

The mayor joined me at the lectern and tried to silence the crowd. At the academy we were taught, sooner or later, every agent would have to face an unruly crowd—the press was generally used as an example—but nothing like this. SLED tried to prepare us, as did the FBI. However, the show-and-tell we'd practiced in front of our peers was nothing compared to men standing up and hollering, hurling questions or talking among themselves. But all that training did keep me from wetting my pants.

I couldn't calm them. Neither could the mayor, or the Myrtle Beach chief of police, or Chief Jennings. The Season was approaching, and down deep inside, there was always the fear "They" might not come, and without "Them," no nuts would be cracked. Along the East Coast, a recreational area second only to Disney World had been built, but that didn't mean merchants still didn't wake up in the middle of the night wondering if the tourists would come. When they finished worrying about the current season, they went on to worry about how they'd survive the off-season. It was a never-ending misery.

"Let Ms. Chase finish," pleaded the director.

Instead, there were questions regarding my résumé. Warden charged to the microphone, shouldered the director and Chief Jennings aside, and asked what did it matter whether it was a serial killer or spree killer, this person had to be stopped. Finally the room quieted, relatively speaking, and I was able to answer the director's next question. He wanted to know what they were to do next. I told him we needed a list of any disgruntled employees who'd left their places of employment or not, during the last three years:

white males ages 20 to 35 were typical suspects.

Restaurant owners groaned. With their turnover that would take some doing. But SLED and the Chamber were adamant. No one would leave without giving us a list, and when patrolmen appeared at the doors, the few who tried to leave cursed and returned to their seats.

Cell phones were brought out and calls made. Pay phones in the outer ring of the convention center were flooded. A couple of dicks threatened lawsuits if they weren't allowed to leave. Warden informed them that local governments had every right to declare a state of emergency. The governor had done just that, and who in the hell did they think were the cadre of suits lining the rear of the convention center?

People turned and stared at the members of SLED who had been pulled from other regions. These men and women had their game faces on and I was part of that . . . family. My heart swelled with pride. Now if I could only regain control of my nerves.

Warden went on to add that lists supplied by the people in the room would be compared with business licenses. Everyone would participate. Minutes later, people crowded the base of the stage, thrusting lists at us. One was my former boss. Marvin Valente had had the coil tower replaced and his truck was running just fine. Flustered, I dropped lists and was cursed when I didn't give their owners exit passes fast enough. Still there were those who wished us luck and asked if there was anything they could do. Among them Alan Putnam. He was invited onstage by the director. Listening over the director's shoulder, I heard him ask Alan to return to his old desk and handle the extra phone traffic.

Alan smiled at me over his replacement's shoulder and said he'd be happy to help out. Then he was gone, as were so many others who'd already turned in their lists.

The Chamber's plan had been to catch the killer or to move him along. Now he was one of us.

17

Just about everyone had left when I joined Warden at the base of the stage. Both of us had had enough of stooping down to retrieve lists and passing out releases to leave the building. Warden held a stack of lists: business cards, index cards, sheets torn from planners. He didn't look up until Heather Jackson approached him. Heather wore a business suit and heels and her hair was up. In her hands was a stack of videotapes.

DeShields followed her to the base of the stage. "Heather says she has something for you, J.D."

Behind them all manner of cops filed through the doors: plainclothes, uniforms, clerks, and jerks, all led by their respective chiefs.

"You could've given them to Sergeant DeShields." As if to make that point, Warden put down his stack, took the videotapes, and handed them to DeShields.

"Is it true you've just alerted everyone that we have a serial killer on our hands?" asked Heather.

Warden took my stack and began going through the lists. "Ms. Jackson, you don't have a serial killer unless you have at least four bodies."

"Some definitions begin with the number 'three.'"

"I'm not going to play word games. You have my answer."

"Who's to say the young woman who disappeared in the parking lot of the Waccamaw Pottery"—a notebook came out of one of the pockets of Heather's jacket— "the one who worked at that shoe outlet—wasn't your first victim, this . . . ." She glanced at the notepad pulled from her pocket.

"M.J. Dawkins," Warden said.

"Then you'd have three."

"Wrong MO."

"How can you say that?"

"Because we found the other bodies."

"Then you're admitting Leslie and Flanagan were killed by the same person?"

Warden found the list he was looking for and handed it to me. It was from the Chamber of Commerce, and Alan Putnam's name wasn't on it.

"What's that?" asked Heather, seeing me scanning the Chamber's list.

"Sorry, Ms. Jackson, but that's all we have." Warden returned to the stage.

Heather tried to follow him up the metal stairs that had been placed there for the occasion, but DeShields took her by the arm.

Shaking off Mickey's hand, Heather asked, "What about the whistles found in the dead girls' mouths?"

I gaped at Heather. So did Mickey Dee. The whistles hadn't been released to the general public.

Warden glanced at me. "Has Ms. Chase told you any part of this investigation involves serial killing?"

"Not in so many words."

"In this case that best mean Ms. Chase told you nothing."

"She didn't have to. I can read between the lines."

Warden gestured at the videotapes held by DeShields. "I appreciate your assistance, but I have work to do."

"Lieutenant, people have a right to know."

"Take it up with your boss."

When Heather turned around she saw her boss coming down the aisle. Behind him came other members of the media, all taking seats behind rows and rows of cops. I'd never seen so many lawmen in one place, and to tell the truth, it made me kind of nervous. Heather's boss took her by the arm and steered her up the aisle. They sat with the other media.

We did it again. The Chamber's director, my boss, and I went through our spiels and passed out the lists we'd received from the businesses. As I said, SLED agents from all over were here, as were members of the FBI. The agent in charge of the Southern District of South Carolina joined us on stage, and in the concourse ringing the convention center, clerks worked collecting more precise addresses or phone numbers of the employees said to be disgruntled. Those who had sat through the first session would soon learn they'd be bugged to death until they finally gave up someone.

"I'm treating this like any other malcontent who wants to get back at the boss," Warden said. "You're to take lists of these young men and conduct field investigations, learning where they've been within the last seventy-two hours. If you get a funny feeling about them, ask them to come downtown for further questioning. If they won't, Mirandize them and put them in your car and move on to the next name."

"What if we can't locate them?" asked a voice from the uniforms.

"Call the name in." Warden gestured at the concourse, where harried clerks worked under the lash of supervisors to compile more comprehensive lists. "We'll get an address, or find out if they've left the Grand Strand. We're going to nail down the location of as many of these men as possible and it will be done tonight." He glanced at the director. "I'm sure the Chamber has ways of making everyone pull his weight."

The director set his jaw and nodded.

"If we don't sleep, neither do they," added Warden.

All the cops nodded. Some muttered in agreement.

"Use land lines for reports, and I don't mean when you've picked up someone who won't cooperate. That's a given. Extra lines are being installed as we speak and repair crews from GTE are making sure all the pay phones along the Boulevard are in working order. Myrtle Beach PD will be our command center, but you may find it easier to get through to your own department. They'll forward your request to us."

"All it takes is one disk jockey on the radio . . . ."

The director of the chamber gestured at the civilians behind the cops. The rows of cops turned around to see who sat behind them, people generally considered to be the enemy.

"As you can see," the director said, "the press is with us on this. They might as well close down if there's no Season. Matter of fact, many of you in uniform will lose your jobs if what Ms. Chase has told us is true and we don't catch this man. If you hear anyone on the air, let us know."

"People are going to talk . . . ."

"Yes," said Warden, "and tell them we have a kidnapped child and we don't need civilians upsetting the kidnapper. Our imaginary little girl is six years old and she didn't come home from school today. It's in the packet, along with ten quarters and ten dimes for phone calls."

Women from the Chamber of Commerce moved down the aisles again. At the beginning of each row an officer took stacks of packets and passed them along. Coming behind these women was another set of clerks who passed out stacks of forms held together by rubber bands. A judge joined us on stage.

"Now . . . everyone . . . on your feet!" shouted Warden, as if the appearance of the judge had the same standing as an officer entering a roomful of soldiers.

Slowly everyone stood, some reluctantly, many looking at their partners, some to their chief.

"That was for the law enforcement officers, not the press."

Most of the press returned to their seats. Some opted to stand to see what would happen. What happened was the judge swore everyone in as a notary public and left the stage. Once he was gone, the first group of women returned to the end of the aisles and began to pass out seals. Word was every city and county building had been stripped of its seals, along with businesses who'd been asked to bring their seals to the briefing.

Once this was finished, Warden continued. "In the course of your work many of you have become notaries, but now there's no question." He tapped a group of forms in his hand. "I want everyone you interview to sign one of these, then you notarize it. This form tells us where they've been during the last seventy-two hours. If the guy won't sign it—"

"Cuff 'em and put 'em in the car," said a voice from the uniforms.

Once the laughter subsided, another voice said, "I don't know if we'll have the room. Some are just plain jerks."

"School buses are available at various pickup points in garages. In your packet are maps of the locations. I really don't think you'll have a problem. They have a choice: either fill out the form or wear the cuffs. Most aren't criminals, just mad at the boss or they said something the boss remembered as hostile." He looked over the rows of men and women. "Any questions?"

"You know," said one of the plainclothesmen, "we could do all this and still miss this guy."

The director leaned toward the mike. "This plan was drawn up by businessmen up and down the Grand Strand in conjunction with the Chamber of Commerce. True, there'll be glitches. If a phone is busy, call back. If there's not a bus at a pickup point, move on to the next location. Above all, remember you have lists of people who may or may not live or work inside your jurisdiction. You may end up running from one end of the Grand Strand to the other."

"That doesn't seem very productive," said Vance, Eddie Tooney's partner in the front row.

The director looked down at her. "A good plan tonight is better than a perfect plan tomorrow. Ms. Chase says the killer could strike anytime, if he's indeed a spree killer. We have to do something and this is all the courts will allow."

That brought mumbles and several boos from the crowd.

"Tonight there is only one jurisdiction," said Warden, taking over the microphone again, "everyone works for SLED. If any civilian has a problem with that, bring him in. We have someone who'll talk with him." Warden glanced at the man sitting beside me on stage. "The FBI will be happy to talk to anyone who thinks his civil rights are being violated."

The agent in charge of the Southern District nodded and flashed a knowing smile.

"Now, get out there and hit these people and hit them hard. We want this guy to know we're on to him. It might be enough to make him stop or even leave town."

I didn't think any of this would stop Alan Putnam, and that's what I wanted to talk with Warden about after everyone left. Instead, I was intercepted by Theresa Hardy.

"Paul would like to see you, Susan." Hardy had arrived during the second pitch and taken a seat behind the media. "When this settles down."

"I'll see what I can do."

"You'll do more than that," said my boss. "We have to work with these people after this is over."

"Paul wants to apologize."

"Find the time to do it, Chase."

"It can't hurt, Susan. Paul knows some important people."

"I'm more worried about what Alan Putnam is up to."

"Was he on the Chamber's list?" asked Warden.

"No, but—"

"Or the King of Hosts Hotel?"

"No, but—"

"And is he going to help us with this?"

"Yes."

"You really buy the idea someone would kill two girls because he was passed over for a job?"

I gestured at the emptying seats. "That's the way it was pitched to them."

"Only because you pitched it."

That stopped me cold. Was I being set up for a fall?

"Look, Chase, if this doesn't work we'll take another look at Putnam."

"Don't worry. I'll handle him."

Mickey DeShields looked stricken. "Susan—"

"Chase, there'll be enough people upset without any of your grandstanding."

"All I meant was I can cover Putnam once he gets home tonight. It's my turn anyway."

Warden gestured at the list I held. "But only after you finish your list."

"No problema." Which was a frigging lie. I'd drawn a list containing the two largest lifeguard operations. "What about Nelson Obie?" I asked.

DeShields shrugged. "Anslow and Austin couldn't find him. He's probably lying low."

"Come on, Chase, do you really think the killer would try something, tonight of all nights?"

Before I could answer, I saw a Horry County policeman leading one of my friends down the aisle toward us. "What's Pick doing here?"

"I asked J.D. to bring him in," explained Hardy. "The clothes he gave you belonged to M.J. Dawkins."

"Pick isn't involved in this."

"Susan, he has a record."

"Peeping Toms aren't usually spree killers."

"Chase," Warden said, "we'd be fools not to bring him in, with everything else we're doing."

"My money's on Nelson Obie," said Mickey Dee.

"What proof do you have the clothes belong to Dawkins?"

"Her roommate ID'd them," Hardy said. "They're in the property room. They're Dawkins', or rather clothing she borrowed from her roommates."

When Pick arrived at the base of the stage, he smiled that innocent smile of his.

"I can't believe you're doing this to him."

"Chase, what's your problem? We're getting as many suspects off the street as possible."

"What about Alan Putnam?"

"Putnam doesn't have a record. He doesn't even have a speeding ticket—"

"Because he worked at the Chamber! It was fixed."

"Susan . . ." started Mickey.

"What do you want, Chase?"

"To make sure Alan remains at the Chamber tonight."

"You can't do that to a civilian."

"Look what you're doing to Pick."

"Your friend has a record."

"He does not. I got it fixed!"

Warden let out a sigh. "DeShields, call the Chamber and tell Putnam to stay put until someone escorts him home tonight." Warden looked at the law enforcement personnel leaving the auditorium. The Chamber's new director was talking to the mayors of Myrtle and North Myrtle Beach. My boss shook his head. "Putnam knows too many people. You'll never tag him for this."

"That's what makes him so dangerous."

"Once we finish this sweep, I'll put a car in front of his house every night and a boat behind it. You have your list and you're wasting time."

"And Pick?"

"He goes downtown."

"If Pick wanted to kill someone, why didn't he kill me? I'm around all the time."

Mickey smiled. "Who's to say he doesn't want to?"

"And who's to say Pick's not the victim here?" My friend wore a jacket, jeans, and running shoes, all light colors and difficult as hell to do any peeping in.

"Susan," he started, "I didn't—"

"Pick, I'll handle this. How long are you going to hold him?"

"As long as it takes to question him."

"He's not competent to answer your questions."

"Then he'll remain in custody until the court appoints someone to represent him."

"With the backlog this operation will create, I don't think so. It's not right for a young man who knows diddly to be put in jail with really bad guys."

"Happens all the time."

"But he's retarded." I felt like a traitor talking like this in front of Pick. "Let me take him with me."

"Under what circumstances?"

"I'll be driving around. Where can he go?"

"Will he be cuffed at all times?"

"If that's what you want."

"That's what I want." To the cop with Pick, Warden said, "Give him a chance to use the facilities. When he's finished, return him to the custody of Agent Chase."

The patrolman nodded, then took Pick by the arm and the two of them headed up the aisle toward the concourse.

"I want him cuffed to the roll bar at all times, do you hear me?"

"That's not safe."

"Then become a better driver or leave him behind."

I was outside before I finally calmed down. A couple of detectives lounging near their unmarked patrol car didn't help my attitude when I exited the convention center.

"This wild goose chase your idea, Chase?"

Not only did I not reply, I didn't even look in their direction.

Austin laughed. Anslow muttered something about me causing trouble wherever I went. My ears roared as I stalked across the parking lot. Alan Putnam was our killer, but I had no proof, and tonight Alan would strike again. How else could you explain the towel from his hotel over Lucy's head? Alan had been in our face from the get-go.

"Susan, are you mad at me?" asked Pick as we raced down the Boulevard. And I didn't have him cuffed to the roll bar. Deal with it, J.D.

"If Warden believes in me, then why doesn't he . . . ." I stopped. Not only did Pick not need to hear me whine, but he wouldn't understand. At the next light I leaned over and gave him a peck on the cheek. "Everything's going to be okay."

"Why did you kiss me, Susan?"

"Because I . . . I love you, Pick."

"Does this mean we'll have sex?"

Heat rushed up the sides of my neck. "No, no, it's a different kind of love. Look, Pick, I need to get you back to the landing." I pulled out my phone and speed-dialed Harry Poinsett as I pulled away from the light.

When Dads came on the line, he asked, "Any closer to who the killer might be?"

"It's Alan Putnam."

"The young man who once worked at the Chamber? I find that hard to believe."

"Sorry, but that's why he's doing it. He was passed over for the directorship."

"Susan, you aren't serious?"

"Dads, would you watch Putnam's place tonight?"

"If you think that's really necessary. What about the police?"

"The cops will be busy and I have rabbits of my own to chase. Alan will be at the Chamber fielding calls, then going home."

"He's working at the Chamber again?"

I sighed. "It's a long story. Can you follow him?"

"Why yes, I can do that. Still, I don't understand why you think—"

"Dads, trust me on this, please!"

"All right." There was a pause as Harry must've looked at a clock. "I'll make some sandwiches to take along and something to drink."

"And a pot to piss in."

"Susan, I don't think . . . you're serious, aren't you?"

"I am."

"Do you think I'll need a gun?"

"Just make sure Alan knows you're there. That's all I need." I glanced at the young man beside me. "And I want Pick to watch the rear of Alan's house. By boat."

"He's no longer a suspect, is he?"

"Not with the evidence those jokers have. Dads, can you take Pick off . . . ." I glanced at the slow-witted young man. "Can you pick him up so he'll have time to get ready?"

"Name the place. I'm dressed." Excellent. Harry's very fussy about how he appears in public.

So we met where the road to the landing joins US 17. It saved me a few minutes but almost got me killed. Nelson Obie had been following me in his SUV, the weapon of choice of every soccer mom, and now that I was traveling on a back road and traffic was backed up for a drawbridge, he was ready to take me out.

I didn't want to fight, but when Nelson rammed me, bumping me into a minivan filled with children, I decided to take *him* out. Looking into my rearview mirror, I saw Nelson, and behind him, a Cadillac with his bodyguard Marcel at the wheel. Huey sat beside him. Off to my right, and down below me, were a row of fishing cabins along the waterway. Behind them a shell road.

As Nelson stepped down from his sport-ute—pistol in hand—his two bodyguards climbed out of the Caddy. Ahead of me, the driver of the minivan opened the door and got out, cursing and looking for damage instead of seeing the big picture, you know, like the guy with the pistol. And me? I jammed the Pink Bomb, as my jeep is affectionately known, into reverse and stepped on the gas.

The Bomb smacked into the sport-ute and pushed Nelson's vehicle back, if only slightly, startling him. Both he and the driver of the minivan stepped back. Marcel and Huey's hands went inside their jackets, but that was the last I saw of them. Having enough clearance, I made a sharp turn off the road and down a hill, crashing through grass, weeds, and small trees, to the shell road below.

Something whistled by my ear, smacking a hole in the windshield and causing my foot to slip off the brake. The Bomb and I hit hard, almost pitching me out. Luckily I was scared shitless and gripping the wheel with both hands. Still, the jeep took off on me—before I found the brake—frightening me even more.

Along the road was a line of fishing cabins, sport utility vehicles, minivans, and smaller RVs. People were opening their cabins for the approaching Season. I laid on the horn as I raced by. People replied with shouts and curses as they leaped out of the way. By the time Nelson came down the hill, cell phones were in use and license plates being jotted down.

Good luck. Law enforcement personnel had more important things on their mind.

Like all roads paralleling the river this one ended rather quickly. I broke through another barbed-wire fence and tried to circle back to the blacktop. If I didn't bog down in the low spots. It wasn't easy. Water splashed under my wheels, the ground squished under the jeep's weight, and I almost stalled out a couple of times. Looking in the mirror, I saw Nelson was having similar problems. His was a big black monster of an SUV, and he was having trouble negotiating the pines.

I crushed weeds and bushes, and in one place, slid between pines close enough to take off the last coat of paint. There was a log I didn't see—glancing back to check on Nelson—and it fell to pieces when I hit it. I had to use the compass glued to the windshield to plot my return to the highway. Ahead of me was a small creek.

Shit!

I tried to take it at an angle, plunging through, throwing up water, and frightening wildlife, but I slammed into the far shore. The bank was only a yard high, but it stopped me cold. The engine stalled. Behind me, a dark form bashed its way through the underbrush and slid through trees—you know, like a really pissed-off driver who's decided, since his vehicle is toast, he might as well toast the one responsible for the damage.

Starting the engine, I shifted into four-wheel drive, backed up, tried again. No go. I couldn't go forward or backward. It was as if I had dropped into a slot, and when I tried to back up, I rammed into the other side. Hopefully, I wasn't filling the tailpipe with all kinds of muck. Letting out the clutch, I pulled forward and ran into the bank again. Rocking back and forth, I finally freed myself, then backed into the other side of the creek—and got stuck again! Wheels whirled as I looked in the mirror.

Here came Nelson! He was less than fifty yards away.

I cut hard to the left, leaned over, outside the jeep, and gave it some gas. That didn't work. What was up with the four-wheel drive?

Calm down. Calm down.

Shit! *You* calm down. Have you looked in the rearview mirror lately?

Nelson saw my predicament, slowed to a stop, and stuck his pistol out the window.

I leaned down, trying to get small, and returned to rocking the jeep back and forth. Finally, the four-wheels found the traction and the jeep climbed the bank to the other side. In front of me, a skinny pine exploded in half and the top half fell across my path. Keeping my head down, I bashed through, then used the compass to return to the blacktop.

Another barbed-wire fence stood between me and the road. I shifted into low, driving at an angle, more for speed than traction, and rammed through the barbed wire. A mile down the road I made several turns and lost Nelson without having to shoot him. All in all, I considered it a pretty good career move.

18

My first assigned suspect was an unemployed guy who lived off his wife until he could begin lifeguarding for the new season. Why was he on the list? He'd threatened my former boss with bodily harm. The suspect said he'd been home both nights, and by double-checking with his wife, I learned that was true.

"You'd think he'd go out drinking or run around on me, wouldn't you," asked the wife, "but he's always here when I come home. Drunk as a skunk, but he's here. I only stay with him for the children."

Then there was a suspect who'd moved inland, perhaps as far as the capital, according to a very grateful landlord. I couldn't pin down the guy, even after checking his previous address. Using my cell phone I called the name in to the people at the convention center and told them to get back to me. They didn't.

Next was a dick by the name of Lance Massingale who, while working for Marvin Valente, had lost it when a tourist ragged him about someone taking his spot on the beach. Or was it that the music was too loud from the adjoining umbrella? I forget. Anyway, after having enough of the tourist's mouth, Lance took the fellow's beach gear and dumped it into the surf, then walked off the job.

Marvin made sure Massingale was prosecuted to the fullest extent of the law. But it was a first offense, so the judge let Lance off with a warning. Since the dummy knew I was tight with Marvin and had dated Nelson Obie, Lance blamed me for being banned from beach service.

Now he lived in an RV parked under a tree in the rear of a dirt lot where produce was sold during the Season. Weeds had grown up around the vehicle, the roll-out tarp had rips in it, and the produce stand was boarded up. I stepped down from the jeep and rapped on the RV's door.

Massingale wasn't at home. He was down the street shooting pool, or that's what his girlfriend said. "You'd better leave him alone, Susan."

Guess he *was* down the street shooting pool. "Maybe I'm here to offer him a job." I didn't want Marcy hopping on the phone and alerting Lance to the fact I was hot on his trail. Despite my comment to Dads, this was not a night for chasing rabbits.

"You'd offer Lance a job?"

"Why not?"

"You didn't speak up for him when he lost his job with Marvin or put in a good word with Nelson."

"Marcy, contrary to popular belief, I don't have anything to do with Nelson Obie."

"You two used to be tight."

"In another life."

She gave me the once-over. "Susan, why are you dressed like that?"

"Had to take another job to make ends meet."

"Oh." Clearly Marcy was out of the loop, so she told me where to find Lance.

With cue in hand, Massingale stood among his guy friends, asking what the hell I was doing messing in his business again. At least that's what I got when I asked to speak to him alone. His pals smiled their little smiles and each held his stick like it was his dearest friend in all the world. Next to their dicks, it just might be.

Eddie Tooney was suddenly at my side, asking the assholes which of them wanted to go downtown. "What about you, Massingale? Know what that'll mean this time?"

"Tooney, you fucking with me, too?" asked Lance.

"After the day I've had, yes."

"Eddie," I said, "you're not supposed to be on the street until you're cleared about the shooting."

Tooney was in civies. "You're one to talk."

"My case is different."

Tooney glanced at the guys on the other side of the table. "Different enough to get a cue stick shoved up your ass."

Massingale laughed. His guy pals joined in. They were probably imagining sticking their sticks elsewhere. Smoke hung heavy in the room. The jukebox played country music. That in itself was reason enough to arrest everyone on the premises.

"Who'd you shoot, Tooney?" asked Massingale, with a chuckle. "Yourself? In the foot, the great shot you are?"

"Rex Kilgore."

"You're shitting me. Why?"

"He wouldn't come along."

"I don't believe you."

"Ask Chase. Me and her, we've got a special on assholes this week. Susan even gives you two for one."

The reference to the shoot-out at the Sunnydale was enough to make Massingale step over to a table and fill out the form. As he passed, Eddie took the cue and Massingale's place in the rotation. By the time the former lifeguard finished filling out the form he was down twenty bucks.

"Shit!" Lance said, slapping the stick out of Eddie's hand. "You sure Rex didn't take your gun away and shoot himself?"

Outside I asked Eddie what he thought he was doing.

"I'd planned on getting drunk, but I can't find anyone to join me. Everyone's working." To underscore his point a couple of patrol cars whipped by, heading up and down the Boulevard in opposite directions.

"Weren't you told to go home?"

"But I want to help." •

I climbed in my jeep. "Well, you're certainly not going to help me."

"Susan . . . ." Eddie glanced into the pool hall. The door stood open, allowing in a spring breeze, along with any vermin. "I don't know what to do."

"Even a better reason to turn in for the night." I cranked my engine.

"I should be doing something, working the phones, checking paperwork, coordinating . . . something, but Jennings told me to go home. What's the point? There's no one there."

And that was Eddie's problem. He was such a nice guy that his wife had run over him, run around on him, then left him for another guy, taking the kids with her.

"Deal with it. I do every day of my life." I put the jeep into gear and left him. It was amazing how I thought I could blow off everyone and not think I'd suffer any consequences.

The next guy was Bob Yale, who lived in a garage apartment on the second row. His Harley-Davidson was in the garage, which was spick-and-span. The apartment looked like my place, except for the books. There were books all over the place, and you could see stacks of them littering the floor when Yale opened the door.

"Susan! Come in. I want to clear up what your boss said about my job at the *Tribune*."

I thrust my clipboard at him. "SLED wants to know where you've been."

He took the clipboard and examined it.

"In the last seventy-two hours," I added.

"You know where I've been." He gestured with the clipboard at the interior of an apartment. "I've been writing."

"Alone?"

He smiled again. "Well, most of the time."

Handing him a pen, I said, "Fill out this form."

"What's this all about?"

"What you put on that questionnaire tells us who you've been with and what you've done in the last seventy-two hours. I have to notarize it."

"Why do you need to know?"

"Bob, you're not conducting this interview. I am."

"Why are you even here?"

"Nelson Obie's secretary reported you to SLED."

"Nelson? I haven't talked with that asshole in months."

"His secretary reported you—for Nelson."

"Listen, I was in the right."

My hips swiveled into a position where I could tap my foot. "What's the problem? Nelson screwing Joanie again?"

"And I threw a punch at him."

"Joanie isn't worth the hassle, which continues until this day. I'm here, aren't I?"

He glanced at the questionnaire again. "Would you like to come inside?"

I shook my head. "I'm on the clock, Bob."

Less than five minutes later, he returned to the door and I flipped away the cigarette I'd been smoking.

"Susan, you know I wouldn't kill anyone."

When he handed over the clipboard, I glanced at what he'd written down. "Who were you with last night? I need a name." Bob is hardly ever alone. I really don't know how he gets any work done.

"I'd rather not talk about that."

"Then someone will be by to pick you up." I made for the stairs.

He followed me. "What are you talking about?"

"You have to fill out the questionnaire. Completely."

"Susan, don't do this to me."

Stopping at the foot of the steps, I looked up at him. "She was underage, wasn't she?"

He glanced at his feet.

"Stay where you are. A patrol car will be by in a few minutes."

"Are you serious?"

"As a heart attack."

"But this could ruin me."

"As well it should."

When I reached my jeep, I quickly started the engine. The sun was setting, and up and down this golden coast older men were taking advantage of younger women. A story as old as time, and one I'd been a part of, which meant I should forgive and forget. Not!

"Susan," called Yale, coming down the stairs after me, "what would be my motive for killing those two girls?"

"They turned you down?"

"Do you know how silly that sounds?"

Shifting into gear, I said, "You were at both crime scenes."

"I'm a reporter. I was curious."

"You're no longer a reporter, just a lech."

"Susan, what is it with you?"

I had turned around to back out of his driveway. Now I faced him. "What is what?"

"You're so damn cold."

"Bob, you said you'd teach me how to write. Instead, you tried to seduce me. Hearing you were with another underage girl doesn't encourage me to cut you any slack."

"I never bothered you again."

"You won't leave me alone. You're always there, on my machine, showing up at crime scenes. You've shown up enough that my boss even suspects you."

"That's ridiculous!"

"Not after what he learned in Chicago."

"I can explain that."

I let out the clutch. "Bob, I have to work to do."

"All I've ever done is ask a few questions."

"Bob, we are not going to be friends."

"I don't see what the Rivers boy sees in you."

"Lucky for me that decision's not up to you."

Returning to Kings Highway I pulled into Shoney's and waited for Yale to trail me into the parking lot. When he did I ambled over to his Harley.

"You can't do this, Bob."

"I have a right to go anywhere I wish."

"You don't have a right to stalk me."

"You're a public employee. I can watch anything you do as long as I don't disturb your work."

"Bob, if after picking up something to eat, I come out and

find you're still here, I'm going to bust your ass. I don't have time for this."

"This isn't fair—"

"You're on the list. That's all I have to know."

"Because Nelson Obie put me there."

"I really don't think Nelson gives a damn about you. His secretary reported you. So what'd you promise her? To improve her typing?"

"I could be helping you with this case."

I shook my head, then went into the Shoney's and freshened up in the ladies' room while my eat-it-on-the-run meal was prepared. When I returned, Yale was nowhere to be seen, but four detectives sat at a booth near the door. One of them waved and I waved back. Before the guy's hand was lowered one of his buddies spoke sharply to him. This was not how most law enforcement personnel planned to spend one of the last slow nights before the Season began.

When I returned to my jeep I found I had another stop to make. Yale had left the name and address of the girl he'd been with on a piece of paper under my wiper. I munched on my dinner as I drove over to the kid's house. Glancing into the interior of the house to make sure no one would hear what she had to say, the teenager confirmed she had indeed been with Bob Yale last night. What I couldn't confirm was that for an older guy, Bob was really hot.

It was after dark, and the next guy was a real dandy. Rodrigo Gonzales never met a mirror he didn't like. Called "Hot Rod" for his prowess with women, the bastard lived off any woman proud to be seen on his arm. And Rodrigo had his pick. Women fell all over him. He was tall, dark, and handsome. And absolutely charming.

Rodrigo, now closer to thirty than twenty, would sit in his lifeguard stand and take the measure of the women along the beach, women who wanted a little excitement. By Labor Day, Hot Rod would have targeted one of the locals to spend the winter with. The one he'd targeted last winter was still stuck with him. I wondered if she thought "Hot Rod" was all that attractive after sponging off her, and hogging all the mirrors in the house.

Janet Halsey lived in Conway, where Chad and his father built boats, but certainly not in the same neighborhood. For that reason I was surprised to find a Mercedes parked outside Janet's house. Up and down the street were older model cars, most purchased for speed and looks.

A black Mazda RX-7—Hot Rod's car—was parked in the driveway, itself nothing more than two dirt trails leading to a garage with its double doors locked shut. Weeds grew in the yard, and someone had run a mower over them, making them uniformly level. Janet had probably done that. Hot Rod did very little, but what he did do, he was very good at. Or so I am told.

I gave the Mercedes a good looking-over before heading for the porch. It had a Georgia Tech decal on the rear window. I didn't remember Chad telling me his mother's Mercedes had been boosted. What did it matter? I was about to become a hero to the old bitch.

I opened the screened door and knocked on the interior one.

No answer.

Since there was no window in the door or peephole, I huddled close, making it impossible for anyone to pull back the curtains and see me through a window. When I knocked again, I heard someone coming, muttering they'd be there. My pistol was out and ready. Hot Rod was going down for grand theft auto and Chad's mom would have to say something good about me. For the next few years Hot Rod would be fighting off guys in prison and I'd be happily married.

When he opened the door, I jammed my pistol in his face. He wore jeans and nothing else. "Susan, what the hell do you think you're doing?"

"Just show me the pink slip for that Mercedes and I'll be on my way." I reached into my pack for my ID as he backpedaled and his hands went up.

He eyed the ID. "You're a real cop now?"

Behind him, the door to the bedroom closed. Janet Halsey

Color Me A Killer

getting in her last licks before being abandoned for the long hot summer.

"You don't have the pink slip, do you?"

"It's not my car."

"You're admitting you stole it?"

"I'm not admitting anything." He inclined his head toward the rear of the house. "It belongs to the woman."

I glanced toward the bedroom door. It took a moment before I connected what he had told me with the car out front. Once I understood what that meant, I didn't want to know any more.

"Marvin said . . . er—that you were really pissed when he fired you." Everything was a red blur, especially the door to the bedroom.

"You know very well that Marvin drives a pickup, when it works. Won't drive anything else. Doesn't matter. I've hooked up with Nelson Obie."

I returned my ID to my pack. "Step outside."

"Why?"

I waved the pistol in his face. "Because I fucking say so!" And I could only hope Chad's mother couldn't make out my voice. Yeah. Dream on, girl.

I led him out to my jeep, where he filled out the form on the hood. Then I got the hell out of there, forgetting to notarize it until I was well down the road.

Never in my whole life had I been in such a situation, not since I'd been caught in the bedroom with a married man. The bastard never told me he was married, but that didn't take the sting out of the encounter. And it was his daughter who'd walked in on us! What'd she thought? What was Chad's mother thinking? And what must she think I was thinking?

Shit! Shit! Shit! I needed to collect my thoughts. That was not to be. Dads called and said Alan Putnam was on the move.

Blowing off the remainder of my list, I asked, "Where is he?"

"At the House of Blues."

"Can you stay until I arrive? I have one more stop."

"We'll be here, Susan."

I'd always thought Chad's parents had a solid marriage. What'd I missed? Easy to see what women saw in Hot Rod. The guy was a real hunk, and if he hadn't been laying every girl he could get his hands on, I might've fallen under his spell. I shook my head, trying to remove the image of Chad's mother and "Hot Rod" doing it. *Double ugh!*

It took a few minutes, but finally I worked up the nerve to call my boyfriend, and I'll be damned if his mother didn't answer the phone.

"Er—Mrs. Rivers, this is Susan. Is Chad there?"

"No, my dear, he and his father are still at the shop."

"Oh." And what was this "my dear"? "I . . . I have to work late tonight."

"Why don't you call him? I'm sure he'd be pleased to hear from you."

"I think I will."

"Or I can make the call for you."

"No, no, that's not necessary."

"I insist, Susan. You sound rather distracted. You must be busy. I'll tell Chad you'll call tomorrow . . . after you've sorted yourself out."

"Yes, ma'am."

"Susan, I've always said you can call me 'Lois.'"

Now I did have to pull over and compose myself. In a very short time I had to run a game on Alan Putnam and I needed my wits about me. But buzzing around inside my head was an invitation to join Lois Rivers for brunch at the country club Sunday morning.

I stopped and walked around the jeep a couple of times. A car honked as it passed by, but by the time the jerks had turned around and were coming back, I was headed toward the House of Blues. But first I needed to sign some special equipment out of the property room at the law enforcement center.

Pick and Harry looked me over as I strolled across the patio of the House of Blues. I'd changed into something Pick recognized and something Harry didn't approve of. Dads wrinkled his nose as I approached them.

"Susan," said Pick, "those are the clothes I found."

The outfit was tight in all the best places. "Putnam still inside?"

"Yes, he is, Susan."

"I appreciate this, Dads."

Harry glanced at his watch. "Do you know what time it is?"

"After eleven."

"Don't you think you should call it a night?"

"If Alan's the killer he'll try something tonight, and I need to know what's on his mind."

"I know what he'll have in mind if you go in there dressed like that." Harry gave my skimpy outfit the once-over.

"Will you make sure Pick gets home?"

"Of course."

"Leave him at my place."

The young man's eyes lit up. "Can I watch the satellite?"

"Sure."

"I don't know how to order movies."

"Don't look at me," said Harry, holding up his hands. "I just have it for the music."

"I guess it'll be MTV for you tonight, Pick."

"Not if I have any say in the matter," Harry said. "I'll help him locate the Discovery Channel."

I thanked them again and passed through the courtyard of the restaurant.

Suddenly Pick was running, catching up with me. The bouncer eyed him.

"Susan, will I ever go to this place?"

"Go here?"

"Yes. Dancing."

I took his hands. "When this is over, Chad and I will bring you here." And Chad's mother can be your date.

Running around on her husband! I loved that man! Mr. Rivers thought I'd actually accomplished something by being appointed to the justice academy.

I looked into those innocent blue eyes. "Pick, wherever

you want to go. Just name the place."

The bouncer looked away, a couple of guys nodded in my direction as they crossed the patio, and in the parking lot an unmarked sedan drove by with Anslow and Austin inside. They slowed to a stop. One grinned, the other wagged a finger at me. Somehow, some way, they'd find a way to work this into a conversation with my boss.

Pick was talking to me.

"What?"

"Can I ask a date?"

"Who'd you have in mind?" This kid knew someone?

"There's a girl down the waterway. She works at the marina, you know, the one near the ocean."

I knew her. She'd blown her mind on drugs and now her parents hovered over her, trying to keep her out of trouble. She'd already had one child and was pregnant with another. This kid would be put up for adoption, too, and this time the girl's tubes tied.

"It's a date, Pick."

"Thank you." And he practically skipped back to where Dads waited for him.

To one side of the courtyard is the restaurant, to the other an auditorium lower than ground level where they have festival seating. Upstairs, ringing the auditorium, are the chairs, tables, and additional bars. I didn't see Putnam in the auditorium, so it was up the stairs for me, my borrowed clothing straining to keep me reined in.

Putnam sat at a mezzanine table that had stools around it. Someone spoke to me as I passed by, but I only had eyes for Alan—and the girl sitting across the table. Ruth Tackett. I had to fight my way through a load of Alpha Delta Pis who'd come to the beach to celebrate the end of exams. One girl with brown hair and a cute figure was holding court, guys hanging on her every word. The girl could've been a model. She had the figure for it but was several inches too short. That didn't seem to slow her down with the guys.

Ruth Tackett wore a tube top and shorts. Very short short-

shorts and stubby heels. And she was smoking a joint. I could make out the twisted weed as I wove my way through the sorority girls to Putnam's table.

Startled, Alan looked up, then looked me over, especially where the fabric didn't quite cover me. "What you doing here?"

"Came to party. Too many dead girls make me want to party." I looked over the railing. "And this looks like the place."

"Without Rivers?"

"He and I broke up."

Ruth closed a mouth which had been hanging open. Now she asked, "You broke up with Chad?"

"Good news travels slow." I sat between Ruth and Alan and made sure my hip made contact with his. "Had my whole life planned for me, even down to the number of kids." I reached inside my pack and took out my cigarettes. The ones that fell into my hand were missing their filters.

Oops! Hastily I found another.

"You're shitting me." Putnam slid onto an empty stool, putting one between us. His tie and shirt were loose around the collar and the sleeves of his broadcloth shirt were rolled halfway up.

After sticking a filter tip in my mouth, I snapped the lighter, creating a flame. "See who I go home with tonight. It sure as hell won't be Chad Rivers." I took a long drag and let it out. Smoke drifted across the table toward Ruth. "Waste that much time on one guy and you have a lot of catching up to do. Think I'll get laid tonight if I can pry one of those college boys off those sorority girls."

"My father wants me to attend a Christian school when I go off to college," said Ruth, trying to add something to the conversation.

"I didn't have to go to college to end up with a damn good job and almost married to a rich guy. You don't have to have an education to get ahead in this world. Isn't that right, Alan?"

"I'm not so sure about that."

"Whatever."

"That why you busted in on me and Nelson?" asked Ruth. Nodding, I agreed.

"Nelson absolutely hates you."

I laughed. I really did. I threw back my head and roared. People turned and stared. What did I care? I was playing the role of someone I hadn't been for a long time. A role fools like Ruth Tackett envied for some reason.

"Ruth, Nelson loves screwing girls who play hard to get."

To that she didn't know what to say.

Putnam had recovered. "You'd never give up Chad Rivers," he said.

I took another drag off the cigarette and blew smoke in his face. "Alan, I don't give a damn what you think. I met you when I was working a case and you reminded me of the good times I used to have. Then, Chad jammed me up about getting married, what his mother expected of me, and I see Ruth with Nelson at that sports bar and I get to thinking. I'm only twenty-six—why the hell am I in such a rush to settle down?"

With a grin, I added, "Dragging you out of Nelson's, Ruth, you have to admit that was a nice touch. Just try to go back." I dropped the butt to the floor and snubbed it out. "Got anything stronger?"

Alan shook his head. "Not for someone who works for SLED. Remember, I caught your act this afternoon."

"Hope you liked it since it didn't go over as well with the powers-that-be."

His eyes narrowed. "And why's that?"

"You should know." Now I rolled the dice. "All those phone calls to the Chamber. You were there."

"What phone calls?"

"They weren't all about incomplete lists."

"What lists?" asked Ruth.

"The ones calling for my head, Alan."

Putnam was wary but couldn't fault my logic. "I—er, didn't hear about it."

"Damn, but you really are out of the loop. Warden told me the new guy at the Chamber said they'd have to reevaluate my being assigned to the Grand Strand after this killer was caught. SLED's history with me."

Color Me A Killer

"What killer?" asked Ruth.

I looked over the railing. The sorority girl had taken a fellow down to the ground floor. Grabbing Alan's arm, I pulled him off his stool, down the stairs, and onto the dance floor. Evidently it was a lot more difficult than I had imagined to convince a spree killer you wanted to be his next victim.

Once we were on the dance floor, I snuggled in close, trying to get a rise out of him. Sometimes a guy's wiring will overheat and he'll begin to think with his—

A hand grabbed my shoulder and spun me around, then slapped my face. I fell back, landing on my butt and sliding across the floor. One side of my face went numb, then stung as I sat up, palms down to hold me upright. Hair flopped down in my face. But I could see who had hit me. It was Nelson Obie and Nelson was heading straight for me.

19

Music continued to play, girls screamed, and people backed away. Tears ran down my cheeks. Putnam was as shocked as anyone and just stood there as Nelson closed in on me. In the background someone called for a bouncer. Unfortunately, the bouncer was out front, checking IDs.

Obie bent down, wolfish grin on his face. "But we already have the law here, don't we, Susan?"

My legs were splayed, but that didn't keep me from kicking Nelson in the shins. The blows knocked Nelson's feet from under him. Unfortunately, he landed on top of me.

"You bitch!" he spit out as he got to his hands and knees and hovered over me. "You've fucked with me for the last time!"

Nelson thrust a knee between my legs—that hurt!—forcing them apart and causing me to draw my hands in to protect myself. That made it easy for him to grab both of my wrists. When he tried to hold both hands with his one, I forced a hand free by turning them against the inside of his wrist and jammed my fingers into his throat. His follow-up blow glanced off the side of my head. Still, it stunned me, lights flashing, me blinking, and trying to see through the tears. When he drew back to hit me again, Alan Putnam grabbed his arm.

"Nelson, are you crazy?"

Obie shook free. "If I am, it's because of this bitch."

When Alan reached for the arm again, Nelson threw an elbow, catching Putnam in the sternum and knocking him away. Alan stumbled out of the picture and Nelson returned his attention to me.

Grabbing my wrists with one hand and holding them over my head, Nelson threw a blow I could only dodge by twisting to one side. Again his fist grazed me, the room went dark, and I went limp. Tears ran down my cheeks as I was about to became a punching bag.

Bong! The sound rang through the fog.

"Stacey, get away from there!" shouted someone.

"Then do something for this girl!"

Bong! There was that sound again.

Suddenly my arms were free, but there was no way I could sit up. I lay prone on the floor, then someone picked up my head and cradled it in their arms. I could see three college boys holding Nelson as he thrashed around.

"You bastards! Let me go! I'll fucking kill you!"

"Call the cops!" shouted one of them. "This guy's on something."

But he wasn't. Nelson had simply been pushed over the edge by some idiot. Me. His bodyguards hadn't been along to lend Nelson a hand when he'd rammed me at the drawbridge—Marcel and Huey had been there to make sure Nelson didn't do something crazy. Like this.

The person cradling me in her arms was the sorority girl who'd been receiving all the attention from the college boys. Lying against her hip was a metal serving tray. The tray hitting Nelson's head had been the funny sound I'd heard.

Alan stood in front of Nelson, trying to reason with him. Nelson stopped struggling and the college boys loosened their grip. Bad move. Nelson shook them off, knocked Alan aside, and made for me again. I was being helped to my feet when the sorority girls saw Nelson coming.

Several screamed, the girls let go, and I staggered around with only the one girl holding me on my feet. Before Nelson could reach us, one of the college boys hit him with a flying tackle. Both went sprawling, and when they rolled over, the college boy lay on top of him, forearm across Nelson's throat.

"Give me a hand here!" he shouted.

As Nelson tried to free himself, more guys piled on. For a moment it was assholes and elbows, then everyone had an arm or leg. Two guys straddled Nelson's chest.

Putnam bent down to him. "I don't know what your problem is, Nelson, but take it outside."

Through busted lips and a forearm across his throat, Obie croaked, "Send Chase outside and I'll go."

"What about the cops?" demanded someone.

"On their way," said the bouncer, putting away a cell phone. Evidently, the bastard didn't begin cracking skulls until the Season officially began.

"Nelson," Alan said, still bending over him, "the cops are on the way. You want to wait for them?"

Nelson could hardly draw a breath with that forearm across his throat and two college guys straddling his chest. His bald head had been scraped, his lips split, and blood oozed down into his beard. A long scratch ran down one arm. When he looked at me, I saw pure hatred in his eyes.

I shuddered. The bastard intended to kill me. Then I'd be posed in a lifeguard stand or strapped on someone's surfboard? I wanted out of here. I wanted to go home. Forget the job, forget everything. I needed Chad.

In the rest room, the sorority girls cleaned me up, gathering around and holding me on my feet. Ruth Tackett was there, hanging back as the Alpha Delta Pis held sacks of ice to my lip and temple. The girl who had bashed Nelson over the head with a tray tried to pull together my outfit where it had come apart.

"I'm afraid you need some new clothes."

"Don't . . . worry. These . . ." I cleared my throat, ". . . aren't mine."

"Susan," asked Ruth from where she leaned against the wall, "haven't you got some extra clothes in the footlocker on your jeep?"

"You drive a jeep?" asked the sorority girl who had quite possibly saved my life. "I have a Jeep Cherokee. What do you drive?"

"Nothing . . . like that." Jeez, how quickly Carolina gals think they can relate.

But she was an organizer and she made sure I reached my jeep with an escort. In the hustle and bustle, I learned they had released Nelson Obie, per Alan Putnam's request, and sent the police away. Putnam told them it had been a lovers' quarrel. Mouth cut, back feeling like it was broken in two, ice pack held to a bruised face, I just wanted to lie down. Alan Putnam provided such a place when he stepped off a curb where Ruth made the first turn driving me home.

"What in the hell did you do to set off Nelson?" Alan pushed Ruth out of the driver's seat and she had to move to the rear and sit on the footlocker. "I've never seen him that way." He put the jeep in gear.

Through a swollen eye, I squinted at him. "He's been killing lifeguards, Alan."

The jeep jerked to a stop and Ruth let out a little yelp. "Alan, watch what you're doing! You almost threw me off the footlocker."

"He's the one?" asked Putnam.

"Check my windshield. Nelson did that."

"Yeah," said Alan with a nod, "that'd work. Nelson visited a woman last week at the hotel. He could've taken the towel then."

"Yes, he could've." I hunched over and didn't look up again until we stopped at Alan's house.

Prying open my swollen eyes, I asked, "What's this?"

"You shouldn't be alone tonight."

Ruth gripped my shoulders from behind. "We'll take care of you, Susan. Real good care."

It wasn't both of them caring for me, only Alan, after fixing drinks, tending to my cuts and bruises, and making more ice packs. A half a drink later, Ruth passed out on the sofa. Sometime after midnight, thinking I'd done the same, Alan threw me over his shoulder and lugged me out the back door and down the ramp to his boat. What Alan didn't allow for was my guardian angel.

"You can't do that to Susan." It was Pick in his skiff.

Alan stopped, then finished his descent to the dock, where he dumped me into his boat.

Time to make my move. Alan was kidnapping me and Pick was my witness. It was also whcn things began to go horribly wrong. Though I'd been clever enough to dump my drink into a potted plant, I hadn't considered how Alan might drop me into his boat. My head hit the gunwale, fireworks went off once again, and everything went black.

The next thing I knew Ruth was jabbering something about . . . Jesus coming and he was coming soon. She went on and on about Jesus. I couldn't make any sense of it. We weren't in church. That was for sure. Waves rushed in, the night was moonlit, and off in the distance, stars flickered. When you can see stars along the Grand Strand, you aren't anywhere near civilization.

Ruth was in front of me. At first I thought she lay on her side as I did, but then I realized she'd been planted in the sand up to her neck. And from the water lapping at my feet, the tide was coming in.

The sand felt cool and rough. I didn't have any clothes on and I was lying on my side. I didn't feel molested, but my hands were tied behind me, my feet were free. To one side of Ruth, a figure bent over and stood up, over and over again. The sound of shoveling—growing up at the beach you learn the sound of a shovel hitting the sand—came from the figure laboring to dig another hole. This one for me. If Jesus was coming, I hoped he'd get to stepping!

What the hell was going on? Why was I naked? And why was Ruth planted to her neck in the sand? And who was the guy with the shovel? My lip was split—I could taste the blood in the crack—and my head ached. So did my body, like I'd been in a car wreck.

SLED was looking for a killer. I must've found him. Now, if he'd only turn around so I could see who. I tried to free my hands. Not possible. Tied too tight. I couldn't even feel them. Down a ways, a boat had been run up on shore.

Ruth broke into "Onward Christian Soldiers," and the girl knew more than one verse. Maybe I'd better join her. When the tide came in, I would have a baptism like no other.

The guy doing the shoveling stopped and turned around. I closed my eyes, held my breath, and prayed. Yes, Ruth, I was getting with the program. After wiping his forehead with a cloth, Alan Putnam returned to digging my stand-up grave and me to breathing.

Alan Putnam was the serial killer! And he'd beat the hell out of me? Funny, that didn't seem like Alan.

Get a grip, Susan. Tied up and ready to be planted in the sand up to your neck, does that sound like the Alan Putnam you know?

"This ought to do it," he said.

His voice startled me and I jerked back, feeling the sand on my skin. The sudden movement sent shock waves through my head. Tears formed in my eyes from where Alan had beaten me. I seemed to ache all over, especially around the head and shoulders.

Alan was talking to himself about how well his plan had worked, how we had fallen into his hands, and how all he had to do was slip back into his house and wait and see what the Grand Strand had to say about two more dead lifeguards.

He laughed. Two lifeguards caught playing that old bury-me-in-the-sand game when the tide came in. Too bad he didn't have more whistles, but the cops would think one of them had washed out to sea.

Jeez! We were in the hands of a madman.

Duh, Susan. Does this really come as any big surprise?

Putnam glanced at Ruth, who'd begun singing "Rock of Ages." No, Alan said to himself, he'd stick the whistle in the mouth of the first damn one he had to hit over the head with the shovel and shut up. He was sick and tired of all that singing.

If there was a boat, then Alan had brought us around by the Intracoastal . . . but SLED would have been watching . . . no, no, not tonight.

"Where's Pick?" I blurted out.

Steve Brown

Alan looked at me. "Back with the living, are you? At least for a short while."

"Where's Pick, Alan?" I rolled over to my stomach and folded my legs under me to get to my knees.

He smiled that warm and generous smile which had been his trademark for so many years. "You really stay focused, don't you?"

Heaving myself to my knees, I said, "I'm focused enough to kick your ass if something's happened to Pick."

After thrusting the shovel into the pile of sand that had accumulated alongside the hole, Alan came over and stooped down beside me. I turned away so he wouldn't see my nakedness.

"Sorry, but your friend didn't make it."

"What are you saying? Make sense."

"I hit him over the head with the shovel, tied him to his motor, and opened a hole in his boat. He won't be found as soon as you will."

I tried to stand. "You fucking bastard! I'll kill you for that!"

Alan tapped me on my shoulder, causing me to lose my balance and tumble to the sand. I pulled my legs together and scrunched around to protect myself from him.

"You really think you can get away with this?" I asked.

"Well, let's see. I was seen with you and Ruth at the House of Blues, but do you think people are going to investigate me when they have Nelson Obie, especially after the scene he caused? I plan on leaving your jeep at his place later tonight."

"I told Warden you were the killer."

"Sorry, but from what I've heard, Lucy Leslie and Kitty Flanagan had their differences with Nelson, too."

"It's you, Alan. It was always you. You left the towel on Lucy's head."

He gazed into the semidarkness of the ocean. Reflecting off the water was a streak of light cast by the moon, shimmering on line and disappearing out to sea. Waves rolled in, then out again.

"It's over, Susan. Your side lost. It's on TV: a serial killer is loose at Myrtle Beach."

"Not possible. There's a press blackout."

"Heather Johnson called the story into CNN."

"Then she'll be out of a job."

Alan chuckled as he returned his attention to me. "Is that all you're worried about? This could take all night if I wanted it to." He touched my cheek and I jerked away.

I had to keep this asshole talking while I thought of something. "You'll be out of a job, too."

"I don't have a job. It was given to someone else. But he'll regret the day he took it. For the rest of his career, he'll be associated with the economic ruin of the most popular resort on the East Coast. Just let him try to get a job after this."

Glancing at the boat down a ways, I asked, "So it was you who strangled Lucy and posed her in the lifeguard stand?"

"To tell the truth I hadn't decided if I was going to do this or not, but there was Lucy at Broadway at the Beach and she was headed for a shoe store at Barefoot Landing. It was too good to pass up. All I had to do was motor down the Waterway, surprise her in the parking lot—of course, she let me get too close—and that was that. After leaving her on the beach, it was easy enough to hike back to Barefoot and pick up my boat."

"And Kitty?"

"You know, that might be where SLED should start their investigation. Luther hasn't been seen for several weeks. I wouldn't be surprised if Nelson Obie didn't have him killed."

"What about Kitty, Alan?" I looked around, trying to figure an angle on how to get out of this. To do that, I needed to get to my feet again.

"Kitty fell into my hands like it was preordained. I was driving around, trying to figure out how to make this thing work. Kitty made it possible. A quick follow-up to Lucy and the pressure was on the Chamber again."

"M.J. Dawkins was your first victim, wasn't she?"

It was a moment before he spoke, and as he did, he looked out to sea again. That was when I took the chance to squiggle around and get to my knees.

"I really don't know what happened. Oh, I remember trying to make up my mind what to do with the body, but that whole afternoon is a blur."

"What afternoon?" I was on my knees again.

"The afternoon I was sacked. They gave me a month's wages, and someone from security watched me clean out my desk. I worked my butt off to get an office in that new building and they let me go. Said they'd give me an excellent job recommendation. They even lined up the interview at the Host of Kings."

"Where's Dawkins' body?" I asked, trying to get to my feet. To do that I had to . . . *freeze!*

He looked at me. "Down the Waterway. Somewhere."

"And her clothes?"

"You were wearing them tonight." He was puzzled. "Where'd you find them?"

"Pick found them, held onto them, and when he overheard a conversation about missing girls, remembered he had them."

Alan shook his head. "I really don't remember. I guess I ran across M.J. in the parking lot when I was driving around. We never dated, but she's always had a crush on me. She wanted to fuck and I obliged her." He shrugged. "What can I say? Something snapped. Next thing I knew she was dead."

"With your hands around her throat."

"That, too," he said with a nod. "Anyway, I got in my car and went home. One of the *Jaws* movies was on TV, and that's when I realized what the Grand Strand needed was a serial killer. I took the boat down to where I'd left M.J. The tide had come in and her clothes were gone. There wasn't anything I could do about that. I worried about those clothes all winter."

He straightened up and I shrank back. "Do you know how many times I had to blow that guy to get him to leave that house to me, and the number of butts I had to kiss on county council? All that and I still didn't get the job? It wasn't fair."

"Sweet Jesus, Alan, but you are sick."

"If I were sick I would've done more of this."

He reached over and touched my breasts. I recoiled and rolled away, into the water.

"Really, Susan, aren't you glad I'm not sick?"

"You couldn't get it up!" I shouted as I continued to roll away. "You couldn't be a real serial killer if you wanted to. You couldn't go . . . and you couldn't touch those girls after you'd killed them. You had to use pliers to rip off their ear-rings." Water covered me as I rolled into the surf, then buoyed me enough to get to my knees.

Well, hello there.

"Don't go far, Susan. You're liable to drown."

Then he realized what was happening. I might have my hands tied behind my back, but I could still float, maybe even float away. I was in a yard deep when Alan splashed in after me. He was ten feet from shore when I tried to kick him—not easily done in water—so he grabbed me by the arm, pulled me to my feet, and sent me in a running shove back to shore.

There he probably expected me to stumble and fall, and I did. But tumbled head-over-heels back to my feet; then I was off and running down the beach. As I passed his boat I heard Alan screaming for me to stop.

Sure, Alan, sure. Very quickly I learned that running with your hands tied behind your back, it's almost impossible to get into a rhythm, even if you've given up smoking. Alan caught up with me and knocked me to the ground. I hit hard, then rolled over and tried to return to my feet. Never made it. Alan kept me down, and feeling his hands on me made me shudder. I didn't want this man's hands anywhere near me.

I blinked away tears, tasted blood, and heard a ringing in my head. Still, I was able to get out, "You're determined to make this as difficult as possible for yourself, aren't you?"

Straddling me, he said, "What the hell . . . are you talking about?" Alan was having a hard time catching his breath.

"Knock me out and you'll have to carry me all the way back. Go ahead and do it." I stuck up my jaw, taunting him.

He looked down the beach from where we'd come.

Uh-huh. It appeared there had been enough of this toting

naked girls around for one night. He hauled me to my feet and walked me back to my hole. For some reason the idiot thought I'd come along peacefully. If so, he'd been watching too many Holocaust movies.

Approaching his boat I broke away again and ran around the bow, toward the stern, splashing into the surf, then looped around the other side when Alan came after me. We played catch-me-if-you-can until Alan crossed through the boat and chased me down, landing on top of me and forcing me face-first into the surf. There he held me under, determined to finish this.

He almost did, but I panicked and kicked back and hit him with my heels. This caused him to loosen his grip. More kicks and I broke free, coming up out of the surf and gasping for air.

Alan grabbed my hair and forced me under again. Sand ground into my face; then the wave went out and I could breathe again. Alan had had enough. He dragged me out of the water, dumped me on the beach, and went after the shovel. I really didn't want him to have that shovel.

Rolling to my side I got to my knees again. The pain in my head, side, and neck begged for me to give it up. Then I was on my feet and stumbling after him, coughing to clear my throat, and not really caring whether he heard me or not. When Alan turned around, I kicked him in the balls.

He screamed, dropped the shovel, and sank to his knees. I coughed to clear my head, then kicked him in the face hard enough to hear bones crack: his face, my foot. We both screamed, then I switched feet and kicked him again.

The blow knocked Alan to one side. Before he could get up, I stomped on his back, then his neck. I really went to work on that neck. Behind me, Ruth sang about the virtues of an old rugged cross. It took a minute, but I finally picked up the rhythm. With my foot, that is.

"You . . . son of a bitch! Those girls . . . and now Pick . . . you bastard!"

I kicked him again, trying to force his nose up into his brain. When Alan rolled away, I limped after him, leaping on his back and coming down with both knees. The broken foot caused me to scream, and I fell off his back, crying in frustration, begging for mercy.

When I stopped whining, I noticed there had been no reply. None from the Lord, none from Alan Putnam. Only Ruth's singing. From where I lay I could reach him, so I kicked at him again, and to tell the truth I really enjoyed it. Lucy, Kitty, or even myself—we'd chosen the lives we'd led, but Ruth Tackett had her whole life ahead of her. And poor Pick . . . . When I stopped, I heard breathing louder than any noise the surf could make.

That was me. Alan lay still and the surf lapped at his side, his hair a mess, stringing down his face. His neck was at a funny angle.

"Is he dead?" Ruth's voice was eerily calm, even with the ocean in her face.

I was too exhausted to reply.

"Susan, can you get me out of here?"

I needed to think. Actually I needed a rest. There wasn't a part of my body that didn't ache. Or if there was, I couldn't feel it.

"Susan, the tide's coming in."

I struggled to my feet, stumbled over to the boat, and tried to scrape the nylon rope off my wrists by using the gunwale, then the motor, anything. There was a tackle box in the bow, but no amount of kicking or stomping would break it open.

Damn indestructible plastic! I couldn't pick it up with my feet, and speaking of feet, one of mine was beginning to swell. It hurt like a bitch. Tears ran down my cheeks.

"Susan, help me!"

When I looked, I saw Ruth was having to hold her breath as the surf came in.

I studied the boat. With my hands tied behind me, I couldn't steer. I couldn't do much of anything, pull the cord, shove the craft off the beach, and the oar was wooden. What good was that?

"Susan, if you'll get me out of here I promise I won't ever be bad again."

"Shut up, Ruth, and let me think."

Glancing up and down the beach, I realized I didn't have a clue where we were. There were lights off in the distance. How far I didn't know. It might be a hotel or a house, but it was a long fucking way off.

"Be right back."

But before I left her alone on that deserted stretch of beach, I sat down alongside Alan and pushed and shoved, with my good foot, until his body was in a position to block the waves reaching for Ruth. Then I crawled to my feet and ran like hell toward those lights.

I was under no illusion that Ruth would be alive when I returned. If I could return. My broken foot begged for me to stop. Instead, I screamed and hollered as I ran. This was so unfair! First the father, now the daughter. My whole leg became numb about the time I reached the first house.

Then another, and another, and another. All empty. Son of a bitch! Maybe I should go through a window. But how would I dial a phone, and who's to say the phone wasn't disconnected if the house was closed for the winter. Most windows were shuttered anyway.

Shit, shit, shit!

At the sixth house, a kegger was in progress. It was some college guys and their dates. That'd been the light I'd seen. Fortunately those dates included the girls who'd helped me at the House of Blues. Damn lucky, I'd say, because arriving stark raving naked—with the emphasis on "raving"—the sorority girls were much easier to convince than their dates.

They sent the guys running down the beach. A cell phone reached 911, a knife cut my hands free, and I was wrapped in a blanket and my foot was packed in ice. Still, the pain couldn't keep me conscious after gulping down half a bottle of Scotch. Anyway, who wanted to be conscious when those boys returned and told us Ruth Tackett had drowned?

20

Two weeks after this fiasco I went down to Pawleys Island where I could catch a few fish and be left alone. By then I was in a walking cast and back on cigarettes and most of my stitches had healed. J.D. Warden was already there. Well, nothing else had gone right lately. Why should this be any different?

Sitting on the end of the pier, Warden looked like any other local: long-sleeved shirt with sleeves cut off, an old pair of pants, and unshaven—for several days. Actually, if you acted like you belonged, you could use any of these piers extending beyond the marsh grass and the snobs on Pawleys wouldn't bug you.

Some piers have benches, even shelters from the sun. The pier Warden sat on stopped at the edge of the grass and had no shelter. Yes, yes, I could've used a boat to get there and avoided the driving, and the hassle of the cast, but I wasn't all that excited about being on the water these days.

Warden glanced over his shoulder at the clumping noise. "Chase, what are you doing here?" His nose had orange zinc oxide smeared across the bridge and it made him look absolutely ridiculous. Next to him was a bright new tackle box with an assortment of lures and other fishing gear, and a cardboard carton with shrimp for bait. He was holding a six-foot pole with a spinner. Max the Wonder Dog was with me and the Lab reached Warden before I did, sniffing out the area, starting with the shrimp.

"I gave you my resignation. I'm not coming back."

"Not my decision." As he patted the dog—Max isn't very picky choosing his friends—Warden added, "Greave told me how many piers to count to find this place. I don't know why that was important, which pier, that is. You've heard he's retiring?"

"I also heard that Nelson Obie got probation." My cast and I clumped to a stop and I put down my gear. "Why isn't it your decision if I come back or not?"

"SLED relieved me of my command."

"You're kidding me. We caught the killer."

"But broke the rules."

"Which one?" This oughta be good. Warden was a by-the-book kind of guy.

He helped me sit down. Getting up and down with this frigging cast made me look like an old woman. Max found something in the grass and plunged in after it.

"Chase, I don't think there's a cop around who thinks women should catch calls on their own."

"Do you really want to go there?"

"Every time a female officer catches a call you'll hear some male officer, uniform or detective, say he's in the vicinity and he'll back her up."

"That's their problem." I looked over the side for whatever Max had seen in the grass-infested water.

"There're people at SLED who think it was irresponsible of me to pair you with Earl Tackett."

"Because he would try to protect me."

Max paddled in the direction of the road. Evidently he didn't think I was in any danger with Warden. That remained to be seen.

"SLED thinks I should've known better."

"Another reason I wouldn't want your job. Who has your job anyway?"

"DeShields."

"That won't work. Mickey tries to please everybody."

"Then why don't you take it? That wouldn't be any problem for you."

"I heard Theresa Hardy put in for the job."

He looked at me sharply. "Chase, you know too much for your own damned good."

"If that was true none of this would've happened."

It was several minutes before he said, "So you're returning to private-eyeing?"

"No way," I said, shaking my head. "I give black widows a bad name." For a moment I couldn't swallow or breathe, the number of people who were dead because of my bungling . . . . I stared into the grassy waters. The channel looked so inviting and I wore this heavy cast. It'd be so easy to slip over the side and . . . .

An arm pulled me into a shoulder and I leaned into it. Tears ran down my cheeks.

"There, there, Chase. You'll make it." Warden dug in his pocket and found a handkerchief.

After wiping the tears away, I cleared my throat. "So they canned you. Because of me."

"Once again you inflate your importance in the scheme of things."

"Then what?"

"I didn't keep you on a tight enough leash."

"You never should've recommended me to the academy."

"Don't know about that. You impressed quite a few people, especially that guy at Quantico. Maybe he'll consider you for the FBI."

"The FBI requires a college education or several years' experience on a local police force."

He smiled. "It's good to hear you're keeping up with the requirements." Now that his shoulder was free, he threw his line into the channel. "So, what do you have in mind?"

"Becoming Mrs. Chad Rivers," I said, dabbing away my tears.

"I heard you two were engaged."

"We moved it up from Christmas." I showed him the ring. Chad wasn't much for show. It was only a quarter carat. Going to have to work on the boy there.

"Good for you."

"I have the blessing of his mother."

Warden glanced at me. "And what do you have on her?"

I hit his shoulder. "What kind of question is that?"

"A logical one when it comes to you."

It was time to return his handkerchief. "I'll still pay penance. I'll have to have brunch with her every Sunday morning."

"Yes. I imagine you've got a lot of catching up to do, learning how to be a lady."

"Compliments will get you nowhere. I'm still not coming back."

At the end of his line something snatched the shrimp, but when Warden tried to reel it in, his catch ran for the weeds. Warden fought the line, but the fish used the grass to its advantage and broke free.

He watched it go. "It's the Grand Strand's loss if you don't return. People moving in all the time, and you know this area better than most. And you're focused, or tightly wound." He looked at me. "How could you be sure it was Alan Putnam?"

I stared at the line lying limp in the weeds. "I knew Alan."

"Seriously, what was it about him?"

"When the FBI told me someone had declared war on the Grand Strand, I couldn't believe it, but then I remembered the towel. The towel from where Alan worked. He was taunting us from the very beginning. So, did you find anything in his house?"

"Combat boots two sizes too large for him."

"No earrings. No trophies?"

Warden shook his head. "Behind a false wall was every book that's been written about serial killers, including *The Alienist.*"

I nodded as I looked over the channel again. "Alan planned this like a campaign."

"But killing women in cold blood . . . I never would've guessed." Warden reeled in his line.

"Alan used to brag he was the King of the Grand Strand. More than once I've seen him leaning into the railing of some balcony shouting just that. Alan had access to every party, every grand opening, every major event along this beach. A king doesn't give up his throne without a fight."

Max returned with a stick. I took the stick and whipped it behind me. It landed in the water near the road. Max was off again.

Warden's rod lay limp in his lap. "I'm sorry about your friend. That retarded kid deserved better."

"And I'm sorry about Ruth Tackett."

He looked at me. "I thought she found Jesus."

I'd seen Ruth once or twice since our night on the beach. But that ingratiating smile, those dull clothes, always the finger marking her place in the Bible—I couldn't stand to look at Ruth. "In the most primitive way, yes, she found Jesus."

"Chase, you're as cold-hearted as ever."

"As I said, compliments will get you nowhere. I'm not coming back."

"Would you drop it? Nobody's interested in how you spend the rest of your life." He jerked the line savagely and it flew toward us, landing in the grass only feet from the end of the pier. The bait was gone. So was the hook.

"It's SLED's loss if they don't take you back, J.D."

"But you have a say in your future. Your resignation is still in my briefcase."

"Nope," I said shaking my head. "Chad calls the shots. I hope I get so pregnant I can never work again."

"Think that's the solution? Women struggle with this issue every day."

"I don't think any woman struggles with killing four guys in less than four days."

"Well, if that's bothering you, now's not the time to return to work."

We sat there, Warden fiddling with a hook.

"Look, you want me to show you how to fish or what?"

"I know how to fish."

"You're not using a sinker, and Greave sent you here to bottom fish."

He thrust the rod at me. "Then show me. Or do you have something more important to do while waiting to get pregnant?"

I took the rod and strung the line, this time adding a sinker from the tackle box so the hook could find the bottom. With a flick of the wrist, I returned the line to the channel. About the same place Warden had placed it.

"What'll you do if the fish takes it into the weeds again?"

"J.D., there's a hole out there where spots can be found. That's why Greave recommended this place."

"'Spot' is a fish? It sounds like a dog."

With that Max returned with the stick, shaking off water from his plunge into the shallows. Ducking the spray, I took the stick and prepared to throw it again. Warden took the stick from my hand, turned at the hip, and threw the stick so hard that it landed in the road. Off went Max again.

"To answer your question about my future, I'm learning the boat business. Chad's father thinks I'll make a pretty decent salesperson."

"I'm sure you will, Chase. Who'd have the nerve to turn you down?"

ALSO BY STEVE BROWN
published by ibooks, inc.:

SUSAN CHASE MYSTERIES
Color Her Dead
Color Me Gone
Color Me Guilty
Color Me a Killer

ABOUT THE AUTHOR

A member of the Mystery Writers of America and Sisters in Crime, STEVE BROWN is also the author of *Radio Secrets*, a novel of suspense about a radio psychotherapist with a secret past; *Black Fire*, the story of a modern-day Scarlett and Rhett facing a church-burning in South Georgia; *Woman Against Herself*, a suspense novel in which a single mom takes on a drug kingpin; and six novels in the Susan Chase Mysteries series.

Steve lives with his family in South Carolina. You can contact him through www.chicksprings.com.